YURY TRIFONOV

disappearance

Translated by David Lowe

ARDIS

Copyright © 1991 by Ardis Publishers
All rights reserved under International and
Pan-American Copyright Conventions
Printed in the United States of America

Ardis Publishers
2901 Heatherway
Ann Arbor, Michigan 48104

Jacket Art by Lev Tabenkin, "At the Bus-stop," 1985 from
The Kathleen G. Charla collection.

Jacket & book design by Ross Teasley.

Library of Congress Cataloging-in-Publication Data

Trifonov, IUrii Valentinovich, 1925-1981
[Ischeznovenie. English]
The disappearance / by Yury Trifonov : translated by David Lowe.
p. cm.
Translation of: Ischeznovenie.
ISBN 0-87501-089-X (alk. paper) : $23.95
1. Soviet Union—History—1925-1953—Fiction.
PG3489.R518213 1992
891.73'44—dc20   91-5110
CIP

INTRODUCTION

It is both a strength and weakness of the human mind that it desperately seeks order, pattern, all the more so when that mind belongs to a novelist who must, no matter how innovative his style, impose some sort of order if he is to create a narrative. To seek to make sense of one's experience and the experience of one's generation seems an obviously legitimate task. But in the atmosphere of imposed amnesia which was until recently characteristic of the Soviet Union, very few writers could honestly pursue this seemingly modest course. Yury Trifonov (1925-1981) was not an underground writer, an emigre writer, or even an embattled official writer. He was accepted and published by legitimate journals and publishing houses, he did strike some critics as provocative, but he had relatively few problems with censorship, especially when compared to other writers. Partly this was due to his style which at first tended to mislead both critics and readers alike into thinking they were dealing with a writer who was perhaps unusual, but nonetheless orthodox at his core. As a person, Trifonov inspired confidence: he was indirect, subtle, but appeared to be a familiar Soviet type, the former athlete who had a burly sort of charm. Trifonov, however, was a real writer, the genuine article, not simply a journalist masquerading as a novelist, and his attempts to make sense of the history of his time have the resonance of art.

Despite his fame as the author of the "Moscow novellas" (published in English as *The Exchange and Other Stories),* and the novel *The House on the Embankment,* Trifonov had no hopes of publishing *Disappearance* in his lifetime. A heavily autobiographical account of life in Moscow during the purges, it had to wait until 1987 and the relative freedom of glasnost for publication. Trifonov worked on this novel off and on for twenty years, and its subjects spilled over into other works published in this time. But only here does the reader find the full picture, as Trifonov discusses how the idealism of the Old Bolsheviks was used to justify the Terror, and filters horrifying events through the consciousness of a boy too young to understand what they mean.

In artistic terms, Trifonov's subject is the nature of time and the nature of a given personality within the flow of time. Trifonov's inclination as a psychologist is to let the reader judge for himself, as characters are revealed to be more, or less, than the people around them see.

The novel, as it stands, is unfinished, breaking off as the Bayukov brothers discuss what the future will bring. But in real life there was a real ending: the Trifonov brothers, upon whom these characters were based, both died in the fatal year of 1937, one under arrest, the other of a heart attack, while awaiting arrest. But a member of the next generation survived—to tell their story.

Ellendea Proffer
1991

disappearance

I

I once lived in that building. No—*that* building died, disappeared, a long time ago. I lived in another building, but within those same enormous dark-gray fortress-like concrete walls. The apartment house towered over trivial two-story buildings, private houses, belfries, old factories, and embankments with granite parapets; and the river washed it on both sides. It stood on an island and looked like a ship, unwieldy and ungainly, without masts, rudderless, and without smokestacks, a huge box, an ark, crammed full of people, ready to sail. Where to? No one knew, no one wondered about that. To people who walked down the street past its walls, glimmering with hundreds of small fortress windows, the building seemed indestructible and permanent, like a rock: in thirty years the dark gray color of the walls had not changed.

But I knew that the old apartment building had died. It had died long ago, when I left it. That's what happens to buildings: we leave them, and they die.

II

On an October night in 1942, after eleven days of crawling from one Central Asian station to another, the train reached Kuibyshev. The now scorching, now ice-cold rust-colored Kazakh steppes had receded. The smell of wormwood had ceased wafting into the open doors of the platforms between the cars. Forever gone was the sight of the old women squatting with dozens of bowls in which sheep guts floated in a slimy wash and something else from sheep, something black. The rains had started, the cold had arrived. At Kuibyshev they stood at a dead standstill on a siding. No one knew anything. The rumor spread that they wouldn't be dispatched for Moscow any earlier than Monday. Suddenly, at dawn, it was announced that an unexpected troop train was being dispatched, two cars had been attached to it, and people should transfer to those cars promptly, without losing a moment. People jumped, ran, stumbled, and dragged bundles in the gray, shiver-inducing dark. Igor hauled his father's very heavy thick leather suitcase, stuffed full of things—clothes, jars, fruit, sugar, blankets—Grandmother had crammed in everything she could, so that she and Zhenka would have less to take—and a bag with two winter coats, his and Zhenka's, two pairs of felt boots, and in addition a string bag, in which there were a loaf of dark bread and Ehrenburg's book War, bought at the train station in Tashkent. Igor had read the book on the trip, lying in the closeness and the sour air under the ceiling. Igor had tied the suitcase and bag together with a belt and flung them over his shoulder. He carried the bag with the dark loaf in his hand. The belt broke, unable to withstand the weight. People travelling with Igor walked past, exclaimed sympathetically, but couldn't help: everyone was dragging his own things.

He couldn't manage carrying the suitcase and the bag at the same time. Then Igor decided to move in short relays. Leaving the bag, he carried the suitcase fifteen paces ahead and then went back to the bag. All his travelling companions had already run on ahead. Taking the bag, Igor set off toward the suitcase and saw that a tall figure, hard to make out in the predawn dark, slightly bent over from the weight of the suitcase, was hastily moving away toward the far end of the plat-

form. Abandoning the bag so as to walk faster, Igor went after the re-
treating figure: he did not start running, did not cry out, because both
of those things seemed somewhat shameful and premature to him.
Why raise an alarm? The man with his father's suitcase quickened his
pace, and now everything seemed to become clear—his thoughts had
been working laboriously, everything had reminded him of a distressing morning dream just before awakening—and Igor took off running.
Not very quickly, so as not to look like a panic-monger. The thief dove
to the right, behind the train cars, and disappeared. Igor was a little
too afraid to give chase: he could miss the train. Igor ran back to
where he had left the bag, but the bag was gone. Igor had left in his
hands the bag with the loaf of dark bread and the book of Ehrenburg's
sketches. The platform had emptied. On both sides the walls of freight
cars stood deafly and mutely black.

Igor started running, frightened at the thought that he'd get left behind by his companions. Where had they disappeared to? He ran a
gauntlet of trains, yelling, calling. A freight car door opened with a soft
squealing, and at floor level a head wearing a shaggy cap appeared, a
strange head, lying on its side, its cheek to the floor, and seeming not
to have a body. It barked an obscenity. Igor immediately heard other
voices. A baby started crying, and a woman tried to quiet it. Igor ran
on ahead, not along the platform now, but the ground. But as before,
there were endless trains standing on both sides. He ran as though
down the bottom of a ravine. He suddenly seemed to be swimming
down a river hemmed in by narrow banks, and he was drowning.
There was nothing to breathe. His body had gone limp, and he understood that he needed to act, move, wave his arms, but he couldn't: he
had experienced the same sort of instantaneous, deathly paralysis once
in July when he'd nearly drowned at the Gabay beach. He had taken a
step and could no longer touch the bottom. He stopped, as though
some invisible person had yanked him by the arm—back then, at
Gabay, it had been Volodka—and realized that he needed to go back
to the spot from where he'd started running. He rushed back.
Suddenly he thought: "It's good that I don't have the suitcase and the
bag. I wouldn't be able to run!" He tore along for all he was worth, incredibly quickly, as though at a race, and then would suddenly stop,

pound on the doors of the closed freight cars, and yell: "Hey, anyone there?"

On the platform of one car there arose a figure in a sheepskin coat, clutching a rifle in the crook of the elbow, and a hoarse voice—you couldn't tell whether it was a man's or a woman's—began grumbling mildly: "Why are you yelling, you good-for-nothing?" Igor explained that he was looking for the troop train headed for Moscow. The sheepskin coat said that they were all troop trains here and all headed for Moscow but advised: "Ask that man over there who's walking back and forth on that track tapping the wheels. Hop up here!"

Igor jumped up onto the platform, pushed his way past the sheepskin coat without ever figuring out whether it was a man or a woman wrapped up in it, jumped off onto the other side, and started looking around, trying to find the man tapping the wheels, but he couldn't see anyone anywhere. Igor strained his vision, pulled at the corner of his eye with his finger—he was nearsighted, and his glasses had been left in the suitcase—and then he cried out in despair: "Where the heck is your man?"

At the same time the gentle sound of steel striking steel was heard, and Igor ran over there, toward the sound, still not seeing anyone, completely blinded by the weight crushing his chest: he'd been left behind, left behind! A railway worker with a flashlight, who was down on all fours near a wheel and for that reason could not be seen from the distance, listened to him and waved his arm: "The third track over, and sideways!"

Igor jumped, crawled across under platforms on which there were guns covered with tarpaulins, waited for an endless train consisting of nothing but tank cars to pass, asked for, called, and finally found the car, leapt up onto the footboard, and landed inside—it was a warm, dark car that smelled of habitation and shag tobacco. It lacked compartments, and all the berths seemed to be occupied, but that did not upset Igor in the least. He flopped down joyfully right on the floor, in the aisle.

Igor's travelling companions—there were six of them, four guys and two girls, all Muscovites who had found themselves in Tashkent in evacuation and, just like Igor, had volunteered there for munitions factories so as to return to Moscow—asked what had happened to him and where he had disappeared to, son of a gun. No one knew that he had had his suitcase and bag stolen, and no one would have believed it, seeing with what a joyous look he had stretched out on the floor. When he told his story in detail, however, everyone was amazed. At first they pitied him, but then they started laughing. Soldiers with a flashlight walked around the car, looking for someone. Then two ticket collectors came through, checking tickets and entry permits for Moscow—they laughed too. The train suddenly started moving, and the gaiety became universal. Strangers lying on distant berths laughed, as did people who came up close out of curiosity and those who were making their way into another car and stopped just for a moment, to find out why people were laughing. Igor felt himself to be a celebrity of sorts. Someone found a place for him: "Hey, you comic, come on up here!"

—and someone else sent him a piece of fatback with bread.

Igor climbed up to a berth on the third level, put his bag with the dark bread under his head, and started chewing the fatback. He'd gotten very hungry. Although the fatback wasn't very fresh and for some reason gave off the smell of tobacco, Igor gnawed and sucked it with pleasure. Moreover, the position of celebrity and hussar who couldn't care less about the loss of his baggage obliged him to eat any kind of fatback, even the most questionable. If Igor had been offered a glass of vodka right then, he'd have drunk it down in one gulp, without blinking.

"How old are you, young fellow?" asked someone lying in the berth opposite.

Igor looked over—the man was covered with an overcoat, like a sick or wounded person. With his dark eyes he looked at Igor intently and unpleasantly, and Igor replied unwillingly and not at once: "Sixteen."

"Do you have anyone in Moscow?"

"Yes, I do."

"Are they expecting you?"

Igor asked rudely: "And what does it matter to you?"

"Not at all, of course. I don't care at all about you, fool," the man said softly and closed his eyes.

Igor breathed deeply, producing a whistling sound through his nose, and mulled over whether he should be offended or not. He decided that it wasn't worth it. The man was pitiful. Maybe he was dying. But the hussar feeling disappeared, and he started to feel sad. The wheels rumbled over a bridge—they were crossing the Volga. Down below people were talking about a war communiqué. Someone had heard the six-o'clock radio report at the Kuibyshev train station: there were heavy defensive battles in the vicinity of Stalingrad and Mozdok. The same thing as all the past few days. It was too scant. What was really going on there? They also talked about the battles in Libya, about the English being cunning, but the Americans not knowing how to be. In Moscow, they said, cottonseed oil was being sold as a fat, but not the sort they had had in Tashkent—a lighter kind, less oily. There wasn't any tea; everyone drank black coffee made of acorns or barley.

The voices from below came through in snatches, in the intervals when the wheels rumbled more softly. Suddenly the voices were raised and began sounding cantankerous, cutting each other off:

"Nobody's asking you!"

"No, I'm asking..."

"You're butting into..."

"You're spreading..."

"Cut it out with him! Can't you see..."

Igor thought about the people who were waiting for him in Moscow. He didn't know, though, whether they really were expecting him. Grandmother had written a letter to her cousin Vera, a woman even older than Grandmother and quite frail—for that reason she hadn't been able to leave Moscow—about the fact that Igor had received a permit and would be arriving in October, but there hadn't as yet been a reply from either Grandmother Vera or her daughter, Aunt Dina, so that they didn't know whether he'd be able to stay with them or whether they were even alive and well. Igor could stay alone, of course, in the room on Bolshaya Kaluzhskaya (was the room still intact?), but Grandmother thought that she'd feel better about it if Igor moved in at Grandmother Vera's. These were all meaningless details. The main thing was that he was returning. And that idiotic business with the suitcase and bag—something out of a Chaplin comedy—was but a small price to pay for the return, an insignificant price, a trifle. There was no need to be distressed. But still and all, just what had there been there? Well, really just trifles, junk, just felt boots, a fur winter coat made by altering Father's old-fashioned overcoat. Well, just some women's jackets, blankets, sheets, tablecloths, all sorts of odds and ends. Now the glasses were a pity. Without glasses he was kaput. But he could order new ones. But now what was really a pity were the diaries, his whole school life from the seventh grade to the ninth. Three thick school notebooks. Everything, beginning with the move from that apartment house to Bolshaya Kaluzhskaya, when the three of them were left together—he, Grandmother, and Zhenka—the new school, the guys, the Young Pioneer Center, two summers in Silver Pines and one summer in Shabanovo. How many valuable, precious, funny, wonderful things there were there! How often he'd laughed when rereading certain pages. All the rest was junk. He should fall asleep and forget. Tomorrow evening there would be Moscow. And he fell asleep, although gray light was coming through the cracks in the camouflage paper. Day was dawning.

He dreamed of the old apartment—the one where they had lived with his father. There was the large, rather dark dining room, next to it Grandmother's room, partitioned off from the dining room by a marsh-colored curtain. It was always sunny in Grandmother's room— there was a window the length of the whole wall and a door out onto the balcony. And there was the wardrobe, the same one that the large mirror mounted in the door had once fallen out of and broken, just before New Year's, completely unexpectedly—no one had touched it.

III

The New Year's tree stood almost in the middle of the dining room. The dinner table had been moved up against the piano. The room had grown crowded and begun to smell of the woods, the country house, skis, the dog Morka, the porch with white windows and the dirty, wet floor, where they would knock their felt boots against the boards, throw their mittens down on the bare floor, without an oilcloth—all the things on the porch had a sorry, frozen look—and throwing open the felt-padded door, they would run into the warmth, into the smoky, dry, kitchen coziness with the crackling of the stove. Everything smelled of pine needles—that was the smell of vacations. In two days Gorik and Zhenya were supposed to go to a country house, not to theirs in Silver Pines, however, but to Pyotr Varfolomeevich Snyakin's, Uncle Petya's. He was an old friend of their father's and Grandmother's from as far back as exile and the Civil War. Uncle Petya also had two grandsons, two little boys, but Gorik didn't know them well, and although he was very attracted by the unfamiliar Zvenigorod, which was called the Russian Switzerland, and by the chance to do downhill skiing and stay at the Snyakins' wonderful country house—about which Mother said that it was a palace, not a country house, and Grandmother, with a touch of disapproval, talked about how people change—he was a little sorry to leave the familiar Pines.

A girlfriend of Zhenya's came to the New Year's party—the thin-legged, dark-eyed girl Asya from her class. She gave herself great airs, but Gorik didn't pay any attention to her. Gorik's cousin Valera and his father, Uncle Misha, also came. None of his school friends had come: Lyonya Karas had gone to Leningrad with his mother—he often went to Leningrad to see relatives; Marat Skameykin was having guests over for a New Year's party of his own; and Volodka Sapog had gone to a country house in Valentinovka. But Gorik didn't regret the fact that none of his friends were there. He wasn't opposed to taking a break from them: Lyonya Karas, with his imagination and secrets, sometimes got Gorik down—he felt that he was slipping into dependence, into a sort of slavery to him; Sapog was a companionable fellow, but he liked to fib and brag; and Skameykin was a real fox. Gorik couldn't live

without them; he loved them; they were his best and only friends; but
that friendship made him tired.

Gorik saw Valera rarely—Uncle Misha lived in the country, in the
settlement of Kratovo—but when his cousin did come to Moscow, he
and Gorik made such a "hullabaloo," created such a "commotion,"
such "bedlam," as Mother put it, that the downstairs neighbors' chan-
deliers shook. They could roll around the floor for hours, sit astride
each other, whirl around and pant, squeezing each other with all their
might, trying to extract a cry of pain or at least a scarcely audible
"uncle." And the more they sweated, got their hair and clothing
messed up, rolled around in the dust, the more they gasped and wore
each other out, the happier and better they felt. It was like a narcotic:
they would get drunk from the playing around, would understand
with their heads that it was time to stop, that the matter would end in
a brawl, but they couldn't stop.

The horsing around was taking place next to the New Year's tree, on
the large daybed, which gave off the smell of disinfectant if you
rubbed your nose against it, and its hard, rough material scratched
your cheeks. There were two bolsters on it that the cousins were fighting with, laughing softly, wheezing voluptuously, trying to hit each
other hard in a painful spot. The girls on the other side of the tree
were playing a table game. They were by themselves, and Gorik and
Valera were by themselves. But during a moment's pause Valera whispered into Gorik's ear: "You know why we're horsing around here?"
"Why?" asked Gorik. "Because we're showing off for Asya." Gorik said
nothing, stunned. Gorik was eleven and a half years old, while Valera
was just eleven, and he was not so very quick-witted, read much less,
but he had stated the truth. How on earth had he guessed about Asya?
Stung by another person's insight, Gorik jumped off the daybed and
yelled: "Let's go to the study!" They ran to Father's study. It was dark
there, and they turned on the light. All the adults had gathered in
Grandmother's room for some reason and were talking, having completely forgotten about the children.

The study was large, full of mysterious things. In four cabinets there
were books crowded together, thousands of books. Many of them
were quite uninteresting, in paper covers, torn and tattered, dusty—

old stuff that no one needed. But there were also very beautiful encyclopedias bound in leather, with gold backs and a great number of pictures inside from which Gorik had long since peeled off the transparent cigarette paper for various needs. On the wall there, in the space between one of the cabinets and a window, hung Father's weapons: an English carbine, a small Winchester with a polished green stock, a double-barreled Belgian hunting rifle, a saber in an antique scabbard, a plaited Cossack whip, soft and flexible, with a little tail at the tip, and a broad Chinese sword with two silk ribbons, scarlet and dark green. (Father had brought that sword from China. It had been used to chop off the heads of criminals, and in an album that Father had also brought from there, Gorik had seen a photograph of such an execution. Mornings, and sometimes in the afternoon too, Father did special Chinese exercises with the sword, waving it around, assuming poses. And once, when Aunt Dina came to visit, Gorik took it into his head to show her a rare spectacle—Father waving the sword around, and threw open the door into the study. Aunt Dina shrieked: "Oh, God!"—closed the door softly, and Father gave Gorik a painful smack on the top of his head, after saying "Idiot!") In the corner of the study stood a lance with a long bamboo shaft, a four-sided tip, and a clump of gray hair from a mane attached just a little below the tip. The lance had been given to Father in Mongolia, when he had travelled in the Gobi Desert. The lance was convenient to use for closing transoms, and sometimes Mother used it for other goals: noticing a bedbug somewhere high up on the wall, Mother would take the stick, fasten a ball of cotton soaked in water to it, and the bedbug would be caught. Gorik's mother had wonderfully sharp eyesight. The only person who had sharper eyesight was Grandmother, who practiced with a shooting club at work at the Secretariat and had even received a Voroshilov Marksman badge.

The floor of the study was carpeted with a huge Persian rug the size of the whole room. It was much more convenient to play around on the rug than on the daybed. Gorik and Valera lowered the blinds, so that no light would get into the room even from far-away windows, and held a "Japanese duel"—a duel that usually took place in complete darkness. You had to guess where your opponent was by his rustling, by his breathing. They pounced on each other several times in the darkness and after a short, fierce struggle separated, running off to different corners. Once they rushed at each other so clumsily that they banged their heads and both cried out in pain. The adults came running in and turned on the lights. Gorik had a very large "goose egg" on his forehead, and Valera had blood gushing from his nose.

A commotion arose, people started running around, yelling, giving first aid, and at the same time scolding mercilessly. Uncle Misha scolded most violently of all.

"You big good-for-nothing!" he yelled at Valera. "What were you thinking with? What part of your body? Why couldn't you just sit quietly for a while and read a book?"

"Ours is a fine one too," Mother said, jerking Gorik by the arm to make him turn his other side to her—she was tucking his shirt into his pants. "When kids come over, he always starts behaving like a lunatic. Look what you've done to your white shirt."

"Don't you two have any more interesting things to do?" Grandmother asked.

They took them into the bathroom, continuing to shower them with reproaches. Uncle Misha threatened to take Valera away to Kratovo right then and there. It was clear that the adults were stirred up about something besides the fight (and there hadn't been any fight). They were really in a rage. When all was said and done, Valera rarely came visiting, today was a holiday, and they had the right to kick up a row. Big deal! Gorik turned sullen and answered his mother in words of one syllable. She shouldn't have jerked him by the arm so hard. The more so as he was hurt. Instead of pity they had raised such a hue and cry.

When they returned to the dining room and sat down on the daybed, Uncle Misha started talking about the past. Gorik had noticed that Uncle Misha liked to recall the past when he'd drunk a little. His face would get covered with red spots, turning rough and heavy. Sweat would break out on his bald head. Uncle Misha would pace around the room with an angry look and talk, talk, talk, threatening someone with a finger. Now—specially for Valerka and Gorik—he was talking about how he and his brother, that is, Gorik's father, had lived when they were young, how they knocked about from stranger's house to stranger's house, earning their living, and so on and so forth. Of course they had a hard time of it, no one was arguing about that: after all, they lived in tsarist times. He wasn't revealing anything new. Valera even turned away pointedly and examined the spines of the books on the black bookstand next to the daybed. Gorik admired Uncle Misha, a Civil War hero who had been decorated with the Order of the Red Banner, had fought nationalist insurgents in Central Asia and still bore the rank of regimental commander, and wore a military uniform, a field shirt with a wide commander's belt. But for some reason Gorik sometimes felt sorry for him. Perhaps because he was no longer a field commander but instead worked for the USSR Society for the Support of Defense and Aerochemical Construction, and perhaps because Gorik often heard his father saying to his mother: "I really feel sorry for Misha." Uncle Misha was constantly in trouble, now at work, now at home. He would quarrel with his superiors; he would get involved in lengthy litigation, defending someone from rogues and scoundrels or, on the contrary, unmasking someone; he would quarrel with his wife, driving her out of the house, then bringing her back again; and Valera drifted from apartment to apartment.

Gorik's mother said: "Mikhail doesn't know how to get along with people. He has a difficult personality. It's amazing: two brothers, and completely different!" But Gorik thought that wasn't the point. He'd once seen Uncle Misha and his father playing chess. Uncle Misha had arrived at that time with some sort of trouble too. It seemed that a certain rogue and scoundrel had written a denunciation of him and sent it to the Society of Former Political Prisoners, and Uncle Misha had to defend himself and try to prove something, instead of just going and "punching him in the snout." And Father phoned someone about Uncle Misha and spent a long time explaining, swearing, and calling someone a fool. Then he and Uncle Misha dressed and went over to the next entrance in the apartment house to see an old friend with whom Father had been in exile. They came back two hours later and sat down to play chess. And Uncle Misha lost five games in a row to Father. He got so furious that he struck the playing board with his fist, and all the pieces went flying. "Of course I'm losing to you," he said, "because my head is occupied with other things!"

And now it seemed to Gorik that Uncle Misha's head was always occupied with other things. That was exactly why he had trouble. There was likely some trouble today too. Uncle Misha paced around, his boots squeaking, the lenses of his glasses sparkling, crimson spots glowing on his cheeks and cheekbones—not from rage, but from his having drunk a couple of glasses of vodka in the kitchen, and he spoke angrily and a lot, but it was obvious that he was thinking about something else.

"Although Nikolay and I couldn't even have dreamed about a life like yours, you good-for-nothings..."

"We don't know what kind of a life they're going to have," Father interjected, and, as it seemed to Gorik, interjected very sensibly.

"What do you mean we don't know? A wonderful life—they've been given everything," said Grandmother, putting the saucers and cups for tea around the table. On it there were two bowls with Grandmother's homemade cookies and an open box of round, shell-shaped wafer cookies with chocolate filling. These were favorite wafer cookies, and Zhenka had had already been making off with them on the sly, but as a person under investigation, Gorik was compelled to sit motionless and devour the waffles with his eyes. Zhenka had taken her fifth one. True, she had given two to Asya. "They have every right," Grandmother went on, "except for one: to do poorly at school. Zhenichka, you haven't washed your hands. Asya, Zhenichka, run to the bathroom and wash your hands."

An hour and a half later all the children except Asya, whom Gorik's mother had seen home, were put to bed in the children's room. Valera, poor boy, began snoring at once; Zhenka also fell asleep; but Gorik lay awake a long time, listening closely to the sounds and voices. He heard another uncle arrive, Mama's brother Sergey, a university student, and with him some men and women, probably students too. There were a lot of unfamiliar voices—one of the unfamiliar women's voices laughed very vibrantly and impudently; all of that noise rolled down to the far end of the hall, and from the dining room came the sound of music: someone started playing the piano and then stopped immediately. The delicate, fresh smell of cookies seeped through the door with frosted glass. Grandmother always baked the same kind of cookies, dry, brown, diamond-shaped, cut with a little round serrated cutter. Gorik felt sick at heart: he wanted some cookies. He wanted to go to the dining room, where the students were talking. He wanted to see the dog Morka, smell the snow, ski across the river to the hills, and have Asya see him flying headlong down from the highest hill, where there were two jumps.

An urgent family council had convened in Nikolay Grigorievich's study. What were they to do? Take the kids to the Snyakins' country house? Sergey had brought an alarming rumor about Ivan Varfolomeevich Snyakin, Pyotr's brother. He was allegedly missing. He had allegedly been missing for three days. "But is that for certain?" Nikolay Grigorievich asked doubtfully, "I don't think anyone's said anything in the cafeteria. I haven't heard anything." Sergey said that he had been informed by a person in the know, someone from theatrical circles. What a joke! The old political prisoner, a bomb expert, had agreed to be the director of a musical theater. And it served the fool right: you shouldn't agree to shameful offers, you shouldn't abase yourself. That was what Mikhail Grigorievich, Nikolay Grigorievich's somewhat enraged brother, who had known Ivan as far back as the Alexandrovsky Prison, thought.

From the dining room, where the young people had gathered, voices could be heard. They'd started singing a wonderful new song from a movie: "The Light Blue Globe Turns and Revolves." Grandmother sang along in half-voice.

"Seryozha, go to the dining room," said Nikolay Grigorievich.

"I'm going, I'm going. You don't need the Herzegovinas?" Since Nikolay Grigorievich had given up smoking five months earlier, Sergey took from the desk a pack of Herzegovina Flor cigarettes intended for guests and headed toward the door. He stopped for a second, made a frightful, merry face, and whispered: "Don't stay here too long, boyars, or you'll miss Motya. Motya's going to read poems that will stun you."

He was twenty-two. Mikhail Grigorievich followed him with his eyes with puzzlement: what poems? Yelizaveta Semyonovna, Gorik's mother, said that they should call Pyotr Varfolomeevich immediately, and everything would be clarified. He and his brother were very good friends.

"But of course!" said Grandmother. "In 1926 they both signed the Platform of the 148. But Petya is much more reliable. I can vouch for Petya anywhere you want."

"And Ivan Varfolomeevich's wife is always at their country house, at Uncle Petya's," said Yelizaveta Semyonovna.

She took the phone receiver off the hook, but Grandmother stopped her: "Liza, wait. What if he confirms it?"

"What do you mean 'what if'?"

"Will you take the children or not?"

"I don't know." Yelizaveta Semyonovna stood there, hesitating. "They probably won't be in any mood for that."

"Then don't call. Petya hasn't called us, and we shouldn't force ourselves on them," said Grandmother. "He would have called yesterday or even today if they were expecting us. You definitely shouldn't call!"

Nikolay Grigorievich walked over to the telephone.

"Why shouldn't we? Nonsense!" With abrupt movements of his finger he dialed the number. "Perhaps it just so happens that because..." He fell silent. All four could hear the phone ringing. "I think it's nonsense. David could have known, and I saw him in the cafeteria. No one came up to me, and that means he's at the country house, and everything is fine." He again fell silent. The phone kept ringing. Suddenly he asked, "Is that you, Varfolomeich? I was beginning to think you'd all died or been burned out, damn it. Yes, yes. We kept waiting and waiting, and now here you are. All right. Relatively, yes. What?" Nikolay Grigorievich looked at his brother, then at Grandmother, and made a movement with his lips that meant "It's bad." He continued listening to what he was being told, keeping the same expression of tightly pursed and somewhat pouting lips. Then his lips parted, he heaved a sigh, straightened up, and said in a different voice: "How about all six of us coming out, including Liza and me. The kids have their hearts set on it. How about it, shall we come? The weather is being wasted. Well, however you want. All right. Regards to everyone. But I'll drop by tomorrow."

Nikolay Grigorievich scratched the back of his head with the receiver, gave a whistle, and hung up the phone. Yelizaveta Semyonovna looked at her husband, her eyes narrowed.

"What exactly did he say?" asked Grandmother.

"He said that there had been a misunderstanding with Ivan. Nothing specific. He's already called David. David tried to find out— without any luck."

"Lord, what a misfortune! What on earth could it have been with Vanya?" asked Yelizaveta Semyonovna.

"It was something," said Grandmother. "As you know, things like this don't happen for no good reason. By the way, I never liked Ivan Snyakin. First, that whole business with changing wives. Second, his treatment of the children. After all, he refused to raise his eldest son, from his first wife, and sent him to a country boarding school. At the insistence of his present wife, the actress. We were all of us outraged at that time, including Ivan Ivanovich, Berta, and Kolya Latsis. Berta helped get him into the boarding school—after all, she's in the People's Commissariat of Education—but she was also outraged."

Nikolay Grigorievich, smiling ironically, wanted to say something, but just shook his head from side to side and left the study. Mikhail Grigorievich took off his glasses—without his glasses his face seemed unwell, tired, with bags under his eyes—and he said in a weak voice: "You're talking rot, Mother. Bourgeois little conversations instead of a real Party-minded appraisal."

The door opened softly, and Gorik's mother came in. She stood motionless in the darkness for a bit, listening intently and trying to figure out whether the children were asleep or not. Zhenya and Valerka were asleep, but Gorik was lying with his eyes open. He said in a whisper: "Mom, I'm not asleep." Mother tiptoed over and sat down on the edge of the bed. With the palm of her hand she touched Gorik's forehead, where the bump was: her hand was cold.

"Son, the day after tomorrow we're going to our place, to Silver Pines."

"Really?" Gorik said, happy. "That's great! I so much didn't want to go to that old Zvenigorod! Will you be going?"

"Of course. Both Father and I. And maybe we'll take Valerka, if Misha will let him go and if you two will give your word to behave."

"Of course we will! Sure we will! You bet we will! Hurrah! Hurrah! Hurrah! Long live our favorite, incomparable, precious Silver Pines!" Gorik exclaimed in an excited whisper. He fell asleep happy.

On the morning of the next day, December 31, when everyone was sitting at breakfast in the dining room, there suddenly came a deafening crash from Grandmother's room. It sounded as though someone had broken the balcony window. They ran there and saw that it was the mirror, not the window, that had broken. The whole parquet floor was strewn with sparkling slivers of broken glass. No one could understand how and why the thick antique mirror had fallen out of the wardrobe door, moreover, when it was locked. It was a mysterious business. The servant Maria Ivanovna said that it meant war. Gorik's father said that of course there would be a war with Hitler and Mussolini, but not soon. And Gorik thought about the fact—and this struck him—that things happened in the world that no one could explain: not even his father, the smartest person on earth, or his mother, who was also very smart and the kindest person on earth. Not a single person—no one—was ever able to explain to Gorik why the mirror fell down that morning.

IV

Igor walked from the train station to Strastnoy Boulevard, where Aunt Dina lived, without any baggage at all: he had eaten the rest of the bread and put Ehrenburg's book in his pocket. Moscow struck him with its quiet, the absence of people—there were hardly any people even on the train station square, the trolleys ran empty—and it moved him deeply and painfully in some way. It was as though he had seen a dear face, but one that had changed and had its fill of suffering during a long separation. On the square in front of the Kirov Gate subway station a few people were standing and listening to the radio over a loudspeaker set up on a lamppost. "The Germans are getting sick from Hitler's ersatz products," the announcer read in an exultant voice, "as a Dutch doctor who had practiced for a long time in one of Dresden's clinics declared in Geneva after arriving from Germany." The listeners' faces expressed a concentrated, somewhat torpid attention. Perhaps they weren't even listening, but were thinking their own thoughts. Or they were patiently waiting for something important that the announcer was supposed to say.

A light rain started falling. Igor didn't feel like taking a streetcar. He went down the boulevard, which was covered with rotting fallen leaves, and stopped at the newspaper cases, reading. The artist Nesterov had died. The District of Ryazan had completed its potato harvest. There were riots in France. The Executive Committee of the Moscow Soviet had approved the initiative of the residents of 16 Novaya Basmannaya Street and 19 Spartakovskaya Street for active participation in preparations for the winter: participation in maintenance work on the heating, roofs, and winterizing of the buildings, the delivery of fuel, its storage and use. Christopher Columbus had discovered America 450 years ago. An exhibit that had opened a few days ago at a library was devoted to this important event. And fascist monsters had driven a Byelorussian partisan woman's daughter, Tatyana, and grandson, Yura, into a cellar and tossed in grenades after them.

Familiar, enormous, the building on Strastnoy loomed black through the rainy fog. Inside, in the cubicles of courtyards, it was deserted. This chain of communicating courtyards had once been a lively place: people took a shortcut through them from Bolshaya Dmitrovka to Strastnaya Square, and in the mornings crowds of women came through here on their way to shop at the Yeliseev store, and in the opposite direction, from below, came others—to the Palashev Market. Igor turned to the right, into a blind courtyard, and went up to an entrance. It wasn't really an entrance, however, but a small, rather dirty old door, painted many times, with an iron handle. The stairway behind it was just as dirty and old. It went up in short zigzags and in its steepness reminded one of a spiral staircase. The stairway went around an empty vertical space so narrow that if someone were to take it into his head to settle accounts with life here, he would have to fly down upright, at attention. On the third floor the railing was knocked out, and the edge of the stairway hung over a precipice; Igor walked up those several steps with caution, pressing up against the wall. "Well, well! How on earth does Grandmother Vera walk here?" he thought with consternation.

He pressed the doorbell button and smiled.

This raw day, the empty courtyards, the windows crisscrossed with paper tape made him happy. This was Moscow. He had returned. He rang again and waited, continuing to smile. Then, when it dawned on him that the bell didn't work, he knocked hard. At once there was a shuffling, a fumbling with the lock. A woman's voice asked: "Who's there?"

"It's me—to see Dina Alexandrovna."

For a second he failed to recognize Aunt Dina: a thin old woman. What a yellow, sunken face! Aunt Dina had a terry cloth robe thrown over her shoulders, like boxers going out into the ring, and it bowed her down completely and made her stretch out her neck. Aunt Dina had a frightened look on her face. She exclaimed: "Oh, Gorik!" And immediately, turning around, she said very loudly and unnaturally: "Mother, Gorik has arrived! It's Go-rik!"

Grandmother Vera came out. She hadn't changed at all. She walked down the hallway, along the wall, raising her thin, nodding, childlike little face with its halo of small gray curls, and smiled from afar. After coming up to him, she hugged Igor with her light arms, bent his head down and kissed him, and he remembered that old woman's smell of chest of drawers, mustiness, and dried-up perfume. They both started in fussing around him, taking off his coat.

"I'll bring the teapot."

"Mother, don't do any fussing and bustling. You'd do better to bring a towel. Walk slowly!"

"I'm not fussing and bustling at all. That expression is so alien to me that I don't even know how you spell it: b-u-s-s-l-e or b-u-s-t-l-e."

"Grandmother Vera, you're terrific," Igor said joyfully.

He sat on a chair and pulled off his shoes, which had gotten rather worn. In Tashkent, where it sometimes didn't rain for months at a time, they had served him well, but in Moscow they had caved in during the very first hour. His feet had gotten soaked.

"Why did you walk?" Aunt Dina asked.

"I was so hungry, so homesick for Moscow! I read the posters and announcements. I know, for instance, that apprentice pharmacists are being recruited for Moscow pharmacies. And why not? If worst comes to worst? There's Khenkin's concert, at the Variety Theater—nearby, on the Malaya Dmitrovka—"

"Wait a minute, Gorik. Where's your baggage?"

He told the story. Aunt Dina's face turned pale. She sank onto a trunk and said: "I got a letter three days ago. Aunt Nyuta wrote in great detail what she was sending with you—you don't know your grandmother—point by point."

"Yes, there was a lot of stuff."

"And food too, she wrote."

"Yes," said Igor, "food too."

Aunt Dina sat on the trunk, examining the floor with a surprised look."How can that be? I don't understand," she said softly and made a helpless gestures.

"How could you be so absent-minded? How could you do that, knowing that you were coming to a hungry city?"

Igor stood before her barefoot, in an agonizing stupor. In his right hand he clenched his damp socks. Only now did he suddenly recognize the horror and irreparable cruelty of what had happened to him and what he was of course to blame for. As always, the recognition came to him later than it should have, and all the more crushingly. He was ready right then, barefoot, to rush out of the house. Grandmother Vera came shuffling into the entrance hall with a towel and stopped, not understanding why Igor had frozen in such a strange pose and Aunt Dina was sitting on the trunk.

"Dina, what's happened?" she asked. "Something to do with Nyuta?"

"No, no, nothing to do with your Nyuta," said Aunt Dina. "Go to your room, please. He's going to wash, and then we'll have tea, and I'll call you."

Grandmother Vera felt with her hand for the nail in the wall on which some receipts were stuck, hung the towel on it, and shuffled back to her room.

"Mother can hardly see," said Aunt Dina. "And recently she's begun to hear very badly. All in all, we live—I don't know how we live. We live on *a single* white-collar ration card! Can you imagine? Marinka has enrolled in foreign language courses at a military department. Getting her in was unbelievably complicated. I pulled every possible string and got her in. She was accepted, but they didn't have time to give her ration cards or anything, and she got sick. She's been sick in bed for over a month. Some sort of smoldering pneumonia. She has a temperature every day. She's there, in her room. Go in and see her later. You won't recognize her. She needs to have honey. But where can you get it? I was waiting for you so anxiously—I'll tell you in all honesty—in addition because Aunt Nyuta wrote that she was sending a jar of honey with you."

"I'll get you honey," Igor mumbled through his teeth.

"Where will you get it, my dear? You can't imagine how Moscow lives. You have to have big connections or very big money. I no longer have either. There's one thing I still can't understand: how could you allow, right before your eyes—oh, to hell with it!" She got up from the trunk abruptly. "I'll go heat up the water. You'll wash, and we'll have tea. What happened, happened. We won't get upset, right, Gorik?" She patted Igor on the cheek. It was a pat of reconciliation and forgiveness, but nonetheless it turned out to be a little harder than necessary, like a weak slap in the face. "Sit down on the chair. I'll go look for some of Boris Afanasievich's socks."

In a half an hour Igor had washed, changed into dry clothes, and was having tea in the kitchen with Aunt Dina and Grandmother Vera. Actually, they weren't drinking real tea, but rosehip tea with saccharin.

"It's good that the neighbors are gone. We can sit in the kitchen for a while," said Aunt Dina. "They put an awful couple in here with us, a year ago now. In Rozalia Viktorovna's room. Do you remember Rozalia Viktorovna?"

How could he not remember Rozalia Viktorovna? She had a low voice, dark bangs, long fingers covered with knotty joints, a way of constantly smiling with dry, colorless lips—her mouth was unpleasant, squashed, all covered with wrinkles, like a piece of paper wadded up in a fist—and a rare ability to torment people. For two winters she tormented Igor and Zhenka with music lessons, but then Mother suddenly broke off with her. She said she was dirty.

"And what happened to Rozalia Viktorovna?"

"She moved somewhere. Maybe she left Moscow altogether. I don't know exactly. She was strange, full of whims, but the ones they moved in here with us are horrible!"

Thin slices of dark bread lay on a beautiful porcelain serving board in the shape of a trowel with a short handle. Aunt Dina had always had a lot of beautiful antique china. The cups that they were drinking rosehip tea from were probably a hundred years old. Intricate monograms decorated the bottoms of them. Dina took slices of bread, with an exquisite little silver knife put an almost invisible layer of butter on them, and gave them to Igor and Grandmother Vera.

Aunt Dina was still bothered. First, giving it up as hopeless, she would say: "Well, of course! We're not going to be upset. The first person to talk about it gets a fine." And she would tell about the new neighbors, the awful couple, about her work at the music publishing house, about a colonel who was courting Marina, and suddenly, in the middle of the story, would begin smiling ironically and interrupt herself: "But what if we look at the whole business in its comic aspect? Imagine: an impractical person is walking along..." Then rage would awake in her, and she would curse the scoundrels and swine who took advantage of people's trouble. Then unexpected ideas would arise: she would suggest writing a declaration to the Ministry of Internal Affairs or to the head of the police at the Kuibyshev train station. "What difference does it make that there's a war on? They are obliged to take up the matter and start an investigation."

Grandmother Vera drank her rosehip tea and chewed her bread in silence. She probably had hardly any teeth left, and she chewed continually, helping with her gums and even with her lips. Her face contracted and expanded, like a concertina, and when it contracted, acquired an amusingly pompous expression. Grandmother Vera put her cup aside and began getting up from the table slowly, her hunched back raised.

"Dinochka," she said, "for a whole hour you've been unable to get away from those suitcases. You should be ashamed, honest to God. What difference does it make whether he brought food or not? Ten days from now we'd have eaten it up all anyway."

Aunt Dina looked at her mother aloofly.

"You're right, Mother. Of course, Mother. I'm ashamed, shamed, too ashamed for words!" She covered her face with her hands. "Ashamed that I can't talk about anything else. Ashamed that I've become so unfeeling. I'm very ashamed, but I think Gorik will forgive me. Will you, Gorik?" Her voice began shaking. "After all, I'm the only one seeing to it that everyone gets fed. I'm the only one bringing bread into the house. Do you understand, Gorik? I have to run from line to line, getting, selling—kerosene, medicine, a doctor, potatoes, the last day for the coupon for groats, trade the tobacco coupon for soap—my head spins! I don't get any sleep. And everyone cheats me, I lose everything, I don't get anything done." Aunt Dina's face was distorted by a grimace, her mouth stretched, and she began howling, continuing to speak in an absurd, bawling voice: "It's fine for you, you're an old woman! You can sit home and wait. And say: 'You should be ashamed of this, but not of that!' Do you understand? Because I have to fight! I have to try to save my daughter! And you! Not for a single second can I be ashamed, you horrid person."

At a leisurely pace, hugging the wall, and nodding her head just the slightest bit, Grandmother Vera went from the kitchen into the hall. Aunt Dina yelled after her: "How do you have the nerve? You're a wicked, wicked woman!"

Aunt Dina yelled out the last sentence especially violently and loudly, so that Grandmother Vera, who was already out of sight in the hallway, would hear. Then Aunt Dina went up to the kitchen sink, turned on the faucet, and began washing her face with cold water and blowing her nose.

Igor, who had sat at the table the whole time, got up and went into the hall. He didn't know whether he could go into the room now, and in indecision marked time in the entrance hall, pretending to look for something in the pockets of his coat. After standing around idly for a while, he sat down on the trunk. Aunt Dina didn't appear. He heard her rattling dishes in the kitchen, moving chairs. She was probably embarrassed after all of this. Now she really was ashamed. What if he put on his coat and quietly left? Igor thought about Aunt Dina with pity. He remembered her as quite different. No, it would be simplest of all to leave.

He looked at the old photographs and prints in dark frames hanging in the entrance hall. He couldn't see well without glasses, and he had to get up from the trunk so as to get closer to the pictures. He had seen them all before, but had completely forgotten them, and now they surfaced in his memory—the old man in a top hat, the woman in a fluffy white dress with such a thin waist that the woman resembled an hourglass, the poet Baratynsky, a view of the city of Parma. All these pictures belonged to a vanished time, that hot summer three years before the war, when he had stayed in Shabanovo, on a country estate turned into a museum. The country house in Silver Pines no longer existed then, and Grandmother had asked Aunt Dina to take him to her place for the summer. Zhenya had left for the Ukraine then with another female relative. Aunt Dina lived right in the composer's house on the estate, in a little room on the first floor, with windows looking out on the garden, a damp gray garden with hundred-year-old fir trees, with a linden-lined promenade that went down to the river; in the mornings an artist, a pale woman with a haughty face, stood on the lawn and painted the lilac bushes. On the canvas they were pink, although they had long since faded, and for some reason the sky was green, but Igor was afraid to ask what that meant. He wandered around the museum rooms, where the floors crackled all by themselves, where old book covers gleamed in cases behind glass. In the evenings they had tea from a samovar on the porch; there were always warmed-up white rolls and black currant jam on the table; and the composer's grandnephew, who looked very much like him, with the same little beard, told about how they lived in Paris just before the First World War. There were other people, too. They also told interesting stories. There was a musicologist, a drunkard, but the kindest soul. There was an Austrian who had fled Vienna to escape the fascists. He could balance a plate on his forehead, and he courted the woman artist with the haughty expression. And Aunt Dina played "The Seasons" on the piano. Sometimes, very rarely, Marina came by bicycle. She didn't interest Igor very much. He was twelve, and she was seventeen. She was heavy, full of herself, and there were always male admirers with her. She called Shabanovo "a hick place." Aunt Dina suffered because of her and said that she was full of "tricks." And Igor liked living at the museum-estate, sitting on the porch until late at night—except that the mosquitoes pestered him—and listening to the not very comprehensible conversations. Once he heard Aunt Dina and the composer's grandnephew arguing about something on a bench in the garden. Aunt Dina was angry, and he was trying to calm her down and suddenly yelled at Igor: "Why do you always hang around when adults are talking?" A few days passed. Igor and the musicologist had gone swimming in the river—it was then that Igor had dropped his shoes in the water when he was swimming across the river, and the musicologist saved them by diving and getting them—and as a secret, and also when he was under the influence, he told Igor that Aunt Dina had renounced her husband. "Forgive me, Yegor, but as far as I'm concerned your aunt has been beneath contempt since then," said the drunken musicologist. Igor knew that Aunt Dina didn't get along well with her husband, Marina's father. Everyone said that in her youth Aunt Dina had been very beautiful, but she got an unfortunate husband. Once Igor found Aunt Dina crying. Later she left for Moscow, came back, and again there were walks, swimming in the cold river with a clayey bank. In the evenings they again sat over tea from the samovar, ate warmed-up rolls, and Aunt Dina played "The Seasons" on the grand piano. Soon Boris Afanasievich, a very large, heavy man, wearing glasses, with a black beard and moustache, appeared. Igor was moved to the room next to the garret, and Aunt Dina became cheerful, sang songs and played chess with Boris Afanasievich. Marina stopped coming, and the musicologist created a drunken scene once, and they called the police.

"This is what Gorik looks like now? Oho! Fantastic!" Igor saw a pale, red-haired girl with a big nose standing in the doorway of the entrance hall. The girl was wearing a tasseled robe. She held her arms crossed on her chest, hugging her thin shoulders with her hands, as though she were shivering. "I would never have recognized you."

"Nor I you..." He stopped short, having sensed that he was saying something wrong, but he concluded gamely: "I surely wouldn't have recognized you!"

"I've changed so horribly?"

"No, but you—you're ill."

"Yes, yes. I'm ill. I completely forgot that I was sick. But why was Mother yelling so at poor Grandmother?"

Igor shrugged his shoulders.

"Maybe because of the funny thing that happened to your baggage? Grandmother told me. Lord, what a brilliant story! You're a genius, Gorik. Oh, still and all, it's such a pity that you didn't manage to be late for the train."

Aunt Dina came out of the kitchen carrying something on a tray covered with a towel.

"Why did you get out of bed?" she asked her daughter. "I'm bringing you something to drink and your medicine."

"But why were you yelling? I thought it was robbers, an air raid warning, or that Bochkin had come back. You woke me up. I was asleep!"

She spoke the last sentence with provocative defiance and walked past her Mother and Igor into the bathroom, haughtily raising her large nose and fluffing out her red hair with a movement of her head. The wave of her smell—medicine and a naked body—passed by behind her. Igor sensed that there was tension between mother and daughter and that he had for some reason increased the tension.

Looking at him with a slight smile, Aunt Dina said: "What non-sense, huh? I have some suitcases on my mind, while the Germans are at the Volga, Leningrad is surrounded. Do you remember Slavsky? He lived at Shabanovo one summer when you were there. A musicologist from Leningrad, a wonderful person. He got caught in artillery fire in August and was killed. Come here, and I'll show you where you'll be sleeping. There hasn't been any news from Boris Afanasievich in four-teen months."

Marina could be heard yelling from the bathroom: "Make up his bed on the couch in my room. We'll talk."

"Don't be ridiculous!" Aunt Dina made an irritated dismissive ges-ture with her hand. "He's a working person, and you're a lazybones. He'll be getting up at six in the morning. Let's go, Gorik."

A hallway, crammed with plywood boxes, bags, jars, a trough, and crates, led from the entrance hall. That junk hadn't been there before. Apparently it had been brought by the mysterious Bochkins, who had taken Rozalia Viktorovna's room. That room was at the far end of the hall, and a large padlock shone black on its whitewashed door. Down the hall to the right were two doors. Igor followed Aunt Dina through the first. He saw the room and remembered that right under the win-dow the iron slope of the roof should be visible, but now the window was covered over with dark blackout paper. Grandmother was sitting at the table and, holding a magnifying glass close to her eye, reading a book.

Dreariest of all is the first hour in the morning, from eight to nine. Outside it's still as dark as night. In the shop the lights burn, or, rather, glimmer: two barely alive bulbs swing on long wires over the draw-bench. There's a third by the forging furnace, but it's usually bright there even as it is because of the burning hearth. And one more bulb barely gleams through the smoked glass of the partition, further over, in the distance, above the fitter's bench. For such a huge place as a blanking shop it's too little light, of course, but where can more be gotten? And then—they're used to it. It's only the cold in the morn-ings. You can't get used to the cold. The severe prewinter wind freezes feet and blows incessantly through the wide-open gate; in the morning pipes are delivered. Two women loaders and an old fellow, an unskilled worker nicknamed Uryuk, lug the pipes, clutching them to their sides with their elbows six at a time, first over the cement floor, then over the concrete floor, and the pipes first rattle, then clatter, then fall with a thud onto a pile near near the annealing furnace.

But neither the rattling and thudding of the pipes nor the cold that roams through the shop—the gate remains open for a long time because the women loaders and Uryuk don't especially hurry—can make Igor really wake up. His thoughts work clearly, though slowly, while his body is limp, paralyzed. His motions bog down in semidrowsiness.

Igor goes back and forth on the gangway beside the pipe draw-bench and pushes a cart with steel teeth along the rails, holding it by the handle. With those teeth the cart seizes the tip of an iron pipe that has been shoved into a matrix with a rectangular opening and stretches the pipe, which has already become square, and is no longer a pipe, but a section, down the length of the bench. The job is simple: you have to walk back and forth. You go up to the matrix, pull the handle up, grab it with the teeth, and pull it along. When you get to the end of the gangway, and again pull the handle up, the teeth unclench, the section falls out, and you toss it to the side. And so on all day long, with a break for lunch from twelve to half past one. Igor's partner, Kolka, drags the pipes from the furnace to the bench and and carries away the ready sections, while the worker Nastya shoves pipes into the matrix and smears the tips with an oily compound to reduce the friction.

Igor has been here twelve days now, in the "blanker," and he likes it here. But in the beginning he worked his tail off as rigger, that is, simply as a loader—that had been the decision in the personnel department. Reading his reference from the Tashkent factory, where it said that I. N. Bayukov was a third-class machine-tool operator-puncher, Major Oganov either laughed or got angry—you couldn't tell which, and made his dark eyes big and round: "What kind of a profession is that? Where from? Punchers and tinsmiths! Shitsmiths, damn you! This is a military factory, not a stall at a bazaar. Oh, the crooks, the swindlers, they've recruited a bunch of crap! And of course you're down as a machine-tool operator, qualified labor. You'll be a rigger in the transport shop; you look like a strong guy. Push and shove there for a while, punch for a while, if you're such a puncher." And for a week he "punched" crates, unloaded trucks, sent shipments off to train stations, other factories, and the riverport. Then a person was needed for a drawbench in the blanking shop, and none of the loaders wanted it; they had all bunched together there, formed a gang, five women, two men, and two young guys Igor's age. They liked the loading work because there were sometimes hours of idleness when you could sit around and smoke, while you couldn't sit around in the "blanker." Igor was in fact chucked out—the new guy should clear out, they felt. And so Igor went from being a puncher to being a drawer.

This is how he was defined: "pipe drawbench machine-tool operator, fourth class." On the very first day he'd been processed as a new employee at the factory he was given a ration card for 700 grams of bread, a grocery ration card, and in addition a new quilted jacket, a very good one, for sixty rubles. They'd also promised to issue him shoes, but not any earlier than the November Holidays. What's good about working at the drawbench? There's no running around. You walk and think your own thoughts, back and forth, pull here, pull there. You pull with your right hand, and in your left one you have a home-rolled cigarette made of shag tobacco—Igor had started smoking as far back as in Tashkent, he'd learned at the pig iron foundry—and when your right hand goes numb, you turn sideways and pull with the left. And you just keep on walking sideways.

At the beginning Kolka had greeted Igor spitefully, never calling him anything but Squint-Eyed or Four Eyes (Aunt Dina found Boris Afanasievich's glasses for Igor. True, they were a little weak, minus three, while he needed minus five), screaming songs in Igor's face such as "I Don't Wear Horned-Toad Glasses the Better to See"—and in the cafeteria he once snatched Igor's ration of bread up off the table and started chewing it calmly, looking at Igor with a smile, as if to say "What are you going to do?" Igor hadn't said anything before, couldn't have given a damn about him, but at that point he suddenly grew furious. He grabbed Kolka by the chest and gave him such a silent shaking that when he let him go, Kolka fell to his knees from fright. And from that point on that was it. No more insolence, no more "Four Eyes."

Kolka is short, absolutely a little kid in appearance, a bowlegged pipsqueak—Igor could deal with him with one hand. But he's not so young: seventeen and a half. In the spring Kolka goes into the army. Having stopped teasing Igor about his glasses, he now torments him with stories—he lies like a rug, of course—about the girls and women he has allegedly conquered. He tells his stories vulgarly, like a hooligan, in Nastya's presence, but she doesn't care—she thinks about her own things and doesn't hear him. Igor, however, is bothered, without showing it. The main thing that's intolerable is that it's in Nastya's presence. She's thirteen or so, homely, sallow, always wrapped up in a gray scarf, always silent, won't smile, and the very feminine meekness and submissiveness, which Kolka jeers at, are just as intolerable to Igor as Kolka's vulgarity.

But Igor lacks the courage to put the lid on Kolka and stand up for the quiet and meek Nastya. He's somehow ashamed to, as though he wouldn't be a man then.

There are two foremen in the "blanker"—Kolesnikov and Chuma. Kolesnikov speaks tonelessly and moves slowly. His face is wan, colorless. He's sick, he coughs. Sometimes he hacks and hacks for hours, unable to get out a word. While Chuma won't stay in one spot for a moment—that's the reason for his nickname—he runs around all day yelling, worrying, instructing, urging on, swearing, and himself slaving away like the devil. He even looks like a devil—undersized, stooped, with long arms, a large, dark face whose skin has absorbed soot and oily fumes permanently, the face of an old monkey, with gimlet eyes hidden deep under a narrow, peaked forehead. Igor thinks that Quasimodo could have looked that way.

"What are you doing there drying your pants? Let's get to work!" Chuma yells.

He always yells. True, in the shop the noise is incessant, the drawing machine whines, the pneumatic hammer blasts away, but Kolesnikov will always be sure to come up close to you and say what he needs to, while Chuma doesn't have any patience—he yells from far away, waving his arms. And even if he does sometimes come running up, he still yells.

The foremen give orders to the drawers and metal workers who file the matrixes on the other side of the partition as well as to the loaders and smiths who work at the forging furnace and the pneumatic hammer finishing the tips of the pipes. And Chuma doesn't just scream, urge on, and order, but sometimes joins in himself: now with a sledgehammer, now stooping over the joiner's bench with the metal workers, now, enraged by the loaders' slowness, grabbing an armful of pipes and dragging them to the forging furnace. He's old, going on fifty or perhaps even more, but he has a lot of strength—you wouldn't even believe how much. A grinder was recently brought for the metal workers and improperly installed. Chuma went into a rage, swore up a storm, and in a fit of temper gave it such a tug that he tore it right out of the floor, like a turnip out of a bed. And the grinder weighed about a hundred kilograms.

No one knows exactly what Chuma's name is. His first name and last name are difficult ones, Jewish. Everyone is used to Chuma. The shop manager, Avdeychik, once let slip seriously: "Comrade Chuma, please..."

"Bayukov, come over here right now!" Chuma shouts from far off. "Kolya, get behind the cart!"

Igor hauls the section the rest of the way—pulls the handle—and the tip of the pipe, bursting free from the steel jaw, jumps up as though it were alive. Wearing mittens, Igor uses both hands to lift the long, heavy, swaying section—you can't lift it from the end with just one hand—and tosses it across the bench, where there is a pile of about fifty metal sections gleaming with oil. Sometimes, while watching a new, neat, cut section make its way out of the matrix's rectangle slowly, with difficulty, with a squeal even, Igor experiences an almost physical feeling of pleasure: a thing has been created, the world has been enriched by a new thing, made with his help, with his hands. Here's what's good about this job: you see a thing being made; you don't just lug things around and load them. The sections are used for the frames of airplane radiators. They are assembled in shop No. 5, and then they're transported not very far, just across the road, to factory No. such-and-such—Igor knew the number, and the whole neighborhood knew it—and there military airplanes are assembled completely, from start to finish. And very soon, a few days, perhaps, after Igor has stretched out the section, an airplane with a radiator containing that section, curved, soldered, and properly painted, is flying off to bomb the Germans.

Hurriedly wiping his hands with cotton rags—although he works in mittens, his palms always manage in some incomprehensible way to get dirty—Igor goes over to Chuma.

"Run up and see Avdeychik. On the second floor."

"Why?" Igor asks.

"Hurry up and get going. Hey, woman, why are you smearing so much on there, huh?" Chuma suddenly yells at Nastya. With his gimlet eyes he can see from far away and in any kind of dark and dusk, like a cat. "How do you spread butter at home? Are you careful with it? Well, answer me. I get 500 grams for the month, and I spread it on like this..."

Igor walks past the pounding pneumatic hammer, past the forging furnace, through the gate into the next shop, and goes up an iron spiral staircase. Why is he needed? In all the time Igor has been there he has spoken to the shop manager twice: the first time when he came to be processed, and the second when Avdeychik came running into the shop for a moment and asked something about the matrixes. The drawers are the dregs of the "blanker." Calling in a drawer to see the manager is as absurd as calling in the loader Pashka or Uryuk. But he's being called in for something! A sudden alarm seizes Igor. Only one explanation is comprehensible to him: something to do with his background—they've uncovered it, found out. Major Oganov has chosen not to talk to him himself, but has ordered Avdeychik to. They can fire him at once. They can do worse: for concealment of the fact with the aim of penetrating a military objective. A strange indifference comes over him instead of alarm. He walks leisurely over the second floor's planked gangway, slapping the iron handrail, thinking calmly: "But what's the big deal? I wrote the truth. Died in such-and-such a year. After all, I was told officially that he died of pneumonia. Mother is working in Kazakhstan in her profession. She's a livestock specialist. She works as a livestock specialist at a state farm. What's the big deal?" He hadn't consulted with anyone, either with Aunt Dina or with Marina—he'd decided by himself. He had consulted once—that was enough. In Tashkent in the spring, after he'd graduated from high school, a few guys were invited to apply to a special military school— including him, although he was younger than the others, sixteen. The school was considered a closed one. It trained some sort of wily radio operators, and the biographical part of the application ran to three pages. That was the first one in his life. Grandmother said: "Write the facts as they are. You should always write and speak the truth, and then there's nothing to fear." He wasn't accepted. Grandmother said: "From their point of view they're right." In August a recruiter came to recruit teenagers and young people for Moscow factories. There was a biographical part of the application there too, but a short one, just one page. He didn't write anything. He had to conceal that from Grandmother. She asked him: "Did you write the truth?" There hadn't even been that kind of a question on that sheet, so that it could be said that he'd written the truth. And—he went. And in addition, with a profound, mysterious, and even alien intelligence—one for that reason probably genuine—he realized that the truth that one was required to write was not the truth. And therefore the deception was not a real deception. It was only the deceit of a deception. No one is as yet aware of that, and perhaps will not be for a long time yet, and he himself is not completely aware of it, but he has sensed that the truth here is not a simple one, but a twofold, secret one.

He has calmed down and resigned himself as he walks the long way, but when he knocks—"May I come in?"—at the manager's plywood coop and sees Avdeychik at his desk, yellow-haired, with a red, dry face that for some reason seems to Igor like a *rooster's*, he feels depressed.

"Bayukov, they say you know how to paint slogans. Is that true or not? Speak up."

"Where did you get that idea from?"

"I'm asking you the questions, not the other way around. Did you go to an art school?"

"Well, yes."

"Go to the shop committee office, get some red calico, and after work paint a slogan quickly and nicely. Here."

Avdeychik hands him a note with the text. Igor reads it with a dull joy, hardly understanding the sense of it: "Workers, engineers, and technicians at aviation factories! Increase the output of fighting machines! Give more fighters, attack planes, and bombers for the Red Army!"

Igor gets home toward midnight. He has supper in his room, because the Bochkins are doing laundry in the kitchen. Aunt brings a bowl of scaldingly hot potato soup from the kitchen. Igor greedily eats the soup with some bread and drinks coffee. Neither Marina nor Grandmother Vera is asleep. They've all been worried because Igor was gone for so long. He usually comes home by nine. The women wouldn't mind some soup, too. Although watery, it's hot. They had their portions in the afternoon, however. Besides, it's essential for them "to keep their figure and not get carried away with soup." But Igor needs to eat a lot, he's a man. And the women drink coffee, a substitute, of course, without chicory, smelling like a sodden pine board, but very hot and with saccharin. It's much better to drink that kind of coffee, Aunt Dina says. It doesn't give you insomnia, but on the contrary, makes you sleepy.

And really, as soon as Igor has his fill of the coffee-and-soup slop and his stomach experiences a false, stupefying, and pleasant feeling of *being stuffed*, he immediately gets sleepy, can't keep his eyes open, yawns, and replies to the women's questions listlessly and in words of one syllable. Aunt Dina nonetheless gradually manages to get the story of the slogan out of Igor: how Avdeychik called him in, how Igor was surprised but didn't show it, how he sweated for three hours after work, did everything the way it's supposed to be done, stretched the huge canvas, used a string rubbed with chalk to make lines, marked off columns and marked out spaces, wrote out the slogan very beautifully, and suddenly, when he had finished, when he had already added the last exclamation point, he discovered, damn it, that he had made a mistake in the word "fighters." The result was "Increase the output of fightees, attack planes, and bombers for the Red Army!" Disgusting. And why had it turned out that way? Igor really had tried so hard, knowing himself, knowing that at school, when drawing slogans and headlines for wall newspapers, he always got something mixed up, dropped letters. Today he had exerted himself and concentrated harder than ever. He wanted to do a good job. The slogan is to hang over the gate in the shop, and when going to the matrix with his cart, Igor will keep seeing it and reading it. What could he do? Laundering the red calico, drying it, and ironing it would be a lot of trouble. He could have crossed out the "e" and written in the letter "r" neatly above it, of course, the way it's done in school notebooks, but that would have looked awful. While he was racking his brains in a panic Avdeychik came, gave it a cursory look, praised it, and ordered it to be hung up right away. Igor didn't tell him anything. It's hanging there just like that, with the "fightees." No one has noticed yet, though, true. Igor went home at once. There are two kinds of air combat planes: fighters, which attack, and fightees, which get attacked. He wondered what people would say to him tomorrow. And if nothing was said, should he confess himself or just let it stay up?

A discussion begins. Everyone is excited. They've forgotten about sleep and are in a rush to state their point of view regarding the treacherous problem that has suddenly arisen. Igor is also stirred up and his sleepiness has disappeared, just as has the feeling of *being stuffed*, by the way—putting away some more soup and bread wouldn't be a bad idea. The problem is that no matter what you say, there is a political subtext here. There could be trouble. Grandmother Vera thinks that he should make a clean breast of it tomorrow and redo the slogan. Why play with fire? An open-hearted confession. (All grandmothers are heart and soul for confessions. You might imagine that they have already confessed to everything they've done over the course of their long lives.) Aunt Dina clenches her hands nervously: "Lord, Lord, what a numbskull you are, Gorik!"

She thinks it would be stupid to confess—why didn't he confess right away?—but that he should make a new slogan at home—she'll undertake to get some red calico—and replace it without anyone's noticing. In Marina's opinion, however, there's no need to be in a dither. Let it go on hanging there the way it is—nobody reads those slogans.

"I'll bet you a thousand rubles that it hangs there untouched until the end of the war!"

"Marina, how can you?!" Aunt Dina is outraged not by her daughter's suggestion, but by her shortsightedness and frivolousness.

Igor finally agrees with Aunt Dina's crafty plan to draw a new slogan and substitute it without anyone's seeing. Aunt Dina suggests doing it on Sunday at a friend's. This friend of hers lives in Gnezdikovskoe, in Nierensee's former home. The halls are large there, and you can spread out a piece of calico of any length.

"All right," says Igor. "But I'm surprised by one thing. How did he find out that I had gone to art school?"

"Gorik, you'll scold me, but that's probably my fault," Aunt Dina says with a somewhat solemn and timid smile. And she sits up straight with a look of readiness to accept any reproach and blow at all.

"How so?"

"Gorik, I couldn't bear your stories. I worried myself sick, didn't sleep for two nights. In her only letter to me Liza wrote: 'Take care to see that Gorik's talents aren't wasted.' And there is Gorik *drawing* pipes, coming home filthy, covered with black oil, twelve-hour shifts."

"Well, all right, all right. What next?"

"Next I started to think. I thought painfully hard, going over what people I had. And I found somebody from the Central Board—he's my good friend Fanya Gromova's brother."

"Dina Alexandrovna in her favorite repertoire," Marina says mockingly.

"His last name's Gromov. Have you by any chance heard of him?"

"No."

"I asked Fanya, and she introduced me to him. I told him everything. He was very kind."

"What do you mean you told him *everything?*"

"I told him that you were my nephew, a gifted artist."

"I'm no artist, damn it!" Igor exclaims in a rage. "I studied for a year at a visual arts studio in a Pioneer Palace. Big deal! Why did you do

that? Who asked you to? I don't need it at all, damn it, and I don't
want it, I don't!"

"Forgive me, Gorik, but I was only thinking about your good."

"You shouldn't have, Dina. Oh, you shouldn't have!" Grandmother
Vera whispers.

"Mother always thinks about what's good, but the result is zilch,"
says Marina. "It's a typical little story."

"Well, and what about Gromov? Who is he, in the first place?"

"He's from the Central Board, Gorik, an important administrator, in
transportation. He manages transportation, so all factories are depen-
dent upon him. Do you understand? He promised to talk to someone
at your factory, and that person apparently talked to the shop manager."

"And poor Igor was stuck with making posters for three hours after
work. Ha-ha!" Marina laughs. "While we worry here and don't know
what's going on. It turns out that Dina Alexandrovna is to blame for
everything."

Aunt Dina hits the table with the palm of her hand.

"Stop making fun of your mother, you hear?" she cries, her voice
cracking. "Good-for-nothing!" Aunt Dina's face goes pale. "You're always making fun of your mother."

"Me?"

"Yes, you! You make fun of me absolutely openly, impudently, taking advantage of the fact that..."

"I'll be quiet! That's it! Forgive me, Dina Alexandrovna. You're always right. I forgot."

Marina goes to her room. On her way, with a grin, she gives Igor a
pat on the back of his neck. Through the wall she can be heard having
a coughing fit there. Igor, depressed by everything he has just learned,
silently turns down his bedding. He sleeps on the bed by the window,
where Grandmother Vera used to sleep, while Grandmother Vera
sleeps on the couch in Marina's room. After hastily washing up, Igor
flops down on the bed, turns onto his side, bends his knees, and pulls
the bedding up over his head. But conversations, even though they're
quiet, continue in the main room. Igor has noticed that in Aunt Dina's
family people like to talk late at night. Marina appears again, and she

and her mother whisper, sometimes quite softly, and sometimes rather loudly, so that Igor can hear them.

"No, Manya, that's not the reason."

"But why do you think that you're always right about everything? Why not for the sake of variety..."

"Because I wish you all well, you idiots!"

"Mother, just remember: you wrote letters to the Ministry of Higher Education, and how that turned out."

"If it hadn't been for your trouble!"

"Of course, when the director calls you in."

"Why didn't you tell him the same thing you did me?" "My God, I couldn't. How can you not understand?"

Then Grandmother Vera's raspy whisper: "Cut it out! Let him get some sleep.

"He's asleep. He dreams of a winter road that he and his father are walking down on an early January evening. To the right of the road are fences, to the left a grassy plot under snow, all marked up with furrows made by ski tracks, but in the twilight you can't see the ski tracks, and the plot seems virgin white. In the middle of it stands an oak. Further on a thicket of willows stands dimly black on the bank of a marsh rendered invisible by the snow. Still further on, a dark strip of forest sways, and there, in its depths, almost indistinguishable in the dark, seems to be someone's country house with a lonely lighted window. Their felt boots squeak on the hard packed-down road. The sky is clear and green. The smell of the smoking tobacco from Father's pipe carries in the frosty air. "We'll get to the ravine in a moment and do some shooting," Father says, squeezing Igor's hand with his own. And suddenly Igor is walking on alone, and Father is gone. Someone's tall figure looms out ahead on the road. It stands motionless, nearly blending with the darkness of the fence. It seems to Igor that the mysterious person is waiting for him, and a shivery alarm takes hold of Igor, now no longer alarm, but a terror, growing by the second, of the dark figure waiting for him. Igor is completely alone in the deserted clearing, and he has to walk on ahead, but his feet won't obey him, he can't take a single step. He becomes rooted to the spot on the petrified snowy road. The figure standing by the fence suddenly turns out to be next to him, and he sees that it's a woman, a very tall, large woman, wearing a coat that reaches her heels, a coat somewhat reminiscent of an army greatcoat, with a collar made of gray astrakhan, buttoned up tightly under the chin, a figure wearing a gray cap made of that same astrakhan, a cap resembling a short officer's cap, and the woman's face is round, full, and crimson-rosy because of her having been standing out in the cold so long and waiting for him. The woman looks at Igor with her slits of eyes and smiles, and on her face he can clearly see a small, black, turned-up moustache and a black little beard. And his heart stops. It's the woman of his nightmares. She has appeared to him several times already and looked at him the same way, smiling from under a moustache turned up in two black ringlets.

V

It was a Pushkin winter. Everything was imbued with his poetry: the snow, the sky, the frozen river, the garden in front of the school, with the naked black trees and the crows walking around in the snow, and the very old building where a prerevolutionary high school had been located, where there were dark elbow-shaped stairways on which silent fist fights took place, where there were rooms with waxed parquet floors and where on the main staircase the stone steps, yellowish like old ivory, were bowed in the middle, as in a cathedral, worn down by boys running up and down them since time almost immemorial.

Something by Pushkin came over the loudspeaker every day, both in the morning and in the evening. In the newspapers, right beside caricatures of Franco and Hitler, photographs of decorated writers, and Georgian dancers who had come to Moscow for the Festival of Georgian Art, next to the wrathful headlines "No Mercy for Traitors!" and "Wipe Betrayers and Murderers Off the Face of the Earth!" were portraits of a gentle youth in curls and of a gentleman in top hat, sitting on a bench or walking along the Moyka. "Frost and sunshine, what a day!" Gorik declaimed in the mornings. "Yet still you slumber, charming friend..." and he would throw a pillow at Zhenya, who liked to sleep late. "It's time, my beauty..." Gorik would pronounce the word "beauty" with a horrible grimace, practically gnashing his teeth, so that it was obvious that any beauty was out of the question.

Evenings Gorik compiled an album: a gift to the school literature society and an item for the Pushkin exhibition (with the fervent hope of receiving a first prize for it). In a large sketchbook he printed famous poems in India ink and pasted portraits, pictures, and illustrations cut out of magazines, newspapers, and even, on the sly from his mother, several books. For instance: "I have erected to myself a monument not of human making"—and right there was pasted a picture depicting the Pushkin Monument on Tverskoy Boulevard. Gorik had cut it out of the newspaper *For Industrialization*, which his father subscribed to. Unfortunately, all the pictures cut out of newspapers had turned yellow from the paste that soaked through.

Gorik's mother was no less keen on the album than was her son. Yelizaveta Semyonovna loved poetry (especially Mayakovsky's satires, and also poems by Vera Inber, Sasha Chorny, and Agnivtsev, many of which she knew by heart) and herself often took pleasure in writing long, humorous poems that her fellow employees at the People's Commissariat of Agriculture liked and that were posted on the bulletin board.

"The Bayukov Family Prepares for the Pushkin Centenary!"— Yelizaveta Semyonovna proposed that slogan in January, when they were staying at the country house during vacation. Who could memorize the most lines from *Eugene Onegin*? Except for Nikolay Grigorievich, who rarely came to the country house and couldn't remember poetry at all well—he knew only one poem by heart: he had come across it somewhere in exile, and it was about Sakya-Muni: "Through the mountains, mid the gorges, where there raged a mighty storm..."—everyone competed, including Grandmother, Sergey, and Sergey's girlfriend, Valya, who was staying at the country house. From morning to night they repeated verses over and over. Toward the end of the vacation the winner was determined to be Gorik; in second place was Yelizaveta Semyonovna, then Zhenya, Sergey, his girlfriend Valya; and bringing up the rear was Grandmother, who had managed to get only as far as "From her *Monsieur* took on the child; the boy was likable but wild."

Gorik received the prize from his mother: a package of stamps from French colonies. True, he had crammed like crazy. Sometimes in the middle of the night he had awakened in fright: he had forgotten a line! And he would lie in the darkness, agonizing, unable to fall asleep until he remembered. Mainly, he had wanted to win over that braggart Sergey and show his girlfriend Valya that Sergunya wasn't at all as smart as he seemed. Big deal—a university student, smokes cigarettes, and yells "Pipe down!" and "None of your damn business!"

The joy was tempered by the fact that Sergunya was beaten not just by Gorik, but by Mother too, and even by Zhenka. Sergunya's Valya said that she had read somewhere that memory developed at the expense of intelligence. Well, they were just making excuses and trying to sugar their own pill, and Mother pointed out to them quite sensibly that Lenin had possessed a superb memory.

A person who had memorized 320 lines of verse in ten days had to win a school contest. And receive the first prize: a bronze bust of Pushkin. Yelizaveta Semyonovna firmly believed that was just what would happen, although she didn't convey her certainty to Gorik with so much as a single word or look. That was something that went without saying, and Yelizaveta Semyonovna was not given pause even by the fact that Gorik was in the fifth grade, while all grades, up to the tenth, would be participating in the contest. Yelizaveta Semyonovna was distinguished by an optimism and a sincere belief that her family was the best family in the world, and that her children, by virtue of their abilities, upbringing, and the moral fiber instilled in them, were superior to any other children, known or unknown.

When, at the special evening, Gorik heard that the first prize had gone to a boy from the eighth grade for a plasticine statuette entitled "Young Comrade Stalin Reading Pushkin," the second prize had been awarded to a girl who had used silver threads to embroider a pillow cover with a picture inspired by "The Tale of Tsar Saltan," and the third prize had been taken by Lyonya Karas—a fine friend, he had worked on the sly, concealing it from everybody!—for a portrait in colored pencil of Pushkin's friend Kyukhelbeker (true, it has to be said that the portrait was great, the very best at the exhibit), Gorik, stupefied and stung in his heart, nonetheless thought at the very first second about his mother. It was going to be such a blow for her! He decided not to give her the bad news right away, but first to prepare her a bit.

After all, Mother had so hoped that their album—yes, yes, *their* album: she had invested so much time and energy in it, bringing magazines, seeking out everywhere the least little thing connected to Pushkin—she hoped it would take at least some prize, but it hadn't taken any and looked a little sad next to the magnificent junk, sculptures, carvings, embroidery, and wood burnings, which taken all together produced in Gorik a sharp feeling of envy, like a pain in the stomach. One boy had done a devilishly wonderful head (the one that Ruslan met), just like a real one, life-size. It had frozen at the instant just before a sneeze, the mouth open slightly and the brow wrinkled. The helmet was made from a Red Cavalry helmet covered with gold paper. The beard and moustache were real, made from black poodle hair. Everyone was delighted by the head. But the boy who had made it didn't receive any prize because he'd suddenly moved out of his building and was no longer attending school. The head was removed from the exhibit on the second day and thrown out somewhere.

Gorik couldn't stand to look at his little album, which had been stuck in an out-of-the-way spot, in the corner of the room. There were probably dirty spots in it, erased ink blots, the paste protruding from under pictures in a few places, and the most unpleasant thing—on the second page, in the title, printed in watercolor, the letter "i" turned out to have been omitted. Instead of "materials" it said "materals." He wanted to forget all of that. In the evening, hanging out in the courtyard, Gorik tried to think up the best way to prepare his mother for the disagreeable news. Lyonya Karas, who was hanging out with him, couldn't understand what was troubling his friend. Around eight in the evening the temperature turned freezing and a snowstorm started. In the rear courtyard—the so-called "stinkhole"—when Gorik and Lyonya were already ready to go home, some kids from Building 4 came up to them to make trouble. Building 4 was a two-story little apartment house on the embankment where there lived hordes of boys who had been at war with the boys from the big building for eons. No one could understand why the boys from Building 4 were nicknamed "rotten meat."

The "rotten meat" were wary of coming into the big building's huge courtyards, where there were often many adults: drivers walking around by their cars while waiting for officials, concierges coming out from their entrances to breathe some fresh air and stretch their legs, and policemen wandering in from the street. On the embankment, however, by the movie house, under the bridge, "the rotten meat," who always went around in a gang, had their own way. They were led by Kostya Chepets, a ferocious guy always spoiling for a fight. It was said that he carried a lead-filled piece of pipe in his mitten.

A short boy whom Gorik didn't know suddenly materialized before him out of the blizzard and asked clearly and distinctly, "How'd you like a knuckle sandwich?"

Gorik knew that expression, which had become popular in the last few days. Stunned by the nerve of the puny-looking boy, Gorik said threateningly, "Just fine!"

The boy stuck out his arm with his hand made into a fist, and right then someone shoved Gorik in the back with such force that his whole body swayed and his face struck the boy's fist. Behind, smirking, stood Chepets.

"Why'd you do that?"

"You asked for it yourself!"

"Me?"

"Yeah, you!"

Gorik's knees were buckling from fear, but he took a step toward the sinister figure of Chepets, rocklike, nearly square in its black sheepskin coat, and took a swipe. From somewhere—he couldn't tell where—like a bolt of lightning, a blow to the chin knocked Gorik flat on his back. When he got up, with a spinning, foggy head, he saw that Lyonya was fighting with three or four of the "rotten meat," his coat ripped, his cap knocked off. And suddenly the "rotten meat" disappeared in an instant, like a flock of sparrows, and Lyonya was lying in the snow. Gorik ran up to him.

Lyonya got up by himself, holding his hand to his nose.

"I'm missing a toof," he said and spat dark saliva.

They found his cap. Lyonya applied snow to his nose and his eye, but the blood didn't stop. Lyonya swayed unexpectedly and again collapsed on the snow. His head was thrown back. Gorik had once seen Lyonya on the classroom floor having a fit during a break. He was held by his legs and head. His face grew unrecognizably terrifying, crimson, and one cheek twitched. His eyes started rolling and with almost sunken eyeballs looked in opposite directions. All the girls ran out with shrieks at that point, while the boys stayed and watched. In a few minutes Lyonya stopped twitching. They got him up and took him off to the teachers' room. He lay down for a while there, got his breath back, and came back in time for the geography lesson. Later the kids asked him whether he remembered anything, and he said that he couldn't remember anything, only that it was as if there were red horses in front of his eyes: they came flying in from somewhere and hid everything from view—there was nothing but red. And that redness also came over Lyonya during fights: he would *fly into a rage*. The kids knew that, were afraid of him, and even the older ones were wary of touching him. Chepets probably hadn't been able to see in the dark that he had run up against Lyonya, and that was they they had taken off so quickly.

Gorik was afraid that a fit was about to start now, but Lyonya sat for a while in the snow, his head thrown back, his eyes closed, and then extended his hand to Gorik, who raised him and stood beside him, so that Lyonya could put an arm around his shoulder.

"Son of a bitch Chepets. Hit me in the bread basket," Lyonya said through chattering teeth. "Well, I'll fix him."

They couldn't go to Lyonya's, where they'd frighten Lina Arkadievna, so they decided to go to Gorik's. Standing on the landing in front of the open door, Gorik spat it all out: about the fight, about Lyonya's not being able to go home, about Lyonya's third prize, and about his own nothing.

Yelizaveta Semyonovna was so shaken upon seeing Lyonya all bloodied that she seemed not to understand anything and didn't even ask about the contest. But a little bit later she suddenly asked Gorik in a whisper, "Really nothing? Absolutely nothing?"

Lyonya really had had a tooth knocked out. True, the tooth had been loose even before. When leaving, Lyonya told Gorik that he'd decided to take an ironclad oath. He would reveal what it was the next day, after the second class. Gorik had long since noticed that Lyonya Karas was always full of private fantasies entailing oaths and secrets, but he couldn't get used to Lyonya's inexhaustible sense of mystery. It caused him pain. And it made him love his friend jealously and devotedly—his mysterious friend, like Count Cagliostro. Gorik spent the whole evening and part of the night agonizing, trying to guess what oath Lyonya had come up with.

At supper Sergey, a very sarcastic person, joked long and disgustingly about the failure with the album.

"So, you say they more or less scrapped your scrapbook? Is that how it turned out?"

"You couldn't do one even half as good as that one."

"That's another question. You have the patience of a horse. I don't."

"Se-ryo-zha!" Yelizaveta Semyonovna struck the table softly with a finger and gave the brother a wide-eyed look of rebuke. Sergey winked at her in reply. She shook her head ever so slightly. Without paying any attention, he went on: "And I want you to know that I never aimed for prizes, decorations, buns, and honey cakes. Awards only ruin a true artist. You should know that Vereshchagin refused the Academy's title precisely because..."

"But I didn't even want to! Big deal!" Gorik yelled, feeling resentment, pain, and hatred of Sergey rising in him.

"You should never do anything specially to get a prize." Sergey shook his finger didactically. "You should do it for yourself. For your soul. Understand? For your own pleasure."

"I don't know why you've started in moralizing to him. I think Gorik understands everything and is not at all upset," said Yelizaveta Semyonovna. "That's how it seems to me. Right, Gorik? Honest to God, it would be silly to get upset over such trifles. And the time hasn't been spent in vain. Gorik has gotten to know and love Pushkin even better, has learned a lot of poems. He's gotten to know such artists as Benois and Lanceray."

Gorik had restrained himself, but when Zhenya suddenly said that he'd made the best album and that the the girls from the the B group in the third grade had asked today whether it was true that her brother had made it, Gorik couldn't stand it and leapt up from the table, rushing off to the children's room. Everything had suddenly been revealed. He realized that he had been humiliated vilely and irreparably. He remembered the evenings under the lamp, his efforts, hopes, the utterly ruined books. A little boy had come out of the snowstorm and asked "Want a knuckle sandwich?" and treacherously, with brutal force, someone had hit him in the back. Lying on his bed, burying his swollen face in the pillow, Gorik thought about a world where everything was so unjust and precarious. Why? What for? He wanted to avenge himself, but it wasn't yet clear on whom. All in all, everyone—

those who awarded unfair prizes, those who leapt out of snowstorms, those who struck you in the back, those who mocked and gloated over failures.

Riding down on the elevator, where there was a thick, persistent smell of varnish and smoke from good pipe tobacco—since Nikolay Grigorievich had stopped smoking five months earlier he had begun hostilely catching the smell of tobacco smoke everywhere and even figuring out what kind it was—Nikolay Grigorievich suddenly decided that if there was a Rolls-Royce waiting, things were bad, and if they drove up in an M, things would work out all right. He hadn't ever used to try to divine the future. Not even in exile, where divination was just as essential a passion as talking, hunting, or writing letters. But in the last year Liza, with her half-childish and facetious superstitiousness, had taught him this game. He had begun divining, on the basis of glasses, old men, trolley numbers. Simply because he thought a lot about Liza. It was connected with her.

There was a Rolls-Royce there, black as a coffin. The granite socle and white facing reeled backwards, and the faces of passers-by, who had been looking in closely and whose way across Hunters' Row had been blocked for a few seconds by the long automobile, were gloomy in a wintry way. Nikolay Grigorievich was going for a pointless conversation. From the two words that had just been said over the telephone, he realized that David wasn't going to do anything. He probably simply couldn't. And for a person who only recently could have, it was hard to confess that he couldn't. In that case he'd go see Florinsky. On Friday, at a reception in honor of the Finnish Foreign Minister Holsti, Nikolay Grigorievich had overcome his own resistance, and going up to the youthfully ruddy, sleek Florinsky, who was wearing an irreproachable dinner jacket, said that he'd like to speak to him about an urgent matter. "Come on by! We're neighbors now. Come by in the evening," Florinsky had responded in an unpretentious way. "Fine. I'll come by." Nikolay Grigorievich nodded casually and felt relieved. He didn't remember until a minute later that Arseny Florinsky had never spoken to him familiarly, that the last time they had talked was five

years earlier, and that in 1920, when Florinsky worked on the division's military tribunal, he was always called "Arsyushka," and Nikolay Grigorievich had sent him on errands, like a simple orderly.

A week earlier Liza's sister Dina's seventeen-year-old daughter had called to ask for a meeting—but no one was to know. She was probably afraid of her mother. Nikolay Grigorievich guessed that the conversation would be about Nikodimov, Marinka's father, from whom Dina had in essence been divorced for five years. Pavel Ivanovich Nikodimov, nicknamed Papa, was an old comrade from exile in Beryozov and Irkutsk, an outstanding person, honest and principled to the point of foolishness, but a bungler and nitwit with regard to the ways of the everyday world, as a result of which, it seems, the falling out with Dina occurred. During the war years something had given way in him, he became a defender of the bourgeois state, and after April 1917 became completely disheartened, crumbled, and gave himself up entirely and firmly to engineering: he built turbines. His troubles had started long ago, beginning in 1931. Everybody tried to pin something on him. He was called in for questioning, implicated: first the Metro-Vickers Trial, then a trial of Ural engineers along the lines of that of the Industrial Party. David and Nikolay Grigorievich had managed to help. Once, six years earlier, on vacation in Gagra, Nikolay Grigorievich had received a sudden telegram: "Beg you save me lungs very bad won't survive winter—Undine."

With every year it had become harder and harder for Nikolay Grigorievich to make appeals in such cases: the people he'd known when he worked for the Board of Governance had long since ceased to exist; others had disappeared; still others had been shoved aside; and lastly, there were people who still worked at their former jobs but who had changed so strikingly that he didn't have it in him to appeal to them. Only David hadn't changed. But he didn't count for anything anymore. Or hardly anything. The people in charge there were young and unexpected, like Arsyushka Florinsky. Nikolay Grigorievich had nonetheless managed to get Pavel off on the group case and to fix him up with a position within the purview of his own committee, with the Ural Steel Trust. But Dina, who had been so active on her husband's behalf, refused to go to the Urals with him and stayed in Moscow with their daughter. At the end of last year the necessity had arisen of sending a specialist to England to a factory that supplied Ural Steel with turbines. The best candidate was Pavel, of course. Nikolay Grigorievich foresaw difficulties, but nonetheless approved Nikodimov's candidacy, although Musienko, Nikolay Grigorievich's deputy and the supervisor of twenty Ural factories, protested very sharply. The conflict grew, Nikolay Grigorievich didn't give way, Musienko persisted (the theses were elementary: on the one hand, "political untrustworthiness," on the other, "unfounded accusations" and "practical qualities"), the matter reached the Council of People's Commissars, while Pavel lived in Zlatoust without suspecting anything. Nikolay Grigorievich prevailed, and Nikodimov was approved. At the beginning of January he was called to Moscow to get his papers processed for the trip, and on 10 January Nikolay Grigorievich received an official communication—brought by the rapaciously beaming Musienko—about Pavel's having been arrested on the train from Chelyabinsk to Moscow and charged with counterrevolutionary activity. A month had already gone by, but he hadn't managed to learn the details, and a few days ago Marinka had shown him Pavel's notebook with his notes about his trials and tribulations of 1931 and 1932. The notebook was entitled "What I Will Never Forgive Myself For."

Nikolay Grigorievich read the notebook twice. In the detailed formal style in which engineering reports are written Pavel gave an account of how and what he had been accused of in 1931 and why he had then signed a "confession." According to what he'd written, he had simply been duped, or, rather, *seduced*, in the root meaning of the word, close to the notion of confusion, bewitchment of the soul. The method of temptation was interesting. They put pressure on Pavel precisely along the line of his "nitwittedness," that is, his strict and foolish insistence on obeying his conscience. The notebook was brought by a stranger, a woman relative of the people at whose place Pavel had rented a room in Zlatoust. The notes had apparently been written a year or two ago. Why? Most likely it was a sort of confession, memoirs for himself and at the same time a vow: "I have never since signed any false testimony or interrogator's lies, nor, it goes without saying, will I ever do so again."

Nikolay Grigorievich promised to bring the notebook to David, to whom he'd spoken on the phone the day before yesterday and who had said that he'd try to make inquiries about Pavel. And now he was on his way to see the old man—without any hope. He thought about Liza again, and his heart was wrung by tenderness. But this was a tender feeling for something much greater: for the February evening, the snow, and the dark apartment buildings, and Liza was a tiny part of all of that. He took the notebook from out of his briefcase, turned on the ceiling light in his coffin, which was gliding along quietly, over ice-covered streets, and bringing the notebook up close to his nearsighted eyes, began leafing through it, looking for a certain passage. It was an extremely important passage, one he needed very much. In it there glimmered an answer—perhaps the shadow of an answer—to the agonizing perplexity that had been the main anguish and the main mystery of the last few years, of the last month.

"And most vexing of all is that when I wrote the two-line 'confession' in 1931 it wasn't so much that I gave in to fear as that I showed confidence in people who didn't deserve it at all. Now control of myself is all the more essential for me! Let's take a literary example: Lev Tolstoy's Hadji Murad. An absolutely realistic character, taken from nature. He tells a Russian officer about how he went to pieces when the murder of his superior and foster brother began in his presence, and he alone galloped away from the numerous murderers. 'How could you have given in to fear, you, a famous brave?' the officer asked. Yes, he had given in to fear, but he had clenched his teeth and never done so again—never in his whole life!

"Another example: the apostle Peter from the Gospel. Peter probably didn't even exist in reality. But that vivid figure was undoubtedly copied from some living person. He was devoted to Christ, and when they started to arrest him, he grabbed a knife and wounded the person who was trying to carry out the arrest. But Christ up and forbade Peter to defend him! And Peter ceased to understand anything. Not knowing what to do, he even began renouncing his association with Christ, when by the night fire the watchman began recognizing him as a disciple of Christ's. But later he thought better of it and completely justified his name Peter, which means a rock. The solution in both of these cases is the following: it wasn't cowardice that decided everything. Confusion and bewilderment did. And with me, too, astonishment played an enormous role—could these guardians of legality really be capable of dirty tricks? And there was only one conclusion: clench your teeth and say: 'You tricked me once, but you never will again.'"

The car turned, coming down off the bridge. From the direction of the Shock Worker a crowd came in a dark stream—the show had probably just gotten over—a few people were running, trying to jump right past the headlights of the slowly moving Rolls-Royce. The archway, a turn to the left—the courtyard where Nikolay Grigorievich lived was to the right—and the car stopped opposite entrance 14.

With David, as with his brother Mishka, he could speak openly with David. Once and for all, beginning with village of Bayshikhinsk on the Yenisei, when he had first seen the little bearded Jew with bulging eyes and heard his conversation about the letters that fools were then writing in hopes of an amnesty on the occasion of the anniversary of the Romanov dynasty, Nikolay Grigorievich came to believe that the the little bearded guy was a smart fellow.

David lived on the ninth floor in a two-room apartment jammed with bookcases. David had never had a family. About eight years earlier he'd taken in a little boy named Valka from an orphanage. Now Valka was fifteen and a lousy student. He hung out in the courtyard with riffraff. How could David bring anyone up, when until late at night he was educating others, at commissions, on committees, at plenums? The old woman Vasilisa Yevgenievna was left at home. She was forever devoted to David for some "sacred deed" in 1918, when he saved someone from the firing squad. David had saved lots of people. And executed lots of them too. He had worked for the Party Control Commission, on purge commissions, in the State Prosecutor's Office.

The short old man, his large baby's head covered with white fluff, wearing a pince-nez, his thick lips stuck out in dissatisfaction, wearing old pajama bottoms that had slid down from his stomach, pajama tops, too, but of a different color, and slippers over bare feet, met Nikolay Grigorievich in the hall. He nodded, and, without saying a word, turned around and shuffled off to the study. The old man had no use for mere form, all those meaningless phrases like "Come in," "You're welcome," "How are things?" and "Bless you."

He seized the notebook and immediately started to read. The piece was a long one, and it took him a long while to read it. As he read, he made a whistling noise with his nose and throat from time to time, and other sounds as well, like snoring and a light groaning. An old woman wearing a kerchief and with an emaciated, brownish face, Vasilisa Yevgenievna, came in and brought tea. While David read she found a place for her light body, made of airy bones, opposite Nikolay Grigorievich, on the edge of an armchair, and in a whisper asked about home, whether everyone was well, how Yelizaveta Semyonovna was, how Grandmother Anna Genrikhovna was, how the children were and whether he didn't need some cottage cheese, because she had gotten two kilos of it at the distribution center, and that was too much for them, no one ate it.

David suddenly flung the notebook aside. "I can't read this! I'm reminded of a sophism from my school days: a Chinaman said that all Chinese lie. Here he is asserting that he is an honest man and that he told a falsehood only once, declaring himself to be a dishonest man, and that he'll never tell a falsehood again. Right? I was informed this morning—this is absolutely certain—that recently at an interrogation he confessed to having been a member of a terrorist organization, to having worked for German Intelligence since 1929, and named fourteen of his accomplices."

"Lord have mercy." Yawning quietly and making the sign of the cross over her mouth, Vasilisa Yevgenievna wandered out of the room.

"Well?" said Nikolay Grigorievich.

"I don't understand anything anymore. When was he honest? When he first identified himself as a wrecker who was a member of a terrorist organization? Or when he declared that testimony to be false and swore not to lie ever again? You have to agree that in view of the new information that we received this morning, both assertions—although they rule each other out—lead to *the same* conclusion."

"Wait a minute. Can you tell me simply, without pedantry: do you believe that Pavel is an enemy?"

Putting his short hands on his knees, the old man looked Nikolay Grigorievich in the eye sadly and firmly. He had had the same sort of slightly glassy-eyed look—Nikolay Grigorievich recalled—when Putyatin had been tried in 1921. There it was, the great mineralogical trait of his character: decades passed, but he remained himself.

"I've known Pavel for thirty years, the same as you have," said David. "He was a wild fellow. He was a bomb specialist, after all. In Beryozov, I remember, he wrote a very sensible pamphlet about fighting agents provocateurs."

"That was ages ago."

"Kolya, remember: people only change outwardly, put on different clothes, different caps, but their bare essence remains. Why do you think that Pavel should have liked everything that was going on, that nothing should have evoked a protest? I know that he withdrew from politics a long time ago. But precisely because of that he could have retained old-fashioned notions about forms of protest and struggle."

"But I don't believe that!"

"And I don't believe," David suddenly cried, "that you, I, Pavel, any of us, could sign a deliberate lie under pressure."

"But people do! In August, and now in January—you and I talked about it. And you spoke of 'temporary insanity.'"

"That's another matter. Different laws, genres! Those are questions of big-time politics. In the final analysis, you have to admit that neither Kamenev, nor Zinoviev, nor Grisha Brilliant, nor Pyatakov ever regarded Koba with affection. That's well known. And they're politicians to the marrow of their bones. They may have slandered themselves and signed God only knows what—acting, as I have already said, according to the laws of the genre. But that our Papa, Pashka Nikodimov, who has long since stopped playing these games and doesn't want to hear about anything except turbines and boilers, that he should have signed a falsehood under the pressure of fear, promises, blackmail, whatever—*that cannot be*! Absolutely not! Lies! Torture, you say? What the hell? What for? It's nonsense, Kolya, twaddle and an utter absurdity! When an interrogator at Oryol Prison, a scoundrel, tried to make me identify a comrade in an expropriation—we'd taken the bank in Vitkovsky Lane back then, without a single shot, and the comrade, by the way, was George Rapoport—you should remember him—he later fled to America with Zavilchansky—well, so I said to him, the scoundrel: 'There's a better chance of hair growing on the palm of this hand than of my saying a word to you, sir!' And I shoved my hand right up against his nose, just like that!" David brought his palm up close to Nikolay Grigorievich's face. "They put me in solitary, and I went on a hunger strike. And I refused to eat for eighteen days. But here—to give the names of fourteen people! That's what stunned me. Can you imagine what we'd have done to him in Bayshikhinsk if we'd found out such a thing about him? We'd have killed him, like a dog!"

Nikolay Grigorievich thought: "What if David is right? After all, he didn't say that about Ivan Snyakin, although, true, he didn't manage to learn anything about Ivan. A person pushed to the limit, rejected, in anguish, is capable of the Devil only knows what."

"Old impressions settle in in us, like chronic illnesses, like radiculitis or an ulcer, and keep us from understanding things, Kolya."

The thought that David was right gradually bore into Nikolay Grigorievich, turning into a conviction and into a certain spiritual relief even. It was painful to think about Pavel, of course, about his undoing, about Marinka's fate (for some reason Nikolay Grigorievich was not worried about Dina), but at the same time there arose a feeling of calmness, because the world's orderliness, which had been on the point of being destroyed by chaos and inexplicability, was being restored. Nikolay Grigorievich suddenly asked—the emerging feeling of calmness, which wished to be complete, demanded it—"Is my name by any chance among the fourteen that he gave?" He laughed. "It could have been. I got him a job at Ural Steel."

"I don't know. Why ask nonsense?"

"Not long ago I recommended him for a trip to the Jenkins factories, in England. I fought for him fiercely, since I consider him the best in the Urals. In addition, he's a relative of mine, after all, a very distant one." Nikolay Grigorievich again gave a short laugh. He sensed that he was speaking in a degrading way. "Although he isn't one anymore."

"I don't know. I don't know," David said drily.

He was displeased by what had been said by Nikolay Grigorievich, whom he liked and considered a very honest professional. Even the facetious suggestion that Nikolay Grigorievich could have wound up on the list of conspirators seemed outrageous and idiotic to him. He began angrily snuffling and wheezing, exhaling air across his thrust-out lower lip, getting ready to cut Nikolay Grigorievich off right away and very rudely if the latter should should take it into his head to pursue the topic further. But at that moment the long-haired, tow-headed Valka, a head taller than David, came into the room without knocking or asking and said raspingly: "David, give me fifty kopecks for the movies!"

The old man opened the wardrobe and started digging around in his pants pocket, jingling kopecks. Valka stood in the middle of the room, his hands on his hips, impatiently tapping one foot.

"How do you speak to your father? How can you call him David?" Nikolay Grigorievich said, suddenly angry.

"What's the matter?" Valka looked at him innocently. "He's not an Ivan or some Selifan, is he? David—that's his name—David."

Nikolay Grigorievich felt like smacking him on his cucumber-shaped head, that of a student kept back for a second year and of a crafty dullard, but he restrained himself, noting the frightened and submissive look that David gave him. Nikolay Grigorievich stepped over to the window. He heard David ask "What movie is on at the Shock Worker?" and Valka's squeaky laugh: "Why? Were you planning to go?"

David hadn't worked at the State Prosecutor's Office for six months or so. He'd been run out by Vyshinsky. Now David occupied some honorable but inconsequential post at the People's Commissariat of Education, wrote articles, gave lectures. It was retirement, of course. He was now working on an article devoted to the twenty-fifth anniversary of the Lena River Massacre, and Nikolay left him at his desk, which was piled high with books and sheets of paper covered over with the large, hurried handwriting of a man working in a fever of delight. David promised to do anything to help him materially—send money, things. But he didn't sympathize with him morally. To betray! Fourteen people!

The sensation of arising calm suddenly disappeared. Nikolay Grigorievich left, crushed by anguish: it was not a personal anguish concentrated on himself, but a general anguish, vague and without boundaries and for that reason not yielding to treatment. Perhaps that was how he had been affected by David's isolation—on the ninth floor, in a cave of books and old papers, isolation with the old woman Vasilisa Yevgenievna, who sat in the kitchen at night reading *Pioneer Pravda* (they subscribed to the newspaper especially for her), and with the blockhead Valka, who ran off until late at night. Nikolay Grigorievich wanted to get home right away, to Liza, to the children, to what was wholehearted, solid, the only thing he had, but he arrived home late that night.

He met Florinsky.

In the yard, coming back from seeing David, he ran into his car. Florinsky, his son, daughter, and two people who were either friends or adjutants or bodyguards had come from the Dynamo courts, where they had watched a tennis match. Florinsky smelled of brandy, and with exaggerated, fervent cordiality he started pressing Nikolay Grigorievich to come visit him right then.

"You promised to, after all, guy! Take advantage of the chance! I usually come home at four in the morning."

The word "guy" and the unduly familiar tone grated on Nikolay Grigorievich. He had been on the point of coldly refusing, pleading that it was late and he was expected at home—David had said that Florinsky was a dangerous character and that one shouldn't try to get in to see him. But Nikolay Grigorievich hesitated, after thinking that such a chance really might never again present itself. He looked at his apartment windows in the corner of the courtyard. There was an orange light burning in the dining room; it was dark in the children's room. That meant the children had gone to bed; he was too late. Liza knew he was going to call on David and wasn't yet worried. Call on? In this enormous apartment building—a city within itself with a population of ten thousand—there lived many acquaintances of Nikolay Grigorievich's, but he hardly ever called on anyone. David was one of their own; he didn't count. But now he had the urge to go calling, to find out, not even to find out, but *to feel*—Arsyushka wasn't about to tell everything that he knew, of course, and he knew enough. He was there, after all, in the kitchen, where people baked and cooked, and on his hands and clothing the smells of that kitchen were left, the smells of that cooking, boiling, and the hot splashes.

As they walked to the entrance and then rode up in the elevator, they discussed a tennis match between a touring player and a very strong Soviet champion. Nikolay Grigorievich didn't understand anything about these sports matters and listened to the conversation with half an ear. Our champion seemed to have been completely routed, and everyone was indignant about that. Florinsky's son was especially indignant. He was simply pale from rage: "That's not the first time for him! He's a damned saboteur! Father, you should tell..."

"I've already told them," Florinsky nodded, "They've grown completely irresponsible.

"Florinsky's daughter suddenly asked: "Has Igor already done his lessons?"

"I don't know." Smiling, Nikolay Grigorievich looked at the girl. She had auburn hair, a high brow, and a serious and sort of befogged gaze. "Do you know Igor?"

"We're in the same class. We had a Pushkin Evening tonight."

The door was opened by Florinsky's wife, a large Oriental kind of woman who was considered a beauty. People talked about her, but Nikolay Grigorievich had forgotten exactly what they said. Something about her former husbands. He was invited to sit down at the table, and they started offering him drinks. Nikolay Grigorievich drank a glass of brandy; they were very insistent. The conversation was about a concert at the Bolshoy Theater the day before. Kozlovsky had been amazing, Nezhdanova superb, Andrey Sergeevich had delivered a very profound speech. What an analysis, every bit as good as Anatoly Vasilievich. Nikolay Grigorievich was growing sullen. "Worse! Anatoly Vasilievich wouldn't go so far as to conclude a lecture on Pushkin with the words: 'Pushkin's books fill us with a burning love for our country, for the great Stalin.'"

Coming here had been senseless. Florinsky was telling about a reception at Yezhov's the day before yesterday, in honor of a bicycle race for border guards. Agranov had cracked a joke, Nikolay Ivanych had frowned. Nikolay Ivanych had said, Nikolay Ivanych had pro-claimed... A servant, a portly lady wearing a cap, who in some way re-sembled Florinsky's wife—just as dark-haired, sleek, with white skin—carried a tray of hors d'oeuvres that was loaded down like a cart. Shaking, she supported it with her shoulder and chin. Arsyushka wanted first to stun, and then to talk. Nikolay Grigorievich, bored, looked over the dining room, which had the appearance of a museum: very old dark paintings in bronze frames, porcelain, crystal, the essence of everything bourgeois. "Well, how about that!" thought Nikolay Grigorievich, "Who's looking after you? In earlier times your place would have been as an agent in a district office."

Although he had drunk quite a bit in the course of the day, Arseny Yustinovich Florinsky was perfectly sober and through the joking con-versation, hors d'oeuvres, and music (his daughter was playing French records on a wind-up phonograph) he looked at his unexpected guest with secret and thirsty attention. A distinct trait of Arseny Yustino-vich's character, a trait that determined many actions and perhaps the progressive and energetic movement of his life itself, was a rare ability to bear a grudge. Nature's treachery consisted of the fact that it had be-stowed such a repellent characteristic upon a person guileless in ap-pearance, snub-nosed, with a healthy athletic glow, possessing a smile and blue eyes.

Arseny Yustinovich's spiteful memory retained the following episode very well: in the fall of '20 he, a young boy in a leather jacket reaching to his knees, with a Mauser at his side, the secretary of the Revolutionary Tribunal of the city of Vladikavkaz, had come tearing into Rostov on a handcar. There the headquarters for the front were located, and he had gone straight to the former Paramonov mansion, to the second floor, to see the member of the Revolutionary Military Soviet Bayukov. The tribunal of the city of Petrovsk had sentenced to death an inspector of the local Cheka, A. G. Bedemeller, more simply Sashka, Arseny Yustinovich's cousin, for the use of the Cheka mandate for mercenary goals, extortion, and plundering the populace. The sen-tence, as was customary, had been sent to the Revolutionary Military

Tribunal of the Front for confirmation, and Sashka had only a few hours left to live. Bayukov was known to be a liberal among the members of the Revolutionary Military Tribunal. He usually wrote: "Grant reprieve." Moreover, he had known Arseny Yustinovich as early as '19, in Saratov, called him Arsyushka, and had once helped his elderly mother by sending her a bag a flour. To Arseny Yustinovich's amazement, Bayukov told him sharply and roughly: "We can forgive anyone, but not a Chekist." And Sashka Bedemeller, who had not lived to be twenty-three, was shot at dawn in a gully just outside of town. Arseny Yustinovich remembered that day very well—in a dark, stifling November—not because he was terribly sorry about Sashka, but because Bayukov had so mercilessly turned down his confidential and nearly tearful request. This mercilessness was the main thing that stunned him. After all, Bayukov was a kind man and felt toward him, Arsyushka, nearly the way he would to a son or a younger brother! And although there remained in his memory even the thought of that sudden, spiteful hatred: "The Cheka isn't at all what you think it is, you damned jailbird!"—and the feeling that he, a youth, had figured something out and seen further than an old revolutionary with sixteen years' experience, there also remained a great and infectious example of mercilessness—mercilessness *that had a right to be.*

Then they didn't see each other for years. Arseny Yustinovich studied, worked in investigative agencies in the Ukraine, in Transcaucasia. They met in about '25 at a plenum of the Supreme Court in Moscow— "the old revolutionary," Bayukov, was a high-ranking official in the Military Administration by then, had four stripes, called Arseny Yustinovich Arsyushka as before and smiled patronizingly, as to a young person from the provinces. Then Arseny Yustinovich was transferred to Central Asia, where there was bloodshed, people were shooting and killing, but he got out of it unharmed, wound up in Semipalatinsk, after that Moscow, where he rose in position after the closed "Trial of the Military Specialists," where he managed to show his stuff quite brilliantly; he and "the old revolutionary" no longer saw each other; the latter was stuck with work involving goods and distribution, as was to be expected, and he dried up and wasted away there with his political prisoner views, working on who knows what. Now he was vegetating in the Council of People's Commissars, in some crummy, useless committee. And there was nothing left of his former importance except for his bald spot and glasses. He must have thought that he'd been forgotten, and at a couple of rotten receptions—he wasn't invited to big receptions now, of course—who needed him?— he pretended not to notice or recognize Arseny Yustinovich, but Arseny Yustinovich remembered everything exceptionally well. His memory was like a safe where a lot of valuable things were kept. He remembered, for instance, the name of the woman with whom, as rumor had it, "the old revolutionary" had had an affair in Rostov, and whose relative she was, and what a man involved in the Nazarov Rebellion had said about her.

Hardly having settled into his new position, at the rank of commissar of the first category, he immediately made inquiries about a number of people, including Bayukov. The papers were interesting. There was, for instance, a document, compiled more than a year earlier, in January 1936, by the commander of the tenth division of the GUGB of the NKVD, Senior Lieutenant so-and-so, stating that Bayukov was a secret Trotskyite, counterrevolutionary in his sentiments, and linked to Smilga, Zinoviev, and Kamenev, who were already dead men by now. That document alone was enough to deliver a knockout, but the day had not yet arrived. When he came up to him in the Finnish Embassy quite casually, trying to retain what was left of his former grandeur, and, laughing wryly, had requested a meeting, Arseny Yustinovich had even been glad: it wouldn't be bad to study him in greater detail, close up. He should drop in and take a look at the apartment. Arseny Yustinovich was proud of the new apartment to which he had recently moved from the Fourth House of Soviets: 120 meters of a single living area! The study was enormous. It was too bad that he couldn't work there: all you could do at home was have breakfast and sleep. Until the last summer the apartment had belonged to one of the people whose vile names will be cursed by mankind forever. The redecorating had been complete—even the parquet had been changed.

A happy feeling of power, but not of coarse, police power, but of a genuine, secret power that came close to fate and divine providence—

the most subtle enjoyment, which in fact was the only thing that made
living worthwhile, since all the rest of life's orgasms were accessible
one way or another to millions, like the city beach in Yalta, Arseny
Yustinovich's native city, where he had been born at the end of the
century into the family of a court clerk who had become impoverished
through illness and who died the same year as Tolstoy—that feeling
did not abandon Arseny Yustinovich, and he regarded Nikolay Grigorievich with a languid, benevolent smile and nodded to him, ap-
provingly, with his eyes.

"Have some smoked sturgeon, Nikolay Grigorievich! Have some
caviar! Have another shot, Nikolay Grigorievich!"

The snowstorm was over. It was frosty cold, clear. Outside there
was snow that looked orange because of the thousands of lampshades
looking out the windows. The yardmen scraped and pounded, hurrying to clear paths for the walkers who on the advice of their doctors
had come for an evening constitutional so as to get a bit of the frosty
cold air before bedtime. Nikolay Grigorievich also walked slowly,
breathing in the frosty air, dispelling the slight intoxication from the
brandy. That Arsyushka Florinsky was an odd duck! They'd talked for
an hour, and nothing had been clarified, everything had only gotten
murky and confused. He's no fool, then, if he knows how to confuse.
No, he's no fool, no fool. That is, he's a fool, of course, but not in the
sense that you'd think after looking at him and talking to him for ten
minutes or so. People don't wind up accidentally in the sort of position that he'd been elevated to. He asked about Pavel in detail, jotted
things down, promised to make inquiries, *to find out what the problem
was*, but during the conversation Nikolay Grigorievich constantly had
the vile feeling that it wasn't to help Pavel and establish the truth, but
instead somehow and for some reason to fish out of him, worm out of
him, Nikolay Grigorievich, some sort of information that Aryushka
needed, everything that he was asking seemingly with sympathy and
writing down with a thin pencil on sheets of paper in a beautiful red
leather blotting pad in the middle of the desk. And no matter how
hard Nikolay Grigorievich tried to lead the conversation to the tone of
a casually open, friendly chat, Arsyushka coolly but persistently resisted that, and the result resembled the interrogation *of a witness in*

connection with a case. He even had the brazenness to lecture Nikolay Grigorievich and advise him on how to conduct himself nowadays. ("The times are extremely serious. You can believe me—I know. In a few days—I'm telling you in secret—there will be a plenum of the Central Committee to discuss questions of democracy within the Party. In their positions people have become terribly bureaucratized and have forgotten about vigilance. They say that Iosif Vissarionovich will speak. The main point is the struggle against those who are trying to destroy democracy, against enemies who camouflage themselves with Party cards, pseudocommunists. My advice is to break off all ties with the opposition, all personal relations—I know, formally you never were—but you in fact had friendly relations.")

Nikolay Grigorievich seethed with fury, but put up with it, trying to persuade himself that all of this would perhaps result in some benefit for Pavel. And only as he was leaving did he realize that no good would come of it. The vague anguish that had attacked him in David's apartment now seized him with such force that his heart was wrung. Suddenly he saw clearly that Arsyushka was far from being Arsyushka anymore. The time for that dog's name ("Arsyushka, sic him!") had long since passed. Arseny Yustinovich Florinsky, privy councilor, senator, received by the sovereign, one of the ministry department bosses, winters in Nice... And the way he offered his hand in parting, the way his eyes flashed with a ministerial coldness—he didn't even go out into the hall, but said good-bye at the door of his study—was a fact that shouldn't be laughed at, but that should be received silently and coolly.

At home there were guests: Dina and her mother, the wise little old woman Vera Andreevna, and with her her daughter Marina. Marina at once made a sign to Nikolay Grigorievich to tell him not to blab in front of her mother. A few minutes later she ran into the study and asked in a whisper: "Uncle Kolya, how are things?"

Nikolay Grigorievich said only that David Shvarts had promised to help with sending things and money. He couldn't tell about Pavel's shocking confession, of course, and besides, Nikolay Grigorievich didn't even really believe in it.

"Are you in trouble because of Papa?" Marina asked.

"Where did you get that idea?"

"Anna Genrikhovna said so. That you had interceded for him and now..."

"There's no trouble. As you can see, I'm alive and well."

In the dining room the two grandmothers, Anna Genrikhovna and Vera Andreevna, were playing piano pieces for four hands. Thin candles left over from the children's New Year's party burned in the old Becker's candelabras, their double reflections flickered in the dark window, and there was a sweet aroma of candles burning and of homemade cinnamon cookies. Nikolay Grigorievich suddenly had a passionate craving for some strong hot tea.

Before bed Nikolay Grigorievich stood at the window in the study—it was a moment of quiet, the guests had left, Liza was in the bathroom, Grandmother was asleep in her room behind the curtain—and after turning out the light, leaving on only the night light over the daybed, he looked outside, at the thousands of windows, still full of night life, orange ones, yellow ones, red ones—greenish lampshades turned up only rarely—and in one window out of a thousand was a bluish light, and he thought somehow strangely about several things at once. His thoughts formed layers, were made of glass, one showing through the other: he thought about how many residences there had been in his life, beginning with Temernik, Saratov, Yekaterinburg, then in Osypki, in Piter on the Fourteenth Line, in Moscow in the Metropole, in sleeping compartments, in Helsinki on Albert Street, in Dairen, God knows where, but nowhere had there been a home. Everything had been unstable, bowling along somewhere, a continual sleeping compartment. That feeling had only arisen here, with Liza and the children, life being rounded out. That had to happen sometime. After all, it was for the sake of that, for the sake of *that* that revolutions were made. But it suddenly seemed, with an instantaneous and insane force, that this pyramid of coziness, too, glowing in the night, this tower of Babel made of lampshades, was also temporary, was also flying, like dust in the wind. The deputy people's commissars, heads of central boards, public prosecutors, commanders, former political prisoners, members of presidiums, directors, medal bearers, were turning out the lights in their rooms, and enjoying the darkness, flying off somewhere into an even greater darkness—that's what occurred to Nikolay Grigorievich for a second just before bedtime, as he stood at the window.

For as long as Gorik could remember, he had always been secretly and quietly proud of something: his stamp album, his bicycle, his muscles, his ability to tap-dance, his father, uncle, cousin, the apartment house he lived in, and many other things, sometimes quite absurd and insignificant. Two years back he'd been proud of the fact that he could bend his left thumb nearly at a right angle, which no one else in the class was able to do. Moreover, he himself couldn't do the same thing with his right thumb! That surprising peculiarity of his left hand was the object of envy, of course. Some people tormented themselves all through the breaks, trying to bend their thumbs at a right angle, but it was all in vain. And he would leave the classroom jauntily, his right hand thrust into his pocket, and with his left he would wave casually, as though incidentally, as though sending airborne greetings— and his left thumb, arched lightly and irreproachably, would stand like a cocked gun. Gorik was proud of other mysterious peculiarities of his body too. He couldn't tolerate strawberries, for instance—he would break out in a rash right away. With his thick lips he knew how to produce a sound resembling that of a cork flying out of a bottle.

The year before Gorik had been very proud of his proficiency at the game of "cities." No one could beat him either at school or at home. They were once playing at home, and when everyone had caved in at the letter "a," Gorik named Asunción (he had about another ten in reserve, very odd ones, such as Antofagasta, Antananarivo, Acapulco), and his father suddenly started laughing: "Come on, smarty pants, don't make things up!" "Who's making it up?" Gorik was indignant, "It's the capital of Paraguay!" "Give it up, give it up! You made it up here on the spot." Gorik ran to his room and brought the atlas. Father was amazed. But Gorik began to feel disconcerted by the fact that he'd proved to his father too graphically that he knew geography better than he did, and although mentally he found an excuse for that—his father had been an orphan, had been raised in an orphanage and had never in his life collected stamps, while all of Gorik's geography came from stamps—just the same he felt guilty. He shouldn't have run to get the atlas. Father had asked for it himself by starting the argument. And nevertheless Gorik's heart exulted quietly and secretly: there were already things in the world that he knew and that his father didn't!

Gorik realized that it was bad to be vain or to be proud of something, but like a smoker who craves the stupefaction of tobacco and can't live without it even though he understands all its harmfulness, Gorik could no longer exist without the familiar and usual tickle of pride, no matter what in, but a constant, sometimes even unconscious one. It sometimes happened that he bared his pride for show, and that would end in embarrassment. Once, in a German class, instead of simply raising his hand and asking the teacher's permission to step out, Gorik addressed her with the long German sentence "Erlauben Sie mir, bitte, gehen dorthin, wohin der Kaiser zu Fuss geht." The class fell silent. No one had understood a thing. The teacher nodded, and he proudly went out. Of course he knew German much better than anyone else in the class because he had been studying with Maria Adolfovna for three years. When he came back he was greeted by malicious laughter. "Well, how did it go? Is everything all right?" "Did you make it?" Volodka Sapog cried. "Did you get there in time?" While Gorik was absent, the teacher had explained his question, of course, but it was interpreted not as a refined aristocratic joke, which Gorik had counted on, but as vulgar boasting, and vengeance was taken on him immediately.

Another characteristic that secretly exhausted Gorik no less than vanity was jealousy. That was a sanctum sanctorum, hidden so deep that he didn't even admit to himself that it existed. But it did, and it tortured him, and later remained for a long time one of the most stinging, tormenting recollections. Everyone thought that Lyonya Krastyn, or, as he was called at school, Lyonya Karas, was an outstanding talent of our time. Lyonya had a passionate interest in paleontology, jujitsu, science fiction novels (he wrote them himself, in thick all-purpose notebooks), drawing, and building up his will power. He wore short pants until December, building up his will power and body. In addition, he *flew into rages*. He was shortsighted, sometimes came to school in glasses, suffered from flat feet, and was the shortest person in the class, but even such great hulking guys as Tuchin and Meerzon, nicknamed Merzilo, were afraid to touch him, because they knew he *flew into rages*. And such a person was a friend of Gorik's. Was he a real one, though? Perhaps Gorik simply took advantage of the fact that they were neighbors? His entrance was number seven, Lyonya's was eight, and they often walked to school together and came back together. Many people dreamed of being friends with Lyonya. Volodya Sapozhnikov, Marat, and Meerzon lived in the same apartment building, but in other courtyards. Could it really be that the only reason for their long interesting talks on the way home from school and back again, about brontosauruses and pterodactyls, Jeans's theory, events in Spain, and the struggle between the Cardinal's guard and the King's musketeers, was the fortuitous circumstance that Gorik and Lyonya turned out by chance to have entrances next to each other? That's what tormented him!

Lyonya usually called at a quarter after eight: "Are you ready?" "Yes, I am!" Gorik would answer, even if he wasn't quite ready, which happened often, since he was a sleepyhead and a "cunctator," that is, a "procrastinator," as his father said. Dressing hurriedly, finishing breakfast on the run, he would grab his briefcase and run down the stairs. They met under the archway. If Lyonya turned out to be there earlier and had been waiting for Gorik for a minute or half a minute, he would make some sarcastic remark: "Couldn't tear yourself away from the doughnuts?" or "You have fried egg on your chin, my dear boy." Sometimes he was capable of saying something venomous: "Only young bluebloods like you eat pastry in the morning." All in all, Lyonya was quick-tempered, easily boiled over, but just as easily recovered, didn't bear grudges. If he didn't call at a quarter after eight, Gorik sometimes called him himself, but most often his vanity kept him from calling. Once or twice it happened that he called, and Karas said, "You go on. I'm going to be held up for a while," and then Gorik went out and saw Lyonya calmly walking along with Volodka or Marat, or with both of them. Volodka Sapog and Marat Remeyko lived in the courtyard where the movie house was, entrance number fourteen, and they usually went together, but they of course were glad to have Lyonya associate with them. The first time that Lyonya betrayed Gorik that way Gorik was struck by something else: just the day before Lyonya had spoken about both of them practically with contempt. He said of Marat that he was "a clever monkey," that all he ever did was read the entries on reproduction in the encyclopedia, while of Volodka he said that he was a real "boot," a rare dolt, and that he had nothing to talk about with him. But they were walking along the embankment and talking splendidly. Gorik pretended that he wasn't in the least bothered by that and passed them, said hello independently, but at the break asked Lyonya as though by chance: "What were you talking about this morning on the embankment?" "Why, Marat was telling us about Spain. A friend of theirs has arrived there." Damn it, Gorik was offended, and he understood why Lyonya had gone with them. "Really?" he said, "And what did he say?" "You know Marat! He remembers all sorts of nonsense, jokes."

But a week later Lyonya was again walking along with embankment with Remeykin-Skameykin, and Gorik trailed along behind, not wanting to pass them up and say hello independently.

The day after the fight with Chepets, Gorik was shivering under the archway and anxiously waiting for Lyonya. He remembered that Lyonya had hinted at some terrible oath.

Lyonya turned up inscrutable and brisk, sunk in thought as he walked along. Only the fresh, beet-colored shiner gave a certain comic inconsistency to his appearance, serious and pale from the strain of thought.

"Well?" Gorik asked.

"What?" Lyonya said.

"What about the oath?"

"Oh! I told you, at the break after the second class."

The first class was German. Esfir Semyonovna was very nervous. A scandal had occurred in her previous class: no sooner had she started talking about a dictation than a racket and hubbub had arisen. Everyone started stamping their feet and pounding the tops of their desks, as people had done at the State Duma (judging by the wonderful new movie Lenin in 1918). With the help of the monitor Esfir managed to calm the class, again started talking about the imminent dictation, but was again thrown off—organized whistling had started. Esfir ran to the teachers' room and came back with the group leader Yelizaveta Alexandrovna. For some reason all of the wrath fell on Merzilo, who was sent out of the room. That was why Esfir Semyonovna was nervous today, and Gorik even felt something like sympathy for her as he watched her eyes guardedly darting this way and that and her small red head moving jerkily on its red, wrinkled neck that in some way resembled a rooster's. There are teachers whose very appearance, helplessness, awkwardness, ordinariness, and lack of a sense of humor produce the desire to torment them. Such a poor wretch was Esfir Semyonovna. It was her lot to serve as a target for secret mockery and to put her foot in it. The smokestack of the Red Torch factory, located next to the school, behind a brick wall, started to whistle.

"Who's whistling?" Esfir Semyonovna cried.

At the second class they also managed to have a laugh. It was Russian. Volodka Sapozhnikov was called on and asked whether adverbs change form.

"Yes, they do!" the fat boy answered firmly. Sapog always comported himself in an extremely assured way at the board. And this time he noticed that a new student who was sitting at the first desk—as it turned out later, he was a big prankster—nodded barely noticeably.

"Think carefully, Sapozhnikov. Do they change form?"

"Yes!" was the even firmer reply.

"According to what?"

"According...according to person."

"Well then, conjugate for me the adverb 'rarely.'"

"Rarely! I rarely do, you rarely do, he, she, it rarely does..."

Everyone roared, but Sapog was unruffled—there was no way you could fluster him. And only on his way back to his desk did he shake his fist at the new student.

The time for the break after the second class arrived. Gorik received a note from Lyonya written in a very simple number code that it took only a minute to read: "The second-floor window across from the physics lab." The window looked out on the garden. You could see the embankment, the river bank, the Kremlin hill, cold under the snow, part of the wall with a tower, and the palace. Sapog came, sat down on the windowsill, and started eating rolls. At every break he ate something. Sapog's turning up disheartened Gorik; could Lyonya really be such a fool as to have decided to let this blabbermouth in on his secret too? Then Marat came running up and said nonchalantly: "Are you guys already here?"

That meant he had been invited too. Gorik scowled. Lyonya's secret had lost its charm. And after all, as a participant in the fight with Chepets and Karas's closest neighbor he had the right to be informed first.

But Lyonya came, and the hurt feelings disappeared.

Lyonya said: "I propose organizing the SSCUP. What does that mean, you ask? The Society for the Study of Caves and Underground Passages."

The three looked at Lyonya, stunned. Sapog started coughing—his mouth was full of unchewed food.

"I'll inform you of the details at the next break," Lyonya said. "But for now we must pretend that nothing has happened."

Gorik was assigned the task of getting a flashlight, candles, and matches. The candles and matches he simply took out of the kitchen table drawer, where Marusya kept all sorts of household odds and ends, but the flashlight took some doing. Seryozhka had a wonderful squeeze flashlight that Nikolay Grigorievich had brought from Germany and given Seryozha for his birthday. It was a pitch-black, graceful oval that fit comfortably in the palm of the hand. Gorik knew perfectly well where the flashlight was kept: in Seryozhka's room, in the bookcase, up on top. Taking it would be easy, but Seryozha would be sure to notice. He was like a dog on the hay: he didn't use his own things, but he kept a vigilant eye on them. There was only one thing to do: make up some lie and ask for it.

Lyonya set the first cave expedition—along the Paveletsk Road, the Gorki Station—for February 23, Red Army Day. Until then they were to prepare carefully, steeling themselves physically and psychologically. Every evening the four of them took skis, went to the Swamp and skied there, to the point of craziness, over the snow-covered vacant land where there had once been a park but whose trees had been cut down. "Where's the flashlight?" Lyonya would ask daily, holding a little book ready. In that little book he'd noted down point by point what had been assigned to whom, what had been carried out and what not. Sapog, as was his specialty, devoted himself to food: he was saving up sugar, dried bread, chocolate, and buying a few things. He even had more money than the others. His mother, Olga Fyodorovna, was a kind woman, and his father worked for the People's Commissariat of Trade. Skameykin was to provide string and numbers. He was to write three hundred numbers on separate pieces of paper the size of half a notebook page. Lyonya was responsible for everything. He had a compass, a map, and a weapon—a Finnish hunting knife.

"Where's the flashlight?"

"Seryozhka wasn't home. I'll definitely get it today."

"Just expropriate it, and that's that. It's not for yourself, after all, but for the society. For the SSCUP. There's nothing wrong about that. All revolutionaries made expropriations."

Gorik had never yet expropriated anything in his life. Just stamps, perhaps, three or four times. But after all, all stamp collectors indulge in that sort of simple-hearted expropriation. Gorik was taught by Seryozhka himself, who had given Gorik his collection two years earlier: he taught him to lick his palm inconspicuously (it was convenient to do that if you sat and looked sad) and then to put his hand down on a pile of stamps scattered over the table while pointing a finger at one: "So that's the one you want to trade?" After which you calmly took your hand away and stuck it in your pocket: one, two, and sometimes even three stamps would be sure to stick to your moist palm. That little trick could be repeated several times in the course of a meeting to exchange stamps as you gradually stuffed your pocket with other people's stamps. Gorik remembered once getting fourteen stamps from Merzilo that way. True, they were all junk.

But stamps were one thing, and a flashlight, for instance, quite another. Taking it without asking seemed unthinkable to Gorik. He agonized while trying to think up a story to tell. He finally figured out that Zhenka should ask for it. Seryozhka would give it to her without suspecting anything. Zhenka agreed after asking for a mechanical pencil in exchange for her help.

In the evening the family sat in the dining room for a long time after supper. The adults talked about all sorts of things, about war, politics, the ancient Khatti, enemies of the people, Shmidt's polar camp, Karl Radek, the fact that Málaga had fallen and that the attack had been directed by the German Naval Staff from on board the cruiser *Admiral Speer*; as always, Father argued with Grandmother, and Seryozhka argued with everyone. No matter what anyone said, Seryozhka immediately tried to prove the opposite. It was with good reason that Mother said that Seryozhka "argued disgustingly." If Grandmother remarked that an article in *Izvestiya* by a Georgian about the Georgians being descended from the ancient Khatti was very interesting, Seryozhka said that the article was nonsense. If Father said that the fall of Málaga hadn't yet decided anything, Seryozhka declared that the fall of Málaga had decided everything, since Madrid would now be cut off from the sea in a very short time. When Mother said that Lion Feuchtwanger was a very intelligent writer, Seryozhka, just for the sake of argument, said: "Excuse me, but I think he's an idiot."

Grandmother couldn't contain herself, of course, and said that he was not yet a member of the Academy of Sciences or a professor, but just a student in his third year. And moreover, one with less than brilliant grades. Seryozhka, of course, was irritated and fell silent. He liked to reprove others and make sarcastic remarks to them, but God forbid that anyone should tackle him. He and Father were drinking lemon vodka, and Seryozhka was already red, talking too loudly, while Father, having taken off his glasses, was smiling somehow strangely. Father joked by saying that Seryozhka wasn't a member of the Academy of Sciences or a professor, but was on the other hand an eligible bachelor, and that meant quite a bit. And at that point Seryozhka definitely took offense and said that his personal matters were no one's business.

An unpleasant silence fell, and it occurred to Gorik that this was not a particularly convenient moment to ask for the flashlight. But he couldn't especially delay either, because soon they'd be sent off to bed. Gorik was sitting sideways in an armchair, having thrown his legs over the soft elbow rest and leaning up against the other elbow rest with his back. He was leafing through a very old, worn volume of Zhukovsky, pretending to look at the pictures but really looking at Zhenka out of the corner of his eye. He was trying to hypnotize her. Zhenka was sitting at the table with the adults and was embroidering an eight-sided napkin using Maria Adolfovna's method. What a stupid activity! Brings home nothing but "C's" from school, and in the evening indulges in such nonsense. Zhenka was marvelously susceptible to hypnosis. He had noted that long since. Of course, if the hypnotist had a strong will. He would suggest to her: "The flashlight! The flashlight! The flashlight!" and she would answer: "I'm fed up with you. Leave me alone!"

Mother said that Uncle Misha had promised to come but was late for some reason. Father roused himself: "Did Misha really call?" They started talking about a manuscript that Uncle Misha had written and that Father was supposed to give to someone and hadn't. Grandmother started scolding Father. Mother supported her: "It's bad, Kolya, really. Misha called three times. That makes him angry."

Father, upset, paced up and down beside the table, rubbing his bald spot fiercely.

"Damn it, of course I'm at fault. I didn't have the chance to see Sergo. I could have specially arranged to, of course."

"Kolya, how unreliable you are." Grandmother shook her head. "And what about the second copy?"

"He only asked for one thing: to give it to Sergo. The other copies he wanted to deliver himself, in the usual way: to the Politburo, the Presidium. Oh, the devil take me! It's all for nothing. The book won't make it, but I should have..."

"The more so because of Misha right now..."

"That's exactly the point," said Father.

Continuing to grumble and shake her head reproachfully, Grandmother went off to her room and came back with her glasses on her nose, holding a newspaper. She expressed the desire to read aloud a note entitled "A Dangerous Toy" from the issue of the day before yesterday. No one objected, and Mother even said, "Of course, go ahead and read it."

And Grandmother began reading. Grandmother liked reading aloud. She said that in her youth people had suggested that she become an actress, but Grandfather had talked her out of it, saying that she needed to give all her energies to the revolution, and later it turned out that Grandfather withdrew from the revolution himself and even broke up with Grandmother because of the revolution, while Grandmother got so interested in the revolution that she forgot about everything else. But even now she still read well and beautifully.

"'A perfectly healthy, nine-month-old baby suddenly fell ill,'" Grandmother read. "'His sleep was disturbed, his digestion was impaired, strange movements of his mouth appeared, his lips grew cracked and bled. The child started losing weight quickly. Neither the mother nor the doctor observing the child could determine the reason for the illness.'"

"It's the heebie-jeebies," said Seryozhka, taking his cigarette case out of his pocket, taking a cigarette from there, tamping it against the cigarette case and kneading it carefully and leisurely, but without lighting up, because Grandmother didn't allow him to smoke in the dining room. He even took out his matches and stuck the cigarette in his mouth—to irritate her.

"'The doctor assumed the presence of an infection!'" Raising her voice and looking at Seryozhka sternly, but not noticing his cigarette, simply demanding silence, Grandmother continued reading: "'On the third of February, two weeks later, the mother discovered grains of some sort on the diapers. These were sharp fragments of rocks— quartz...'" (Zhenka tiptoed up to Seryozhka and whispered something in his ear. He nodded, and Zhenka went out of the room.) "'...granite, and feldspar, some of them the size of the head of a pin, and rock dust. And the reason for the child's illness became immediately clear.'"

"Very interesting!" Seryozhka said in an insolent tone of voice. "It was probably sabotage?"

"'When the child put the toy in its mouth,'"—for some reason Grandmother pointed at Seryozhka—"'the seams would come apart and the contents find their way into the child's mouth and stomach.' Is it clear to you? 'The toy is so craftily designed that if afterwards one takes the rattle by the handle and shakes it, no rocks spill from it.' And so on."

Father, after saying something to Mother, tiptoed out of the room.

"Next," said Grandmother, "they give the address of the factory that manufactured that truly malicious toy. By the way, it's in Leningrad. That's also noteworthy. It's too bad, by the way, that Nikolay Grigorievich left. He's always saying that I'm inclined to panic."

"You know, Mother!" Seryozhka got up so abruptly that the chair nearly fell over, but Gorik didn't hear what Seryozhka started talking about. He slipped out into the hall, from there to the children's room, where it was dark and from where he could hear a cherished humming sound: Zhenka was having fun with the flashlight. Gorik ran up to her: "Let me have it!"

She hid it behind her back.

"And what about the pencil?"

"I'll give it to you in just a second. Honestly, some people!" He nearly choked with resentment: to so fail to trust your own brother! In the dark—he didn't want to turn on the light, so as not to destroy the charm of the humming and shining booty, and Zhenka didn't want to turn on the lights either, and continued the humming and casting zigzags of light around the walls—he felt around for his briefcase, which was lying on the floor, found the mechanical pencil on the bottom, under his notebooks, and took it out without any regret. "Here," he said, "Now let me have it, and thanks."

"And what should I say if he asks for it tomorrow?"

"Say you forgot it at school."

She ran off, and Gorik stood for a while in the dark, making the humming noise and casting the beam around.

Then everything was ruined by Marat, the windbag and womanizer: he blabbed to Katya Florinskaya and even invited her to go spelunking with them. Lyonya was stunned when Katya suddenly came up to him and asked whether she could bring her older brother along. Before he had yet realized anything, Lyonya answered: "Absolutely not!" Then, after the realization, he grew furious: "What an ass I am! You're all blabbermouths and unreliable people," he said. "You're as cowardly as rabbits and as lascivious as she-cats." Lyonya couldn't stand women. He had never asked any girl even a single question. They were like blank spaces to him. And if a girl by chance asked Lyonya something, he would puff up, turn stony, and mutter something incomprehensible through clenched teeth.

He and Gorik had once been walking outside, and Karas proposed that they swear to each other never to have anything to do with girls. They swore an oath. Gorik regarded the oath lightly. He had no dealings with girls, and such dealings were not even expected, so that the oath didn't cause him any detriment, and in the final analysis the oath couldn't have even the slightest significance for Gorik's life; he'd simply agreed to it so as to be nice to a friend. But once Lyonya gave him his science fiction novel to read, *The Buried Treasure in the Cave*—three thick notebooks in book covers of artificial leather—and Gorik imprudently showed it to Zhenya. She couldn't read more than two pages, but all the same Lyonya was terribly offended, called Gorik a traitor and oath breaker, and didn't talk to him for several days.

Angry now too, Lyonya announced that the expedition was being postponed for an indefinite period—until the weather improved. He said that because of the thaw it was impossible to get to the entrance to the cave—it was all flooded. Perhaps it really was. The dull, uneasy winter dragged on: there were alternately periods of cold, snowstorms, and dampness.

Suddenly, after a Sunday, Lyonya sat down next to Gorik at his desk at the first class and showed him his left palm, which was horribly cut up: it looked as though the skin had been scraped off with a metal comb. Almost the entire palm, from the spot where one felt for the pulse to the upper cross cut, was smeared with antiseptic ointment.

"Keep quiet, understand?" Lyonya whispered. "I was climbing in a cave yesterday. Alone. Oh, it's really beautiful there, honest to gosh! Warm as anything! Just terribly warm, sixteen degrees or so Celsius, and I crawled out all covered with sweat. I got to a second room, left a note, and went back. But got this when I lost a mitten in the first room while jumping. I fell."

Gorik listened, astounded.

"How could you go alone?"

"Why not? It's great alone. You keep quiet, don't tell anyone! You and I will go together—understand?—next Sunday."

At the break Vovka, suspecting something, charged up to Gorik and started trying to find out what Karas has whispered to him.

"Just stuff, nothing special."

"Nothing special? Then why did your eyes bug out? I saw that."

It was unpleasant lying. The main thing was that Gorik didn't understand the point: if anyone was to be punished, then it should be Skameykin, while Sapog had nothing to do with it.

The thaw was replaced by freezing weather. As they walked along the embankment to school, a dark blue icy haze rose over the Kremlin, and on the granite parapet lay a fluffy and thick morning layer of snow, which it was good to knock off with a stick, schoolbag, or simply a mitten.

Katya Florinskaya asked Gorik why Lyonya Karas hated her so much. Gorik, embarrassed—Katya troubled him in some way, she was new, mysterious—was forced to say that Lyonya had a negative attitude toward women in general. Gorik wanted to tell Katya everything and to invite her to go with him the next Sunday, but without Marat, without anyone else, the two of them, but of course he didn't say anything and just looked at Katya, smiling wryly and impudently. She was very distressed. They were standing in the middle courtyard, next to the rear, service entrance to the food store, near which there were always mountains of wooden boxes, dirty paper, shavings, and pieces of cardboard. Gorik held his schoolbag in both hands and banged his knees with it, first one, then the other. Then they parted: Gorik went to his entrance seven, Katya to her ten.

Meanwhile Marat Remeykin-Skameykin was perishing right before everyone's eyes. He carried Katya's knapsack from abroad, holding it awkwardly by the straps, which looked silly, because not a single fool carried knapsacks that way. Having lost all sense of conscience, he waited for Katya at the entrance in the morning. He got into a fight with a giant from the seventh grade who had started pestering Katya in the cloak room, and they had to intervene and save Skameykin. (The three of them knocked the giant to the floor and nearly suffocated him under a pile of coats.) This was all shameless and humiliating. And when Lyonya told Gorik that Marat should be expelled from the ranks of the SSCUP for being a corrupting element, Gorik joyfully agreed. He couldn't exactly quite conceive of the meaning of the phrase "corrupting element." A repellent picture of a dark brown, completely rotten, runny pear arose in his consciousness.

The closer it got to the date set by Lyonya—Sunday—the greater became Gorik's agitation, which he had to conceal. He hardly slept Wednesday night. On the one hand, he was haunted by the pictures of a horrible death in caves and caverns that came back to his memory from books by Hugo, Dumas, and Gustave Aimard, but through strength of will he conquered fear and was, in essence, ready for anything; on the other hand, however, even more agonizing than the fear was the necessity of observing secrecy, which Lyonya demanded. That was an altogether sadistic torture: he was willing to perish, but to perish in obscurity, so that not even his mother would know where and how he had perished! Several times in the middle of the night Gorik decided to get up, go to the study, call his mother, and admit a few things to her, hint at a few things. But each time he lacked the ultimate resolve to show *faint-heartedness.*

Gorik went to school with a headache, sat through classes in a state of torpor, couldn't think well. On the next night Gorik fell asleep quickly, as soon as he lay down, but his sleep was troubled. He dreamed of a river, with rafts near the shore. He was swimming nearby—in a deep place, where it was over his head—and he was being pulled under the rafts by a cold current, was being driven further and further along, into the depths, into the dark.

In the dining room the adults were sitting up late drinking tea. They suddenly saw Gorik, barefoot, in his night shirt, come out of the children's room. Extending his arms and feeling around in the air with his hands, the way one does in the dark, he padded across the whole dining room to the armchair. His eyes were closed; he was asleep. Everyone was terribly frightened. Father snatched Gorik up in his arms—Gorik didn't wake up—carried him to the children's room and put him in bed. Mother was so worried that she didn't want to let Gorik go to school the next day. But all the same she let him go. Gorik didn't remember anything in the morning and was very surprised when they told him. And immediately, as usual for him, he began to take pride in it: he told everyone at school that he had walked around the apartment at night like a real sleepwalker.

Mother said: "His nerves are shot after the Pushkin anniversary."

Grandmother said: "He reads too much. You shouldn't allow him more than a book a week. He devours them like crazy."

Father said: "He's growing. That's all it is. And there's no need for panic."

No one knew what was going on with him. And he steeled himself—didn't say a word to anyone. But then, as luck would have it, Uncle Misha and Valerka turned up and stayed the night. Valerka boasted the whole evening, telling about what Finnish jumping skis his mother had given him and how he and his friends had gone to a very remote station on the Kazan Road to jump from the ski jump. And how he had fibbed to his father and told him that he had gone on a ski trip with the class, while if his father found out the truth, he would give him such a hiding that Heaven help him, and would break the skis in half. He hated the skis even as it was, because they were a gift from Mother. He had even demanded that Valerka refuse them. What a laugh—to refuse Finnish jumping skis! Listening to Valerka's boasting was unbearable. Gorik put up with it, fought with himself for a long time, but after they'd gone to bed, he couldn't stand it and told Valerka everything. He and his jumping skis immediately looked puny. And he started begging Gorik to take him along to the cave. Gorik promised to.

Gorik felt better at heart: now if need be there was someone to tell Mother about how and where her son, a courageous, reserved, and very quiet person, had perished.

When he got back from school the next day, Valerka was already gone. He'd been taken somewhere, to his mother's or his aunt's, but Uncle Misha had stayed. And the first thing that Uncle Misha said— slyly and quietly, whispering in Gorik's ear—was "Well, pal, you're going to have to answer your father today!"

Gorik's stomach even turned cold. Did Valerka, the creep, really blab? Mother had gone to a state farm on a work assignment three days earlier, Father was at work, and so was Grandmother. Thrusting his fingers under his broad, shiny belt, Uncle Misha walked around the room and looked at Gorik mysteriously, without saying anything. He was waiting for Gorik to come out with it all himself. But Gorik was silent. He remembered how Lyonya had once taught him not to admit to anything and to deny everything.

"Here's what it's all about, Igor Nikolaevich," said Uncle Misha. "All your malicious intentions have become known to us. Your father has already called the mother of that hero of yours—what's his name?— who is constantly steeling himself and goes around with bare knees until December so as to catch tuberculosis of the bone."

"Lyonya?" Gorik exclaimed, horrified.

"Maybe. He's got some sort of illness. Your father says that he has fits. How could you go spelunking with an epileptic? Or even worse, allow him to go alone? Well? You're a grown man, you ought to understand. I always thought you were a fellow with a head on his shoulders, Igor Nikolaevich, not someone like my useless son."

"Well at least I'm not a traitor!" Gorik muttered with a shaking voice.

"Do you mean to say that Valery betrayed you? True, but you betrayed your Lyonya by blabbing to Valery. So you're both fine ones. But the point is that this Lyonya's mother... Who is she?"

"An ordinary woman. Works at a printing plant."

"And the father?"

"The father doesn't live with them. He's in the military. A brigade commander, I think. He's somewhere in the Caucasus."

"Brigade commander? What's his name?"

"Krastyn."

"I knew a Krastyn in the Far East. But that's not important. The mother, a strange person, started laughing over the telephone, simply burst out into merry laughter—your father told me—and said that Lyonka lies constantly, you shouldn't believe him, he's altogether a dreamer, she said, and there's no one to whip him. He hasn't been climbing in any caves and won't be, and as for his hand, he hurt in when he tried to get into the movies without a ticket, climbed over the wall here, in your rear courtyard, and fell down. Your father, my dear friend, was outraged by the fact that you were planning on the sly, without telling anyone, to go somewhere on the commuter train."

Gorik listened dumbfounded, then went quietly to the children's room, threw his schoolbag on the floor, and lay down on his bed.

Soon Grandmother came from work, Seryozhka showed up, Zhenka came from her exercise class, and Mother arrived, frozen through, tired, in a tarpaulin coat, white from hoarfrost, over a sheepskin coat, with a backpack, where there were always presents of some sort—this time wooden toys bought at the market in some Godforsaken little town—and as always after being away from home like this, Mother was in a very good mood. She immediately ran to take a bath. It just happened to be Friday, the hot water day.

Like a noble person, Uncle Misha didn't tell either Mother or Grandmother anything. Everyone was waiting for Nikolay Grigorievich, who had gotten held up for some reason. Gorik, after lying for a while with the look of a person in complete despair and thereby producing a pleasant agitation in Zhenka (she came up several times and asked with fright: "What's wrong with you?"—but he kept silent, and besides, to tell the truth, he himself didn't know what was wrong with him), and then with furious energy tackled his lessons: he did Russian, examples, four math problems, drew an outline map, but Father still wasn't home. Uncle Misha was anxiously waiting for him the whole time and even grumbled a bit: "Where the devil can he have gotten to?" Father was supposed to see Ordzhonikidze that day and find out about Uncle Misha's manuscript from him. There had been a lot of conversations about the manuscript. It was called "Waiting for the Battle." About a future war. Grandmother and Mother said that the manuscript was very interesting, Seryozhka said that he disagreed with some of it, and Father, though he praised the manuscript, told Mother—Gorik had accidentally heard it—that Mikhail was in over his head. He and Uncle Misha had once quarreled, and Uncle Misha had yelled: "Your job is to give it to him, while as for what you think of it, I'm not interested!" A great deal depended on what Ordzhonikidze said: whether the manuscript would be published, whether Uncle Misha would be returned to work at the Military Academy, and whether he would finally be allowed to go to Spain, where he had been trying to go for a long time and unsuccessfully.

That was why Uncle Misha was nervous as he waited for Father. In addition, he wanted to return to Kratovo today and was afraid of being too late to catch the last commuter train.

Instead of Father, Grisha, Mother's brother, suddenly arrived. He lived in Kolomna, with his wife Zoya, and worked at a Kolomna plant as an engineer. Grisha told about how just the day before he'd been to see Ordzhonikidze with a delegation from the plant. They invited Sergo to a conference of diesel specialists at Kolomna, but Sergo wouldn't be able to go—the conference was starting the next day. He gave them a written message of greetings. Grisha took a sheet of paper out of his briefcase and showed it to everyone: "I congratulate the diesel specialists of Kolomna! Strive for 240,000 horsepower a year!"

"We'll have it printed up," Grisha said. "There'll be a little portrait of Sergo here, and we'll give them to the delegates as presents."

Seryozhka and Grisha sat down on the daybed to play chess. Gorik settled next to them to watch. Uncle Misha also came up from time to time, watched for a second, and in the tone of a commander ordered: "Chase the officer! Hit him with the rook! Get the queen away, get her the hell out of there!" He stabbed the board with his finger, grabbed pieces, and rearranged them. Seryozhka, smiling contemptuously, but not saying a word, would put the pieces back, and Grisha would ask in his delicate, thin voice: "Mikhail Grigorievich, please..."

Uncle Misha played chess very badly. Probably worse than anyone else. But he loved to interfere and give advice. Seryozhka finally couldn't stand it and said politely, but sarcastically: "Uncle Misha, we'll finish up our game in a bit, and then you and Grandmother can have a quiet game, all right?"

Grandmother did not play the least bit worse than Uncle Misha, but Uncle Misha went into a rage: "Why, you puppy! Of all the impudence! Why, I'll destroy you in a match, grind you into dust, into hamburger!"

Seryozhka immediately proposed playing a set of ten games for money. He often "milked" Uncle Misha that way, but Uncle Misha for some reason stubbornly leapt at the chance to play with him and indignantly rejected odds, while Seryozhka even offered a rook. They'd had time to play five games, Uncle Misha had lost them all, and at that time Father called and said he was on his way home. That meant he'd gotten held up again somewhere, had dropped in to see someone. Perhaps even here, in the building.

A half an hour later he arrived, entered the dining room wearing a fur coat and cap. His face was gray, somehow blind. Not looking at anyone, he said: "Sergo's dead."

Grandmother uttered a shriek. All the others looked at Father in silence. He repeated: "Sergo's dead. Four hours ago. They say it was from paralysis of the heart."

For the first time in his life Gorik was pierced through with compassion, painfully and immediately, as though by electric current, but not compassion for the dead Sergo, but instead for his father, who suddenly seemed old and weak to Gorik, and for Grandmother, who was crying without being ashamed of her tears, and for Uncle Misha, who had frozen on the daybed somehow remotely and stared silently out the window for a long time while everyone was talking. There was something incomprehensible and frightening in the way Sergo's death affected everyone. After all, he wasn't a relative or a close friend, like David Shvarts, for instance. True, Father had told about how he and Sergo had become friends at the Caucasus front, where they were both members of the Revolutionary Military Council. Then their paths had parted. Sergo had risen swiftly, becoming one of the country's leaders, while Nikolay Grigorievich, gradually sinking, had turned into an ordinary *functionary*, the likes of which there were thousands. Making a request of Sergo was not a very simple matter for Nikolay Grigorievich and not even a very pleasant one. And all the same he had known that at some time, on "day X," he would be able to go see him—not with Mikhail's manuscript, not with a request to be supported at the Politburo, but with some last, mortally important question, to which Sergo would reply, definitely stating all the truth of the matter that he would know. It wasn't "day X," however, but death that had made them even and brought them close again.

For three days they didn't think about anything except Sergo. With a red face crumpled from tears Grandmother read the papers. "They made his illness more acute through the most vile treachery... They did our Sergo in... May an eternal curse..." Monday was a day of mourning. There was no school, and Gorik just happened to come down with tonsillitis that day, and he very much regretted that the tonsillitis went for naught, was of no use to him. Uncle Misha and Valerka came again. So that he wouldn't get infected Valerka wasn't allowed into the children's room, and opening the door just slightly, he made various funny faces, did Petrushka, while Uncle Misha and Father would again quarrel, Mother would calm them down, Uncle Misha would grab Valerka by the arm, and they would leave, the door would slam, Father would yell, and they would come back. And the winter dragged on, the river was covered with snow, while the ditch near the Shock Worker Movie Theater didn't freeze, and there was always steam swirling above the dark water.

VI

Icy weather has come swirling in, and the cold has made it horrible in the blanking shop. Kolka runs to the forge and heats a defective matrix there. After making it white-hot he drags it over on a hook and throws it on a bench, and all three of them take off their mittens and warm their hands. If Kolesnikov, or even worse, Chuma, appears, Kolka quickly shoves the matrix onto the floor with the hook, and they set to *drawing* again, with pity looking at the matrix, which hisses on the damp oily floor and expends its heat uselessly.

All in all, with regard to fire it's good and easy in "the blanker." You're always welcome both to get warmed up and to have a smoke: the forge is right nearby, not like in other shops. When they need a light, for instance, they run to the forge, use tongs to pull some white-hot object out of the forge—a matrix or a bolt, and a hundred people could help themselves to a light if they wanted. It's warm by the forge! The hammerers work just in undershirts, and even at that they're all wet, while the drawers wearing quilted jackets can't stop their teeth from chattering.

There had been three hammerers. One of them, a young and strong fellow, had recently been drafted into the army, and the two remaining ones—both from Byelorussia, elderly men who had wound up in Moscow as refugees—can't manage. The smith Uncle Vasya yells at them, calls them "jerk offs." The shop foreman has promised to transfer an unskilled worker to the ranks of the hammerers, but for the meanwhile Chuma is perpetually asking Igor or Kolka to help the smiths out. Kolka purposely strikes with the sledgehammer weakly and clumsily so as to make Uncle Vasya angry and so that he'll send him away, and Kolka sits with his back to the furnace, smoking. But Igor is done in by his unconquerable vanity, his old desire to be proud, no matter of what and before whom. He would like to have everyone—Uncle Vasya, the Byelorussians, Chuma, the women loaders—see and be amazed by how dashingly he swings the sledgehammer and with what force he delivers a blow. Igor has strength, of course, but not so much as to be amazed by it.

Uncle Vasya takes a pipe with a glowing, white-hot tip out of the forge and places the tip on the anvil, and with a few blows Igor is supposed to smash the tip, turn it into a narrow, flat little end capable of sticking into the matrix opening and convenient for being grabbed by the cart with its teeth. That's all there is to it. With a savage look on his face Igor tosses the sledgehammer high and brings it down with such fury that Uncle Vasya frowns: not so hard, not so hard. The Byelorussians don't even look at Igor's efforts at all. And in a quarter of an hour he himself feels that he's about to expire, and he can't understand how those bony little men, on whom you can't even see any biceps, can swing a sledgehammer twelves hours a day.

On the night shift, if you sit down by the stove to smoke, you can even fall asleep inadvertently—the warmth overcomes you. Igor dozes for a minute or two, thinking in his sleep about something colored and vivid that never existed, about something that resembles a plot of grass in the forest, where mushrooms are growing, where he himself is lying in his shorts on an old cloth blanket warmed by the sunlight and through which pine needles poke him. He is reading a book and gradually dropping off in a doze, deafened by the quiet, the sun, and the woods. And suddenly—as though something were shooting inside him—he wakes up. A log has burst in the fire with a bang. A homemade shag-tobacco cigarette still smolders in his hand.

Sections crawl along, the steel being bent creaks, the cart's teeth chatter, a tug forward, a tug back. And slowly, lengthily, like a damp homemade cigarette, the night smolders...

Kolka hasn't worked for three days. He has created a medical excuse for himself: he's used a chisel to dig an open sore on his right hand. He sits on his bed in the dormitory from morning on and plays cards, either twenty-one or "three leaves," with the same kind of slippery ailing characters as himself. In place of Kolka Chuma has put an Uzbek auxiliary worker nicknamed Uryuk on the drawing machine. He is a taciturn, obliging, and strong fellow. No one really knows anything about him. "Hey, Uryuk! How much are the dried apricots?" the boys in the courtyard yell at him. Uryuk doesn't say anything, doesn't hear. He's about fifty years old, or maybe even sixty or more. "I was mob'lized," he says of himself. Igor's heart always contracted sadly when he would happen to see Uryuk from afar. He who would wander along amid the women loaders, lagging behind them, immersed in thoughts of some sort, absurd in his robe donned over a quilted jacket, in his soldier boots and black sheepskin hat. He would position his feet with the toes to the sides, look down, and spread his arms out slightly. As a result he seemed ready to tackle any job right away. And really, he was meek. He was ordered about by everyone: by the women loaders, by the hammerers, who made him cart firewood to the stove, and even by Kolka, who yelled in the tone of a boss: "Hey, Uryuk, get that there out of here!" Uryuk would submissively drag "that there" away.

Now, just as submissively, silently, and easily he carries pipes from the forging furnace to the bench and then drags the ready sections to the gates, where the women loaders pile them onto carts.

In two days Uryuk has exchanged perhaps ten words with Igor. On the third day, rather, the third night—Igor has been working the night shift all week—people are getting ready to go to the cafeteria at midnight. Igor slams the knife switch down with the palm of his hand, turning off the machine. Nastya hurriedly wipes her hands with cotton rags and sheds her coveralls. They're hurrying so that after coming back after eating they'll have at least a quarter of an hour to sit in peace and smoke. Uryuk doesn't hurry off anywhere: he sits down by the stove, wraps himself in his robe, and looks as though he intends to doze.

"What are you doing?" Igor asks, surprised. "Aren't you going to the cafeteria?"

"Nope." Uryuk shakes his head.

"Why are you being like that?" Nastya says, yawning. And she and Igor leave.

Uryuk doesn't go to the cafeteria the next night or the third. While Igor and Nastya gulp pearl barley soup and eat potato patties fried in cottonseed soil, Uryuk dozes by the stove. They come back, wake him, Igor turns on the knife switch, and the sections crawl along, the steel squeals, the cart clicks its teeth.

Finally a morning comes when Uryuk doesn't want to go anywhere, neither to the cafeteria nor home to the dormitory. He sits down by the stove and says that he's going to sleep there until the evening. It's cold in the dormitory, he says, but here it's warm.

"How do you like that!" Nastya says, yawning, and leaves. She has two children and an elderly mother. She doesn't have time to talk.

Igor sits down next to Uryuk, leans up against the brickwork on the stove, his back feeling the broad, relaxing warmth that is not very hot—precisely what he needs.

"What happened to you?" Igor asks.

Uryuk mumbles something incomprehensible.

"Listen, I've brought you something here for fun..."

Igor digs around in his pants pockets, in his quilted jacket—he's looking for the dried apricot that he discovered yesterday in his Tashkent jacket and that he has saved specially so as to show to Uryuk. Uryuk will probably be very pleased to see a dried apricot. It will be like a greeting from home. Such a tiny, hard, almost ossified little round thing, it had slipped through a hole in the pocket and gotten stuck under the lining. That apparently was when Igor was coming back from the Yangi-Yulsky construction project at the end of August, when he had fled from there after hearing that in Tashkent young people were being recruited for Moscow factories. In August it was unbearably hot there. At night in the tents the oppressive heat didn't let up. Sun scorpions hissed: they came suddenly in great numbers from all over the steppe, smelling remains of rotting meat, although those remains were buried in the sand. But neither the oppressive heat nor the sun scorpions kept him from sleeping. Igor slept the sleep of the dead there, without dreams, as never before. His back and arms ached from long hours of swinging a hoe. After all, he had had to demonstrate his strength, be a *palvan*, a hero, and once, all fired up, he swung without looking, and a fool turned up under the hoe—a fellow from the nearby school—and the hoe struck him on the noggin. Igor's legs gave way out of horror, and the fellow remained lying on the sandy slope. He was taken away on a stretcher, but everything turned out all right, he survived. One night deserters dragged a girl off into the steppe, and she nearly died. She was found unconscious, all battered, as though she has been attacked by dogs. She was a fat Jewish girl who had been evacuated from Odessa. The next morning everyone armed himself anyway he could, and they ran off into the steppe to look for the deserters so as to wreak vengeance, but they didn't find anyone. And all the same it had been all right there. There was plenty to eat. They were given mutton and pilaf, a thick pilaf, sometimes a meat one, and sometimes Bokharan, with apricots. There were tons of apricots there, but the grapes had not yet ripened, and when Igor fled from there, with a young fellow, also a Muscovite, they walked through the steppe all day, and at night they reached a collective farm orchard and ate their fill of apricots and apples there. Like boa constrictors, they stuffed their stomachs, couldn't move. The dried apricot under the lining was probably left from that supper in the orchard at night, when the sky was already turning dark, and the frogs had started singing.

"Here!" says Igor, joyfully extending his palm, on which the apricot, which has turned into a stone, lies. "Did you see? Take it!"

The bearded Uzbek takes the apricot, looks at it indifferently, and throws it on the floor.

...Grandmother was very irate when she found out that he had left the canal without permission. "What? The construction project wasn't yet finished, and you ran away! When the entire populace is straining its energy..." She had even wanted to go to school and complain to the director. She was completely out of her mind. What did the school have to do with Igor? He had graduated from it and said good riddance to it. The director there was a dimwit who busied himself only with his garden and selling things at the market. True, he hated evacuees and was capable of doing any sort of vile thing out of hatred, but at that time, in August, he no longer had any power over Igor. Igor could have told him everything that had piled up in him, and several times, when they met nose to nose on the street, he could hardly keep himself from speaking his mind, but he restrained himself: he was afraid that the director would revenge himself on Zhenya, who still had studying in the eighth grade ahead of her. And it was to such a person that the old woman was planning to go complain. She had simply gone off her rocker. She didn't want him to leave for Moscow. That was the whole point. It was getting harder and harder with her, especially since she'd taken David Shvarts into her room and another old woman, who lived in the same room, had protested.

This other woman, Sinyakova, who also had a record of service dating back to before the Revolution, was a repulsive person. She was constantly puffed up, took pride in some meritorious actions, and regarded other old people, including Grandmother and David Shvarts, with haughty contempt. But Grandmother told about how at one time, when Grandmother still worked in the Secretariat, that woman had tried to curry favor with her, and in 1920-something, during a purge, David Shvarts had saved her from expulsion. But now Grandmother was an ordinary unhappy old woman living on a pension and living in poverty, just like other people, and from a fearsome, nationally-known judge David Shvarts had turned into a sick, half-crazed old man, and Sinyakova could have contempt for them and make fun of them. She called them opportunists and continually made sarcastic remarks such as "This isn't the Government House, you know," "This isn't Silver Pines, you know." Once collective farmers brought a gift of honey. For some reason Sinyakova didn't get any, and she ran to the regional Party committee to complain that opportunists had gotten honey instead of her, a crystal-pure member of the Party who had not once signed any opposition platform...

Sometimes Sinyakova drew Grandmother into political arguments. She did so craftily: she would start slowly, from afar, would gradually grow brazen, say vile things, lies, and Grandmother, unable to contain herself, would enter into a skirmish with her. Sinyakova's final exultant argument was "Well, I'm here, an honest person. But where's your son-in-law? Where's your daughter?" She was a big, fat old lady, with a red, leathery face and little blue slits for eyes. Her left arm was missing. She said she lost her arm in the Civil War. But Igor didn't believe her.

Grandmother said of her that she was a Party member by chance. In spite of the fact that she was missing an arm, she knew how to fight and liked to. She had once had a fight with an old man near the boiler; either she had wanted to get some hot water without standing in line or else he was trying to do the same thing. She hit him in the back with her teapot and yelled: "You're a Bundist! I know you're a

Bundist!" She also called David Shvarts a Bundist, although Grandmother said that was a ridiculous lie, Shvarts had never been a
Bundist, and, on the contrary, had always sharply criticized the
Bundists. Once Sinyakova raised her hand against Grandmother.
Zhenya just happened to be coming into the room, and grabbing a
pair of scissors off the windowsill, she ran up to the enormous old
woman. "If you so much as lay a finger on my grandmother, I'll run
this through your stomach!" After that Sinyakova carried on for a long
time, threatened to go to the police, called Zhenya "enemy blood," but
nonetheless Zhenya turned out to be the only person in the room, and
perhaps in the settlement, whom she rather feared. With some sort of
instinct she sensed that Zhenya really could stick a pair of scissors in
her stomach. Igor knew that she could; Zhenya was prone to violence,
she "pitched fits," just as Lyonya Karas did.

Sinyakova hated David Shvarts especially fiercely. No doubt precisely because he had once done her a good turn. She tried to drive
him out of the room; she said vile things about him and about
Grandmother, laughed at his wretched appearance, purposely opened
the windows so as to cause him to catch cold. Grandmother suffered
most of all from this mockery of Shvarts by Sinyakova, and that was
why scenes with shouting and reciprocal threats flared up: "You'll answer for your words!" "I'll file a complaint against you with the CPC!"
Igor couldn't stand to hear the yelling, couldn't stand to see Grandmother's white face. He would leave. If Sinyakova had been a man, he
would have struck her. But he didn't know what to do with an old
woman.

Other old men and old women would slowly gather round in response to the yelling. An investigation, an examination of all the dirty
laundry, comradely reproaches and admonitions would start, all the
more prolonged and with loving attention because all these old men
and old women had absolutely nothing to do. Sinyakova would repeat
her side of it: "I want this immoral person to be removed from the
room!" David Shvarts's immorality consisted of the fact that he'd declared that he would neither wash nor shave "until his return to
Moscow." In his deranged mind there was some link here with the
pledges of his youth, when he would announce hunger strikes in pris-

ons or refuse to answer the investigator. That was his response to the war, the fascists, evacuation, the adversities and horrors of life, his humiliating position, which he did not fully understand but probably sensed, the way people sense the weather, a change in the atmospheric pressure. Only Grandmother could get Shvarts to wash, and even she had a hard time managing to do that and didn't always succeed. Except for Grandmother no one needed him. David Shvarts's only sister had died just before the war. It wasn't clear where his adopted son Valka was, at a military school or at the front. He didn't write anything. And the old lady Vasilisa Yevgenievna was left in Moscow and didn't write anything either. Grandmother couldn't let him out of her room, no matter how Sinyakova raged, because she knew that without her he would perish.

David Shvarts didn't notice, see, or hear what passions seethed around him. An investigation of his "case" in the presence of several loudmouthed old people took place sometimes right above his head, but he would lie on the bed indifferently and silently and look at the people arguing exactly as though they were on another planet. His brain was busy with some persistent reflection. Suddenly his face would be illuminated with the reflection of another thought, one from *here.* He would suddenly frown, sit up on the bed, and scream sternly and wrathfully, as he had done once upon a time: "Stop making noise! Idiots!" But his earlier meditation would immediately overcome him, and he would again sink into a half-sleep, lie flat on his back, and look at the loudmouths from afar. The old man suffered greatly from the heat, would cast off his clothes, and spent almost the whole day in his underwear. He was capable of going to the cafeteria in his underwear. Igor himself twice intercepted him on the way and forcibly dragged him back to the house. Grandmother would cry: "If only you knew what a man he used to be! What a mind!" She considered that the person was no longer there, that all that was left was an insignificant, slovenly shell. And all the same Grandmother loved David Shvarts and felt unbearably sorry for him. It sometimes seemed to Igor that she loved the old man more than she did him, Igor, and even more than Zhenya.

Grandmother never got angry at Shvarts, but Igor and Zhenya often irritated her. She would scold them because of trifles, and once she even slapped Igor's face. With ease she could call Igor a scoundrel, a liar, a no-good bum. Her irritation would flare up especially quickly after a conversation with Sinyakova. Igor in fact knew that if she had a quarrel with Sinyakova in the morning, that meant that in the afternoon Grandmother would be sure to start carping at him and Zhenya. With Sinyakova she restrained herself with all her might, but with them she gave her nerves completely free rein. No, these weren't hysterics, they were vicious injustices. True, Grandmother never tormented Igor and Zhenya in front of Sinyakova. In the presence of "that female bandit" the family had to look united and harmonious.

Among the old people there were some decent people too. Some sympathized with Grandmother in her struggle with Sinyakova. Others felt bad for David Shvarts, visited him, brought him fruits and nuts—he liked walnuts very much. One old woman came up to Igor once when he was sitting by himself on the bank of the Boz-su and said quietly: "I knew your father on the Caucasus front. I respected him very much. He was a real Bolshevik." And without waiting for a response, looking around fearfully, she went away and never came up to Igor again, didn't even say hello to him.

Almost all the old people thought that David Shvarts was beyond help. Three years before the start of the war he had been put in an insane asylum, kept there several months, and released, but Grandmother had said that he "was no longer the same person." He was even given work as a staff assistant in an ethnography museum. Igor remembered the conversations at that time. Some people were indignant: "It's a mockery to stick David Shvarts in a museum!" Others, Grandmother among them, objected: "On the contrary, it's a humane act. They gave him a job so that he would feel like a human being. Work will cure him." Even now Grandmother believed that something would cure him. "David needs to go back to Moscow," she would say. "As soon as he gets back, he'll recover."

It sometimes seemed to Igor that the old man was hopeless, but sometimes he happened to catch an intelligent, concentrated, and profound look in his bulging eyes—that occurred when Shvarts was "working," that is, lying on his bed, he would be writing some endless series of figures on long sheets of paper—and for a moment it would strike Igor that the old man was pretending to be a little crazy, fooling everyone. But at the next moment he would realize that it was an empty hope. Shvarts kept the papers covered over with lines of figures hidden under his pillow, but they often remained on the bed or lay scattered on the floor, and Grandmother, Igor, and Zhenya always picked them up, while Sinyakova, of course, would tear them up and burn them. She would sadistically stick some of the sheets on a nail in the bathroom. No one could understand what the figures meant. Grandmother asked Shvarts many times, both gently and very sternly, and unexpectedly, so as to catch him red-handed: "David, what are you writing?" He would answer angrily: "It's no business of yours." And nevertheless, while knowing that he wasn't in his right mind, Grandmother believed there was something important in his notes. She thought he was writing his memoirs in an old underground code and therefore she tried to keep the papers, gathering them and hiding them in a suitcase. All of those papers were lost together with the suitcase that disappeared right before Igor's eyes at the Kuibyshev platform.

"Well, what's with you?" Igor says and stands up. He can feel that his back has gotten very hot. "Why aren't you going home?"

"Aw!" Uryuk waves his hand. "It's a long way home."

"You really could stay here and sleep," Igor thinks and again leans his back against the stove, closing his eyes. He sees the river Boz-su, yellow from silt, the curved little suspension bridge that creaks and sways and where bandits lie in wait for people in the evening. Late in the evening he is seeing home a young woman, the doctor who came to give Grandmother shots. They are carefully coming down the steps carved out in the rocky soil. Igor holds the young woman by the elbow so that she won't stumble, and suddenly someone cries out in the dark: "Kirghiz, stop!" Terror bathes his insides in a hot wave—Igor knows what that voice means. It's a signal to someone standing on the other bank of the river. But with firm steps he leads the woman across the creaking, swaying bridge. It's dark all around. They cross to the opposite bank and go up the rocky steps. Now they are saved. In the distance streetlights and a tram car at the last stop can be seen. "You helped me out. Thank you!" says the woman, and unexpectedly putting her arms around his head, she kisses him on the lips. He feels a soft mouth, opened lips, their vegetable, eggplant taste. She leaves. He can't come to his senses. It's the first kiss in his life, and now he knows that a kiss can have a vegetable, eggplant taste. He runs back skipping along, swings on the bridge, whistles while flying up the steps, and no one touches him. And even higher up between the two banks there stretches a wooden flume that water for irrigation flows in. And some bold fellows who are too lazy to go down to the bridge make their way across the river on the flume.

The river banks are overgrown with *dzhida* and nut trees. When you sidle along the girder supporting the flume, you make tiny little steps with your trembling legs, and bending over, you cling to the flume with your hands, and down below the dense foliage of the *dzhida* shows green, the nut tree silver, while the water is brown as clay, the sun's brilliance blinds you, and you mustn't look down, you have to look at the girder or at your hands hanging onto the flume. After going across on the flume for the first time, Igor feels proud of himself: great going, he didn't chicken out! He doesn't tell Grandmother and Zhenya about his feat, of course. Why frighten people? And then, during the rainy winter, while running home from school, he sees Grandmother creeping along the flume. In her hand is a milk can. She had gone to get milk. She walks along the girder very slowly, hardly moving. After waiting for her to finally reach the bank safely, he yells in fury: "What are you doing? You're out of your mind! Don't you dare ever do that again!" Grandmother is embarrassed, she mumbles about the wet weather, slippery steps, and the fact that with her heart getting up the steps is hard...

Uryuk has been talking about something for a long time. Igor tries to understand the end of his speech. What's he doing here? Where is he from? Men like him stand at the market with bags of nuts, with dried melons, with eggs, onions, and shake their pitiless beards "No!"

"How many thousand of people there is here, and they all looks at me and all they can say is 'Uryuk!' Uryuk comes, and they'll say 'the dirty devil,' they'll say. 'Why did you come here?' they'll say. I was mob'lized! Why did I come? I was mob'lized, and I came..."

"But you have to understand: little boys used to tease you, and now that's just what they call you! Yesterday Kolesnikov said to the chief: 'Uryuk,' he said, 'is a good worker. He held up for twice the daily work quota.' And the chief said to the secretary: 'Give Uryuk a bonus for this month. And issue him some shoes, a pair.' Well, what do you think they were doing—teasing you?"

"I was mob'lized. I came to work. Of course, I don't know the words..."

"Why don't you go home, for crissake?"

At the market, where you could go play hooky from school, where people wade through the February mud, where invalids without legs, on crutches, on carts, sell shag tobacco, show magic tricks on suitcases, talk hoarsely and sing, where people trade used linen for sugar, where old Jewish women sell old gilt coverlets with the gilt peeling off, where there roam thieves and people who were recently members of robber bands, recuperating patients from the nearby hospital, hungry girls, unfortunate women, profiteers dressed like beggars, elderly, shabbily-dressed dandies in fur coats of prerevolutionary vintage and without a kopeck in their pockets, where you can sell patched galoshes, which Igor manages to do toward the end of the day, and he walks up and down the rows with forty rubles, not knowing what to buy until an old Uzbek sitting under an awning beckons him: "Hey, *bacha*, come here! Want some melon? Oh, it's sweet, try some!" He reaches to offer a heavy chunk of wonderful dried melon. You could cut it into little pieces and have it with tea for a long time, for two weeks or so. "How much does it cost?" "Here, try some," says the old Uzbek, and his eyes grow transparent, like a cat's, his mouth melts into a smile, and you can see several black teeth. "*Bacha!*" says the Uzbek and puts his hand around Igor's leg above the knee. Igor kicks in some direction, the melon seller yells and falls over on his side. Igor runs, and people yell after him "*Ur! Ur!*"—the way they shout when they catch thieves and beat them to death. He shouldn't have run. He should have walked off with dignity, like a man who has been insulted. But then all those melon sellers...

He has lost his dinner card. He played cards in the dormitory and lost the card. Oh, it's nothing, five days are left, and then another month starts, another card.

"What did you play? 'Three leaves'?"

"I don't know," Uryuk says, "Kolka was playing."

"How can you play a game that you can't win, silly man? After all, they play 'three leaves' at our market in Tashkent!"

Uryuk hasn't been to the market in Tashkent. He hasn't even been in Tashkent proper, has only seen it through the train car window.

Igor goes to the second floor to see the shop foreman. The man has to be saved: what kind of a day is it without a dinner! Avdeychik has no time to talk about the petty details of the lives of auxiliary workers living in the dormitory. He sends Igor to the tool shop to see Valya Kotlyar, the Komsomol organizer. There is only one Komsomol organization here, because the shops are next to each other, in the same building, with the only difference that there are about forty Komsomol members in the tool shop, while in the blanking shop there is perhaps only a total of five people in the metal-worker group where they saw matrixes. Valya Kotlyar is a technologist. She's very short, like a gnome, has white ringlets and a penetrating voice. Boots and a quilted jacket make her tiny figure square. The whole business with the cards outrages her, but she isn't anxious to help Uryuk.

"There's no end to helping out fools! We have more important worries here. Three guys in our shop—can you imagine, the scoundrels—have started up production. Making knives. Like in America. And they were selling them at the Tishinsky Market. I mean, cigarette lighters—all right, I mean, fancy cigarette holders—all right, but making Finnish hunting knives like that out of files on the night shift..."

And nevertheless they go to the dormitory. For assistance Valya takes a big strapping fellow from the shop.

"For some reason this is the first time I've ever seen you," Valya suddenly says to Igor suspiciously. "Where are you registered?"

Igor explains that he's not registered anywhere because he's not a Komsomol member, and he works as a pipe drawer.

"Get ready. We'll be taking you in," Valya declares even more suddenly. "We need people like you. Are you planning to join?"

"Of course! Why not?" Igor shrugs his shoulders. He has thought about joining the Komsomol even earlier, has thought often and a lot about it, but each time stops short of doing anything. He has lacked decisiveness. The fact that he had answered Valya so calmly and seemingly indifferently wasn't the truth. He had tensed up completely when he heard the sudden proposal. And again without doing anything, again the decision is put off until "later," until "sometime," when there will be no way to retreat—from his own timidity.

Kolka is sitting on the floor surrounded by guys and is cheating someone at "three leaves."

"Just who is it that lied?" Kolka yells and bores into Uryuk with a nobly angry, incinerating gaze.

He doesn't know anything about any dinner card, of course. He doesn't even have his own. It must have been stolen by sons of bitches, thieves who took it right out of his pants. It must have been in the cafeteria. When he eats his dinner he becomes crazy, like a deaf person, doesn't hear anything or notice anything, especially when he's eating the first course, soup, for instance, with dumplings, or cabbage soup with meat. When he's on the second course, he's already normal, he's recovered, but when it's the first they could easily have stolen it. Here! Search the place! From out of the nightstand fly rags, pieces of iron, a fragment of whetstone, pieces of wire. Pockets are turned inside out to the accompaniment of cursing. A blanket under which there is a gray, stained mattress takes flight. There! There! Here! Take a look! Why did you lie? Evil devil!

Uryuk says nothing in reply and behaves as though he doesn't understand the meaning of the whole scene and Kolka's yelling.

"He spoke the truth!" Igor says, with disgust sensing his voice trembling. "And you shut up. I'll deal with you later." Kolka answers without looking.

"Ugh..." says Uryuk.

He lies down on his bed and turns his face to the wall.

"If we see cards once more," says Valya, pointing her childlike index finger at Kolka like a pistol, "we'll expel you from the dormitory. I want you to know that!"

"You've really scared me! As it is, it will be hut-hut, left-right, left-right for me in the spring."

Two days later Igor gets his pay, a large amount, for "the end of the month": 620 rubles. Igor has never before received so much money at once. In Tashkent, when he worked at the iron foundry, he once earned 703 rubles, but for a whole month. But here it's 620 for two weeks! In his excitement Igor practically runs down the lane, thinking over how to spend the money, what to buy. There are lots of essential things: he needs, first, to get some mittens at the market, because it's embarrassing to wear the the government-issue ones from the factory. How long can you stand it—you can't take your hand out of your pocket in the subway or on the trolleys. Second, his socks have holes in them. They also have those at the market, knitted ones, for sixty rubles a pair, at the Minaev Market. He should give Aunt Dina 400 tugriks for "feed." He should get some honey for Marina. He saw that at the Minaev Market too, for a hundred rubles a glass jar. He should buy a whole jar. What else? Seems like that's all. A comb, too, because he lost his. Although the comb isn't obligatory, he can make one himself. The guys make excellent ones from aluminum, like a thin little hacksaw. He should also stop in at a book store, buy some books out of his pay. On the history of art, for instance. A collection of pictures from the Tretyakov Gallery, an album—a valuable thing! There was also a very valuable book in one store—*The History of Hypnotism.*

At the end of the factory fence, at the corner where the lane forks—right to the subway, left to the dormitory, to the Butyrsky Embankment—there's a newspaper hanging on a board, and Igor stops to read what's playing at the movies. It's already rather light, and by bringing your face close to the glass and straining, you can read. Behind him, with a murmur of voices, noise, stomping along the wooden planking of the sidewalk, the night shift runs to the subway. An American comedy, *The Three Musketeers*, is playing at the Moscow, *A Masked Ball* at the Central. But Igor will definitely go to the News of the Day Theater, on the boulevard! What about going straight to the market to get the honey, and to buy some tobacco in addition, and from there go home, to sleep? An English offensive in Lebanon. Fighting on the approaches to Bizerta. The consumption of 20-30 grams of dry yeast a day assures a healthy person the necessary diet of protein. A kilo of edible yeast produces 4250 calories, a kilo of fatty meat, 1720 calories. The technology of yeast production is very simple...

A sudden listlessness overcomes Igor. He crosses to the other side of the lane, where there are no people, and he can walk slowly. He doesn't feel like hurrying anywhere, neither to the movies, nor to the market, nor home. If only he could go home! But the place where he'll arrive in an hour is not his home. There are good people, kind-hearted people there, and it's *their* home; *his* home is somewhere else. No, not where an uninhabited room with frozen books stands under lock and key, and not a thousand kilometers away, where an old woman and a girl live in a clay-surfaced hut. They hate that hut, they dream of running away from there. And not where an empty hulk rises, glimmering with hundreds of fortress walls. Does he have a home on Earth? In the steppe, where there's unbearable heat, where there's freezing cold, where he's never been, there's a little house, guarded by machine guns, where a kindred soul languishes. Perhaps there? He doesn't feel like going anywhere, and he stops and stands there, leaning up against the fence. He can see the white snow on the roofs. Beyond the brick wall that the lane dead ends into can be seen the black boxes of warehouses, beyond them some apartment buildings, smokestacks, smoke in the gray predawn sky, further on—concealed by apartment buildings, the invisible circuit railway line, which comes out at the suburban platform of the Byelorussian Station—and again, beyond the Butyrsky Embankment, apartment buildings, smokestacks, columns of smoke, an endless city. A deserted city, where there's not a single apartment building, where there's not even a small room, essential for life.

The road along the brick wall leads to the dormitory. Valya Kotlyar talked about Kolka and the other guys from the dormitory: they're called "the guys from Vitebsk." They're from on orphanage, from Vitebsk District. They're all orphans, and Kolka is too. The orphanage was bombarded during the very first days, and the counselors were killed. They managed to evacuate some of the kids. They say: "We have lost our parents for a second time."

What if he runs as far as Kolka's? To visit the fool? He's still on sick leave, but now Kolka has fallen sick for real. Igor doesn't feel any hostility or enmity toward him. The whole thing with the cards and the interrogation turned out stupidly. Valya grabbed the cards and started tearing them up. Kolka went at her with his fists, and Igor and the guy from the tool shop went for Kolka and roughed him up. And why on earth does he, the puny thing, try to fight? His friends stood there watching, no one made a move. Perhaps they were losing and didn't object to the game being stopped. And Uryuk just continued lying with his face to the wall, didn't even turn around. And then, when they were coming back down the lane, Valya talked about the orphanage, and Igor suddenly had a complete change of heart. Valya had said then: "You were great, you did right! What kind of a family do you come from? What background?" "What do you mean 'what background'?" Igor asked. He more or less understood the sense of the question, but he wanted to understand it more precisely. In addition, for some reason it was pleasant to look a little dense, not very quick. "Well, what are your parents—workers, professionals, white-collar workers?" "Professionals. That is, rather, white-collar workers. But my father was a worker..." Valya said: "We need people like you. Get ready, we'll be taking you in!"

Igor quickly crosses the snow-covered roadway, reaches the brick wall, and turns left. The way to the dormitory leads past the rear factory yard. Three guys come out from around the corner. They arise, like three trees, right before his eyes. One takes Igor by the scarf and silently pulls him lightly to the side, into the lane. Igor follows him obediently. Resisting would mean displaying cowardice. They want to have a fight with him and for that purpose choose the lane, where's it's dark, where no one will see, and he follows them, since his pride doesn't permit him either to resist or yell or run. He hurriedly tears off his glasses and hides them in the pocket of his pants: that's the most important thing to do before a fight. The only thing he can't understand is who they are and why they want to beat him up. The guy holding Igor by the scarf brings his face close to Igor's—it's squint-eyed, pale, one eye greenish, the other light blue—and says, through clenched teeth: "Why did you rat on Kolya Kolyvanov, son of a bitch?

You know what happens when you rat?" And it's unclear to whom he orders: "Give it to him!" A fist comes flying out from behind the guy's back, and a pain strikes the middle of his face, a very great pain, as though someone had struck him with a log in the face with all his might. Igor topples over backwards, strains, trying to push away the fellow holding him by the scarf, holding him firmly, bending his head down, but a new blow from the other side knocks Igor to his knees, the scarf unwinds all by itself, and Igor, sensing liberation for a second, manages to leap up and hit back. He swings wildly, and they pummel him with six fists, on the ear, in the stomach. He bends over—for some reason he's still standing on his feet—and sees red fists and realizes that it's his blood. "You'll remember this, son of a bitch! Get his money!" Somebody from behind rips the coat off his back. His cap has already been knocked off. They knock him to the ground. One holds his head, the others hold his arms down, digging around in his quilted jacket, turning his pockets out. Suddenly there is a deafening roar from nearby overhead.

"Just come in!" a radio thunders. "A successful... offensive... by our forces... in the area of Stalingrad!"

All four of them freeze for a moment. The fellow who was holding Igor's arms down doesn't unclasp his own, and the one squeezing his head throws himself on Igor's face, covering it with his stomach so that Igor can't wriggle free. And freezing, they listen.

"In the last few days our forces, located on the outskirts of Stalingrad, have gone over to the offensive against the German fascist forces. An offensive has begun in two directions: from the northwest and from the south of Stalingrad. Having broken through the enemy's defenses along a line of thirty kilometers in the northwest, in the area of the city of Serafimovich..."

The one sitting on Igor's legs gets up, and the other two also get up, and silently, without looking at Igor, who is lying there with a bloodied mug, they leave. Igor sits up against the brick wall, first of all carefully, with fear, thrusts his hand into the pants pocket to get his glasses—they're intact, they didn't break!—and presses snow to his lips, to his eyes, and listens. And he's joyous, his joy is immense, he's happy. He gets up on unsteady legs so as to get closer to the speaker, which is up there, on a pole.

"In three days of intense fighting," the announcer reads with a voice full of bliss, "overcoming enemy resistance, they have advanced from sixty to seventy kilometers... Our forces have taken the city of Kalach, the village of Krivomuzginskaya... Thirteen thousand prisoners... three hundred and sixty artillery pieces..."

And the day is now totally white and snowy. The lane is empty. In the distance a man is standing and also listening, or perhaps looking at Igor. Never before has Igor experienced such a strange sensation: he is happy, immensely, infinitely, and sincerely happy, but this feeling of his seems to exist separately, as though *outside of him* and *apart from him*. This feeling lives an independent life. It's visible. One can see it, just as one can see, for instance, a cloud formed from one's breath in freezing weather, and it has no connection to the person in the torn coat, who walks along, staggering, and spitting out blood.

He has to present the gifts nonchalantly, casually, and most important, without at all revealing the pleasant excitement and pride in oneself that one experiences in so doing. He has to take off his coat without hurrying, and ask, "Well, how are you doing here?" Then he should wash up, clean his hands carefully, in some places with pumice, use a small pair of scissors to dig the grease out from under his nails, walk around the room a little. He can have a cup of tea or acorn coffee, smoke a home-rolled cigarette, and then, at last, say offhandedly: "Oh, yes! I've brought you some silly little things." Then go to the entrance way, where on the trunk, as though forgotten, under a newspaper, he has left a jar of honey, a paper cone with 300 grams of rice, and thick knitted socks for Grandmother Vera, who complains that her feet get cold. Rake this all up and put it on the table in the room with the words "All sorts of stuff from out of our pay!"—and sit down to the side and, puffing away at the home-rolled cigarette, immerse himself in the newspaper.

The rice was bought for Aunt Dina: the doctor had prescribed rice water for her.

Grandmother Vera joyously reproaches Igor for being a spendthrift, but immediately puts on the socks and pads around in them back and forth, as though in new shoes. Marina comes out of her room, manages to say, "My Lord, what a luxurious life..."—and freezes, looking at Igor with horror. He puts his finger to his lips. Grandmother has almost completely lost her sight, and, thank God, can't see his face. And his face really is awful, bruises all over, his mouth covered with congealed blood. He took fright himself when he looked in the bathroom mirror. True, thanks to that ugly mug he earned indulgence at the market: one old woman let him have the socks for just four rubles, and he bought the jar of honey for eight.

"What happened to you?" Marina whispers and draws Igor into her room.

They sit down on the bed, which is sloppily covered by a blanket. Igor tells her, propped up against the wall, one leg on the other, a home-rolled cigarette in his mouth: "Well, I gave him an uppercut... He aimed a direct blow at me... I ducked... Then they launched into a series, one after the other. I covered myself..." In Marina's room it's always stuffy and smells of medicine. Marina never raises the dark blackout curtain—why raise it if the window looks out on a narrow slit of a courtyard, the sky can't be seen, opposite is the wall of another building, one so close that if you want to you can reach it by sticking out your arm with a long stick, with a mop handle, for instance—and in Marina's room the electricity, a little night light above the headboard, doesn't go off. "Once upon a time there was a pale knight," Marina says, touching his cheek, his lips with her hand. "He looked gloomy and pale..." Her hand lingers near his lips, barely touching them, as though waiting for something. He falls silent and sits, his eyes closed, immersed in the sensation of that palm, near and light, smelling of medicine. When he opens his eyes a few seconds later, he sees Marina's face next to his own, quite close, and hears her frightened whispering. "My poor maimed cousin... Lie down right now and rest." Is she making fun or does she pity him? She looks closely at the bruises under his eyes and demands that he take off his glasses. He does so. He stubs out the home-rolled cigarette in an ashtray. She touches her lips to one bruise, then another. Grandmother Vera can be heard padding down the hall. She stops at the doorway into the room and asks, "Gorik, why don't you go and rest?"

"He's sleeping!" Marina whispers. "He's more relaxed here. Let him sleep."

Marina doesn't move away from Igor. On the contrary, she cuddles up to him. She lies on her stomach across the bed, her legs hanging over the side, and presses her lips to his bruises. No, these are not kisses, they're gentle healing touches. Marina has a very kind heart. She loves Igor like an elder sister, and now, it's obvious, feels great compassion for him. But all the same it's a good thing that Grandmother Vera can't see anything. From the side one might think that Marina is kissing him, but she's just breathing, blowing, cooling his inflamed skin. Her lips touch his swollen, broken lips, press themselves to them for a moment. Grandmother Vera pads back, to her room.

"Does it hurt? Is it unpleasant?" Marina inquires.

He shakes his head. No, of course it doesn't hurt and it isn't unpleasant. On the contrary even—he finds it pleasant, unusually and surprisingly pleasant, but it's not seemly for a man to admit such things. That's why, after shaking his head, he freezes and, just in case, closes his eyes.

Marina leaves, first arranging the bedding for him and then turning off the night light. He breathes the scent of her pillow, which smells of her face and her hair. And, lying in the dark, he thinks about her: "What a strange woman! It's as easy as anything for her to hug a person, cuddle up to him, and even kiss him, and then right away vanish, disappear, forget about him." From the next room her capricious voice can be heard: "Grandmother, you've mislaid the needle case again!" She considers him a child, and that's the whole problem. Of course, she's five years older than he is. She's already twenty-two, thank God, she has a fiancé, a military engineer stationed in the North, and she has two admirers who visit her and bring gifts. One of them is especially zealous—a plump major with the hairstyle of a sheep. He always smells of eau de cologne. The other, a pathetic university student, is lame, uses a cane, and is named Yasha. Marina regards him much more highly than she does the major, pities him, considers him talented and unfortunate and always tries to feed him. But, really, Igor

isn't a little boy either! Thank God, he hears such stories from Kolka
every day that it would knock you off your feet. In two weeks he'll
turn seventeen. With his right hand he can press a square twenty-kilo
weight fourteen times. If she tries to cuddle up to him again—she's
not at all to his taste, he doesn't like such thin long faces with big
noses—but if she tries it again, he'll hug her so hard that her bones
will crack. Because of imagining so distinctly how that will happen
he's suddenly thrown into a fever and begins tossing under the blanket, unable to find a comfortable position: he can't lie on his right side
because a rib aches, or on the left because the pillow touches a bruise
under his eye. He finally lies on his back. Once upon a time Mother
used to come into the children's room, and if he was lying on his back,
she would turn him on his side: lying on one's back causes the cere-
bellum to heat up and you can have nightmares. He flies into sleep
more and more swiftly, happily. The last thought that penetrates this
happiness, this swiftness, is the following: they've broken through the
front near Stalingrad, have freed Kalach, there are thirteen thousand
prisoners.

He doesn't know when he wakes up: there's quiet and dark all
around. Perhaps it's already late at night, perhaps noon. His whole
body hurts, his shoulders and back ache. Igor takes two steps, and he
staggers. What devilishness! It means he hasn't slept enough. He's
slept very little. It can't be any later than one in the afternoon. Grandmother is sitting at the table, and looking through the magnifying
glass, is cleaning the rice on the oilcloth. Aunt Dina hasn't come home
from work yet. Marina is at the institute, there's an evening lecture
there tonight. It's a quarter after six.

"Gorik, there's a letter for you. You slept, slept, and finally came
out."

It's from Tashkent, from Grandmother. It's her angular handwriting
on the homemade envelope, made from a notebook cover: "To Igor
Nikolaevich Bayukov." As always, Grandmother writes extremely drily
and conspiratorially! "Our efforts aimed at what we have been dream-
ing about have not yet produced any results. They say it won't happen
any sooner than in a half a year. The reason I initiated the effort remains the same as before... He had the flu. Several people here were

sick...." To be read as follows: her arrival in Moscow is being postponed. David Shvarts's health is bad, just as it had been before. They had a severe epidemic of flu there. (Grandmother had written the Central Committee about the fact that in order to recover his health it was essential for David Shvarts to return to Moscow, and she, a close friend and his only one, should accompany him.) "I'm working at home now for a small producers' cooperative. I knit nets. It's important work, of strategic significance. We listened to Comrade Stalin's speech on the radio November 6 and envied your being in Moscow." (What is there to envy? We also listened to it on the radio.) "He put it wonderfully well about the fascist butchers not being able to escape retribution... In the second drawer of the desk on the right there should be a black file. Zhenya's birth certificate and Vasya's bonds should be there. Hide them. Has there by any chance been any news from Vasya? Be sure to write whether there has, because we're worried. The last letter from him was in August..."

"Vasya" is Grandmother's code name for Mother. There really hasn't been a letter from Mother in a long time. She is allowed to write once a month, but it's been three and a half months now without a word from her. But Grandmother Vera thinks it would be strange if letters from a camp were delivered without interruption during the war.

"I can just imagine how worried Nyuta is!" Grandmother Vera says. "But you could never tell it from the letter, could you? What strength of character! I'm constantly amazed..."

Grandmother Vera always speaks of her cousin with respectful rapture, but somewhere deep inside is a shade of the slightest and most usual derision. "She's not a person, she's an iron strongbox. When the misfortune happened to your mother, for a month and a half she concealed it from us—from me and from Dina, people near and dear to her. She said that Liza was on a work assignment. Do you by any chance know why she had to do that? We're not the Grinbergs or the Volodichevs, who started crossing to the other side of the street and turning away when they met Nyuta at the store. We're relatives. And when Grisha, your uncle, came down with tuberculosis and was sent to a sanitarium—and everyone knew about it—she assured us that he had gone away on a training assignment."

Grandmother Vera loves to talk about the other grandmother, sort through the past, her youth, their life together in Petersburg and Rostov, their husbands, who were friendly with each other and who were killed almost at the same time during the revolution. Igor enjoys listening, although he realizes that all this information is useless, unneeded. His own grandmother never reminisces about anything. She once said something that stunned Igor: "I don't remember what my real first and last names are. And I'm not interested." For forty years now she's been living under the name she got in the underground—Anna Genrikhovna Virskaya—and even her cousin, Grandmother Vera, calls her Nyuta.

"Nyuta is knitting nets! Lord have mercy! In the first place, the poor nets. Second, poor Nyuta: she's completely unused to physical work. After all, in the last few years she worked at that, what's it called, Secretariat, I think? Yes, yes, she was an important person, an administrator. And I was proud: my cousin was such an important person! Huh? I was very proud, yes, I was, yes, I was!"

Grandmother Vera laughs, nodding her weak-sighted head. In her sympathy and her laughter Igor recognizes a trace of that old secret cousinly envy that has now disappeared. And it makes him feel slightly uncomfortable.

"I always liked Nyuta. We were very close in our youth. But our lives worked out in such a way that we were almost never in an equal position at the same time. When I was here, she was there. When I turned out to be there, she would have risen to here." Grandmother Vera, continuing to smile because her narration gives her pleasure, points out with movements of her arms some symbolic "heres" and "theres." "That complicated our relations, of course. But just the same I liked Nyuta, admired her as a person, as an unusual personality, although I never understood her enthusiasms. I was very far from politics. But my husband, Alexander Ionovich, on the contrary, was a very lively, passionate person with a civic temperament, as befits a lawyer. He was also a *Social Democrat*, but of some special variety, I don't know exactly. After February, for example, he worked in the Provisional Government's commission for the exposing of double agents. We lived on Liteyny for several years. We had a wonderful seven-room apartment. I remember that your Grandmother came to see me in about 1912, for instance—in November Alexander Ionovich and I happened to be planning to go to Paris, we went there almost every winter—she came to ask me to help two comrades. She was so poorly dressed, so wretched and thin. I felt terribly sorry for her, I can remember that now. She had a boil on her lip. I wanted to feed her, to have her stay at our home, but she refused. Alexander Ionovich helped her in some way. He was the most noble person. And you know, Gorik, for my whole life, like a pain, there is imprinted on me the memory of Nyuta going off somewhere to a train station, at night, in the rain, while I stayed in a warm apartment with suitcases packed for Paris."

To judge by her nodding face with its blind smile you would never say that she was experiencing any pain from that memory right now. On the contrary, she seems to enjoy recalling it, and she has even put aside the magnifying glass and stopped picking through the rice so as to give herself up completely to the pleasant experience.

"And then the roles changed. In 1920 Alexander Ionovich got stuck in Novorossisk, didn't manage to get evacuated. He hadn't served in the Volunteer Army, but had retreated with it. He was a profoundly civilian person. And I was in Rostov, where I received the tragic news from him that he was threatened with being shot. I raced off to see Nyuta. She worked at the Political Department of the front. I implored her, wept, and she did everything she could, of course. She went to see your father, Nikolay Grigorievich sent a telegram, and Alexander Ionovich was saved. Then in Novorossisk they selected out of those 'volunteers' a large group of jurists for work in Soviet organs—people who agreed to work honestly. Nikolay Grigorievich was a humane person, he knew how to believe people. Alexander Ionovich worked very well with him, at the Tribunal for the Front, I think, I don't remember exactly where, on Bolshaya Sadovaya Street. And then there was some large insurrection, Alexander Ionovich was sent to investigate the matter. He wanted to sort things out in good conscience, of course, but he was accused of showing indulgence. They said that he, you know, was not a specialist from a proletarian background. He was taken off the job and threatened with all sorts of punishments, and at that point he fled to the Crimea. To his brother, the professor. Of course he made a mistake. He shouldn't have fled. I was left with the children in Rostov without any means at all. But he was dealt with cruelly. After the taking of the Crimea he was shot, and so was his brother. Your father couldn't do anything, while Nyuta said, when I came to see her: 'If my son Grisha had committed an act of desertion, I would have given the order without a second's hesitation. It's another matter when people are shot by mistake—that's a tragedy.' I remember that sentence: 'That's a tragedy.' But what happened to Alexander Ionovich was *not* a tragedy. I understand, she was talking about her husband, your grandfather, who had died a tragic death not long before that in Baku. He was shot for absolutely nothing, he had long since left politics, worked as an engineer in the oil fields. He was an amazing person, of unusual kindness, unselfishness. I always regretted that Nyuta broke up with him. Alexander Ionovich was friends with him in 1905, 1906, before he left for Baku, and I remember he told me: 'Andrian Pavlovich is a true revolutionary, he wouldn't hurt a fly.' How about that?" Grandmother Vera's dark, watery little eyes squint as she tries to look into Igor's face and make out what sort of impression those words have made on him. "How do you like that definition? A little unusual, isn't it? Alexander Ionovich was a great jokester, I have to tell you... In 1920 we had a very hard time of it, and Nyuta helped us... And five years ago she came to see me late at night and said: 'Vera, if anything happens to me, promise you won't abandon Gorik and Zhenichka.' And you know, I again felt terribly sorry for her when she was leaving. It was also raining, by the way. She was so old, wearing an old coat. She didn't have an umbrella. I gave her my umbrella."

Grandmother Vera's finger moves a black, bad grain of rice across the oilcloth into the little heap of white rice. So, she can't see anything though the magnifying glass either.

"Stop straining your eyes," Igor says. For some inexplicable reason he feels a slight irritation. "Here, let me clean it."

He makes an abrupt movement toward the table. Grandmother Vera, startled, covers the little pile of rice with her hands.

"No, no! I'll do it myself!"

"But you should give your eyes a rest today. Rather than pitying Grandmother, you should have pity on yourself, your eyes."

"It's my work. I'll do it myself."

"Why do senseless work? A labor of Sisyphus," he says, getting into a temper. "A labor of Sisyphus with the help of a magnifying glass!" He falters and falls silent.

Grandmother Vera is also silent. She is silent for a long time. Igor realizes that the old woman has been offended. It was very rude: "senseless work, a labor of Sisyphus!" She should be allowed to do the only thing she can, and she should be allowed to think that it's important. Igor squirms on the chair and has even broken into a sweat: he's ashamed and wants to make up for his rudeness. But he can't find the words for making up for it, and he continues to be silent, scowling sullenly. The entrance door slams, someone stamps down the hall, the lock on the next room clicks. Judging by the stamping—it's Bochkin. Very slowly, using her finger, Grandmother Vera moves a grain of rice at a time from one little pile to the other. Her face, with the magnifying glass placed over her eye, is inclined low. Igor sees her greenish crown, the white hair. He suddenly recalls that once in his childhood he had crawled into caves and seen a white grass there, under the ground.

"Was Sisyphus a slave?" Grandmother Vera asks unexpectedly.

"Who? Sisyphus? First a tsar, then a slave. Somewhere in the underworld."

"Like any person. First he's a tsar, then a slave. Old age is slavery." She falls silent, dropping her head lower. "Especially such a useless old age as mine. Why am I alive? Who gets any good out of this, out of my vegetable existence?"

"What are you saying?"

"Me? Not in a long time. Those near and dear to me? I can't do anything. I just eat bread and irritate people with my conversations. I irritate myself—by the fact that I'm helpless, sightless."

"But everybody loves you, Granny Vera!"

"I know." She nods, nods, can't stop. Her short bony finger crawls slowly over the oilcloth. "Perhaps it's in fact for them that I live."

———

And another conversation with Grandmother Vera. Also in the evening, and also when they're alone in the room. Igor has just finished having supper—he had a bowl of soup and drank a cup of coffee—and is lying on the daybed with the newspaper.

Grandmother Vera, sitting down next to him on the daybed, makes an unexpected request of him: to talk to Marina about her behavior.

"She respects you. Although I don't know what for..." Grandmother Vera jabs him in the side jokingly with a light fist. "Perhaps just because she isn't accustomed to respecting anyone else in the family. And you're a man, for what it's worth. You should tell her. Give examples from history, literature. You like literature, after all."

Igor wrinkles his brow. Tell her about what? What examples?

"That for thousands of years a woman's main virtue," Grandmother Vera whispers, "was considered her faithfulness to a fiancé away at war. Volodya writes tender letters, sends money. But here—there's that Yasha, that Vsevolod Vasilievich. I can't understand. I'm not asked, of course. Who am I?"

"But it's awkward for me," Igor says. "It's your and Aunt Dina's business."

"Aunt Dina and I are powerless. I haven't had the right to a voice for a long time, and she simply doesn't respect Dina. No, no! She simply doesn't listen to her. She feels sorry for her, of course, and loves her as a mother, but there's no respect. When Dina tried to say something, she snaps at her: 'Mama, you renounced a live husband, so don't try to teach me noble behavior.' So you see! I'm not defending Dina. She acted against her conscience. But, first, she was thinking about that Marina, about her fate. And, second, Dina and Pavel Ivanovich lived in disharmony even before all of that happened. I know what your mother went through. I know that at the People's Commissariat of Agriculture they demanded that she renounce him. And Nyuta, by the way, for all her firmness, said to Liza: 'Kolya would praise you. You must save the children. And your signing some piece of paper is absolutely nonsense, a trifle. Kolya will understand. Everyone will understand.' But Liza couldn't do it."

Igor thinks: she couldn't have become another woman. Turn into another person. He sees that summer long ago at the summer house, the arrival of Aunt Dina and a tall man with a moustache, Pavel Ivanovich. Father wrestled with him at the Gabay beach. It was a hot August day. They had arrived there in two rowboats. On the way they had had a contest to see which boat was faster, and Igor sat at the helm. And Father dropped his glasses in the water that day, and Mother dived for a long time until she found them on the bottom.

"You say they'll understand. But after all, Marina chose not to understand Aunt Dina. Although it was done for her sake."

"I didn't say that! Nyuta said that. True, I'm not certain that she said that just..."

"Well?"

"Well, you know your grandmother. She's not like ordinary people. Above all, she's a person devoted to discipline."

Bochkin has gone into the bathroom, rattling the washbasins there. The noise of water running has started up. Now he'll proceed with his disgusting business: he'll put pieces of hide in the basins, drag out jars of acid and blubber oil. You won't be able to get into the bathroom.

"Gorik, please go put on the soup. Dina will be home soon. And I beg you: not a word to Marina or Dina about my... But you..." Grandmother Vera covers her face with her hands. "Talk to Marina! She's perishing! Surely you can see that the girl is perishing. After all, she's been dismissed from the Institute. She's fooling people, not going to any..."

Grandmother Vera sobs. She cries without tears, the way very old people cry.

Igor promises to talk to Marina. What else can he do? But he can't manage to talk to her: she isn't home evenings, and in the morning he leaves too early.

Once he wakes up in the middle of the night from hunger. Perhaps not even from real hunger, the hunger that claws at a person with the ferocious desire to eat anything, as long as one can eat one's fill, stuff one's stomach. No, it's not all the same to him what he eats and what he stuffs his stomach with. He wouldn't eat the sauerkraut soup, for instance, that they serve in the cafeteria. The vegetable "unlimited" either, probably. He wakes up from a perfectly distinct and potent desire that comes from inside: to have a piece of black bread. He wants to get up quietly, tiptoe up to the buffet, open the glass door with maximum carefulness, so as not to wake up Grandmother and Aunt Dina, get the bread basket, and cut off a piece about ten millimeters thick from yesterday's loaf. Sprinkle it with salt and follow it with water from the faucet. For several seconds Igor lies motionless, looking into the dark and wondering at this bread whim that has awakened him in the middle of the night.

He's not the slightest bit sleepy, and the desire to feel the familiar, glutinous acidity of black bread burns in him more and more strongly. But he continues lying. No, he can't go to the cupboard and commit a theft. And what else is it but theft: under the cover of night biting off a piece from the common loaf? And besides, he'll be ashamed if Aunt Dina wakes up. Grandmother Vera won't hear anything, even if cannons were fired. That's what so awful, so shameful, that it's happening at night, when the others are asleep. If in the evening, in full view of everyone, he were to go up to the cupboard and with the words "I seem to bit a little hungry" calmly cut off a little piece of bread, that would be quite decent and natural. But in the middle of the night now, on the sly... No, it's impossible! At ten o'clock it would have been possible, but now—he reaches for the alarm clock, looks closely at the glowing figures—at three o'clock in the morning it's absolutely unthinkable. Better to die from starvation. Just imagine: Aunt Dina suddenly wakes up, for any number of reasons, a stitch in her side, and sees her nephew, standing in his white underwear, by the buffet... Meanwhile the desire for black bread—nothing more, no pastries, pickles, liverwurst, nothing except plain black bread—is becoming unbearable. There's a burning sensation inside, as though a mustard plaster had been put there, in his stomach. Igor begins unconsciously calculating how to throw back the blanket as quietly as possible and how to lower his left foot to the floor without knocking into anything. What nonsense comes into people's heads when they're half awake, though! Will the good people who love him like a son really begrudge him a little slice of bread, forty or fifty grams? The only awkward thing is that it's nighttime. But after all, waking them up in the middle of the night so as to inform them of his unconquerable desire to have some bread would be even more awkward. It would be simply a vile act, the more so as Grandmother is tormented by insomnia and has trouble getting to sleep. And when all is said and done, he's the main person in this household, the "German, the reliable breadwinner, in a cotton nightcap," so to speak. He earns 700 grams on his worker's ration card, Aunt Dina earns 500 on her office worker's card, Grandmother Vera doesn't earn anything, and Marina doesn't either.

The last foul thought enters his head as he is already sneaking barefoot to the buffet. With a piece of bread, sprinkled with salt, and a glass he then glides into the kitchen.

He turns on the light, fills the glass with water, sits down at the table—so that his bare feet will not be on the cold floor, but will dangle in the air—and digs into his feast. His thoughts don't manage to concentrate on anything, drifting from Kolka, Avdeychik, the new matrixes, which give out too quickly, and Chuma's complaints about that (yesterday they redrew the previous day's whole batch of sections, which had been rejected by the quality controllers; the matrixes had gotten "flabby" unusually quickly, and no one had noticed), from rumors that many people will soon be returned from the Urals, that there will be reassignments in the shops, that coupons for caps with earflaps will be issued for New Year's, from everything at the plant, which has become tormenting and part of him, to the offense west of Rzhev, to the breach of the front, to yesterday's rally at the shop, to Stalingrad and Toulon, where the French sailors blew up their ships, but the captains remained on the bridges and almost all of them were killed. And suddenly he clearly hears a key grating lightly in the entrance door.

Someone is turning the key just as slowly and carefully as he had just acted himself when opening the door on the buffet.

Igor turns out the light in the kitchen and just in case arms himself with a kitchen knife. The key continues grating. The door finally opens; whispering and stamping at the doorway can be heard; something heavy is put down. Marina's voice: "Don't bother, it can stay here." More fumbling of some sort; the heavy thing is moved across the floor; two people whisper. "No. We mustn't, because..." "Please!" "Come here. Here, to the kitchen."

They enter the kitchen. The light goes on. Igor squeezes up against the wall, screens himself off with the cupboard, but he's still in plain view. For the first second he experiences shame, piercing and murderous, like a bolt of lightning, but then he begins not to care, his feelings are deadened, and he sinks into a benumbed and dull indifference. He hears Marina shriek, laugh, then sees her collapse on a stool, sees red patches break out on her cheeks, tears stream from her eyes. He sees Vsevolod Vasilievich's leather coat, his bulging blue eyes, and his mouth, yelling: "Idiot! Frightening a woman like that!"

Then Vsevolod Vasilievich disappears. Marina sits on the stool, but Igor still can't come out from behind the cupboard, because then he'll be revealed entirely, from head to toe. Marina, clutching her head in her hands, mumbles something about "a horrible spectacle," about not being able to stand seeing "that disgusting filth," "what shame," and something else. He doesn't understand anything.

She suddenly says in a clear, sober voice: "Young men should wear underwear even in the winter, not those disgusting things."

Then he realizes that she's drunk. She covers her eyes with her fingers, and walking unsteadily, bumping into the walls with her elbows spread wide, she makes her way out of the kitchen. From the hall her mumbling can be heard. She is talking to herself: "Careful here, you little fool... Don't trip, my dear... Here are the potatoes, a bag of potatoes, forty kil..." He stands motionless, listening closely, clenching his fists. The blood, which was about to stop, again seethes in his veins and throws him into a fever. He so hates the man with the bulging blue eyes, and so loves the drunken girl, and is so humiliatingly aware of himself, his insignificance, that he wants to fall down, to die.

And he pours some water into the glass, sits down at the table, eats the rest of his black bread. Then he goes down the hall to Marina's room, opens the door without knocking, and says into the darkness: "Marinka, I've got to have a talk with you."

VII

They left the skis at the entrance, for camouflage they covered them with snow and put branches on top. Lyonya crawled in first. The opening, cleared of mushy snow, mud, and last year's leaves, was small and unappealing. It was impossible to believe that this hole led to giant catacombs. First you had to stick your feet in the opening, and then force your way in with your whole body. Lyonya said that after the first passage, about five or six meters down, there would be a little ledge that it would be most convenient to climb down from just like that: feet first. "Adieu!" said Lyonya, and his head, covered by his leather flyer's helmet, disappeared in the black hole.

"With his hams, Sapog wouldn't have gotten through here anyway-ay-ay-ay-ay." Marat made his teeth chatter on purpose and shook as though from fright. But although he was fooling, his face really was pale.

His cap with earflaps slid away too. Gorik thrust his feet into the hole, and pushing off with his hands and elbows, helping with his shoulders, began boring into the tight and narrow hole. If you didn't know that this confinement would soon end and spacious passages and rooms begin, as Lyonya had promised, you could be seized by despair. Gorik moved too quickly, because he heard Marat's half-muffled voice from below: "Hey, careful... My head..." Oh, so that was it! Gorik's foot had twice bumped into something unsteady that slipped away. From even further away Lyonya's voice could be heard: "Jump!" Marat apparently jumped down. Gorik could feel that the confinement had ended, and his feet were in the empty space above the ledge. Jumping without knowing the true height was frightening. Gorik dangled his legs in the air for several moments, moving down millimeter by millimeter and trying in vain to touch the bottom with the tips of his shoes. "Come on, jump!" someone said, pulling Gorik by the foot, and Gorik tumbled to the ground. He didn't have to fall, but could have landed on his feet—the ground turned out to be close, no more than half a meter from his shoes, but because of the tension and shaking in his knees he couldn't stay up and fell down.

All three of them lit their candles and saw a small, semicircular room with a low ceiling and two exits that loomed as black hollows. The room was remarkably cozy. It reminded one of a living room with the windows curtained over. The floor was littered with papers, bones, cans, and the corpse of a little dog. The dog had obviously died long since, because the corpse had dried out, nearly turned into a skeleton wrapped in dark hide, and it didn't give off any bad smell. In the room there was a warm, musty, but very pleasant smell of sandstone walls. Lyonya headed confidently to one of the black hollows, from which a passageway started. It was now clear that Karas had told the truth: he was an old-timer here. And that meant he had lied to his mother about the movies and about having allegedly climbed over a wall and scraping the skin on his palms. He had been here, that was for certain. He hadn't wanted to frighten Lina Arkadievna. But how could he, the monster, have come here alone? To take the train from Moscow, set off on skis, squeeze through that trap, hurting his hands and ruining his coat, and all just so as to be alone for a while—with a candle in his hand—in this sepulchral darkness. That was an act of awful strength. Even the thought of such an act made his flesh creep, and he cast it off, tried not to think about it and not ask Lyonya anything, because for the meantime he could still doubt, but as soon as he found out for certain, he wouldn't be able to treat Lyonya as he had before, as an ordinary person. Therefore it would be better to think that Karas had lied, that he hadn't been here alone, but with some adult, with a professor, for instance, a specialist in the study of caves. He couldn't have, *did not have the right* to come here alone. If he had done so, he would tower over everyone monstrously and excessively, and simultaneously humiliate everyone around.

The passageways and chambers were replaced by new passageways and chambers. Lyonya continually drew a piece of paper out of his map case and marked something on it in pencil: he was making a map of the cave. He wanted to give the map to the Geographic Society, for which, as he calculated, all three of them should be elected members of the society. And perhaps even honorary members. All of that was alluring and wonderful, especially when it was discussed there, on the surface, but now two things nagged at Gorik. The first was that over the course of a rather long section of the way Marat had put down only nine or ten paper numbers. Lyonya had told him to leave numbers only where the passageways forked. That was sensible, of course, but nevertheless some of the passageways were so long, winding, with such complicated turns, that it would have been better for peace of mind to put down numbers more often. That was Gorik's opinion, which he did not state, of course, so as not to look too *careful*. Moreover, the fact that Lyonya had said to save numbers—and they'd made more than a hundred of them!—meant that Karas's appetite had grown and that he intended to walk through his favorite cave for another five hours or so. But Gorik thought that everything was already clear and that they could start making their way gradually to the exit. They had walked some, taken a look, and from there on it would be the same—another chamber, another passageway.

The other thing that nagged at him was the thought of Volodka. At Lyonya's secret insistence the expedition had been kept from him, but Sapog, out of thoughtlessness or malice, could have happened to call home and discover the lie. Gorik had said that he was going with his class on an excursion to Lenin Hills. Most likely, Sapog was not about to call, because he'd guessed that for some reason he'd been barred; on Saturday he'd had such a wan, crushed look that he even felt sorry for him. All in all, Gorik thought that Sapog was a frivolous person, a prattler and a liar, and he shouldn't be let it on secret matters, and for that reason he was even glad when Lyonya suddenly declared that for special reasons Sapog had to be excluded from the SSCUP—Lyonya promised to inform them of the reasons later, after he ascertained the accuracy of the facts. He just said that Marat's crimes—his shameless *running* after Katka Florinskaya, for all to see, and the fact that he had blabbed to her about the caves—were nothing compared to "the special reasons!" But just exactly what the matter was the damned mystifier didn't say.

Gorik was irritated with him. "All right! There's a thing I won't tell you either." There wasn't any "thing," of course. There was a feeling of offense that had stuck in Gorik since the morning, when Karas took it into his head to make fun of him. The nasty desire to make fun of his friends sometimes came over Karas.

At the first break he came up to Gorik and said: "Let's find out who the 'crocodiles' are!" "All right!" Gorik agreed willingly, not imagining a trick.

"Crocodiles" was what Lyonya and Gorik called people who only know what they were taught in school—in short, ignoramuses, dimwits. "Crocodiles" were resisted by "octopuses," well-educated people knowledgeable in many fields. There were plenty of "crocodiles" in the class, but precious few "octopuses." Lyonya, Gorik, and three or so more people, no more. Identifying "octopuses" was a very pleasant business, a very diverting pastime. So Gorik had thought that Karas was suggesting that they have some fun, feel out several people, ask some test questions. Lyonya showed him a picture in a book and asked: "What flower is this?" "Who the hell knows?" "You don't know?" "No." "Amazing! It's a rafflesia. It grows on the islands of Sumatra and Java. Every 'octopus' ought to know a thing like that!" And he walked away, laughing, as though to say: "And it turns out that you're a 'crocodile,' pal!"

Gorik, stunned by such baseness, spent the whole lesson thinking over how to get revenge, and at the next break called to Lyonya: "Lyon," he said as simple-heartedly as possible, "do you by any chance know who the *Mormons* are?" "No." "Amazing! Every 'crocodile' ought to know that. Not to mention 'octopuses.'" At that point the boastful professor got it all, turned red as a crayfish, and making a wry face, said contemptuously: "You're always copying me, you ape!"

And until the end of the class day they didn't speak. Only on the way back did Karas unexpectedly catch up to Gorik on the embankment and said in a dry tone of voice: "You're still a member of the SSCUP and should know that in three days we're going to the cave." And precisely at that point Karas told him about Sapog, and Gorik, who had been on the point of completely forgiving him, got irritated again. If Sapog had come up to Gorik the next day and said, "Guys, what for?"—Gorik would surely have demanded immediate explanations from Lyonya, but Sapog didn't come up. Sapog had fallen silent, didn't talk to anyone, looked incredibly sad. He appeared to understand the hopelessness of his position. That submissiveness to fate was not at all in his, Sapog's, character, and merely confirmed the suspicion that there was something dishonest here.

The fatty was aware of some fault.

After an hour or an hour and a half of wandering through passageways and chambers they at last came out into the Round, or Tsar's Room. This was where Lyonya had been wanting to get to. A halt had been promised here. The chamber was large, the walls and ceiling were lost in the dark, the three candles couldn't illuminate anything except for a patch of the rock floor under foot, and that underground infinity was even more distressing than the darkness. In the middle of the chamber lay huge, flat rocks, one of which they used for a table, spreading out the food: boiled meat, eggs, bread. But they had no appetite. Only Lyonya worked his jaws energetically and while so doing, without stopping speaking, talked about the principle of mining stone in the eighteenth century, when quarries arose. Half of Moscow, it turned out, was built of the white stone that had been extracted here, in these chambers. Then he said that the Tsar's Chamber, where they were sitting, must be near the old main entrance, which was now blocked with stones and walled over, and therefore they had gone a long way from that other hole. That news did not make Gorik and Marat especially happy. They looked at each other as though by chance, wanting to say something, but kept mum. Lyonya thought there must be other exits somewhere. It couldn't be that there existed only one exit from such a gigantic labyrinth. There had to be others. They should look for them.

Marat and Gorik continued chewing listlessly. And suddenly Gorik asked—he didn't mean to ask, it came out all by itself: "Karas, did you really come here alone?"

"Yes, I did," said Lyonya.

"Why on earth am I asking?" Gorik wondered with despair. Something even shuddered and began to hurt in his chest when he heard: "Yes, I did." But it was all over, the arrow was deep in his heart, and its vane quivered slightly.

"Why alone?" Gorik asked in a weak voice.

"So as to test myself," Lyonya answered abruptly and pitilessly.

In the quiet the metallic crunching of his jaws chewing could be heard.

"Well, you're sure a one..." sighed Marat.

"Do you know which caves in Europe are the least studied?" asked Lyonya, not noticing either Gorik's stupefaction or the respectful sigh. "Spain's and Portugal's! Listen—any 'crocodile' should know..."

Now he could be boorish and make fun as much as he wanted. Gorik was vanquished. He couldn't even take offense, let alone answer. A great person: he had tested himself! And been satisfied with the test!

"I would also like to test myself... sometime," Gorik said timidly and enviously.

"Easy as pie. In general you should test yourself not sometime, not once in a hundred years, but constantly. Well, at least once a month," said Lyonya. "We can test ourselves together if you like."

"All right," Gorik agreed.

"And me too! We'll take Sapog, damn him," said Marat. "Let the fatty test himself. It won't hurt him."

Lyonya suddenly told them a stunning piece of news about Sapog: his father, it turned out, was an enemy of the people and a German spy! A few days earlier he had been exposed and arrested. Gorik and Marat hadn't heard anything like that. They couldn't even believe their ears. But Lyonya said that he'd found out for certain, that it had been confirmed by a woman, a friend of his mother's, the seamstress Aunty Taisia, who lived on the same stairway as the Sapozhnikovs. The news was terribly interesting: it meant they knew a real spy! Knew him very well, had shaken his hand many times, talked about this and that. Sapog's father was a fat person who went around in a white shirt and suspenders that for some reason always dangled, weren't worn on his shoulders. He would look at Gorik with a dark unsmiling eye, wink stupidly, and ask in an official voice: "Well, what's new on the Pioneer front?" And such an ordinary man with dangling suspenders was a German spy! You'd never guess. But precisely because it was so incredible Gorik believed it; you could never tell real spies right away. It was only in movies that they showed spies who leapt out at you from the very first moment. To any fool from the fourth grade sitting in the theater it would all be clear long since, while on the screen intelligence agents agonized and racked their brains.

"And for that reason," Lyonya said, "Sapozhnikov must be expelled from the SSCUP."

"Why?" Marat asked, surprised, but immediately added: "But when you come down to it, yes."

But that seemed dishonest to Gorik. After all, Sapog wasn't to blame for the fact that his father was a spy. How could he know? He wasn't interested in his father's affairs, was he?

"You know what my father said," said Lyonya, and in the light of the candle his face turned harsh, with prominent cheekbones, like an Indian's. "He came to Moscow not long ago for a plenum. He saw Stalin, Voroshilov, all the leaders. And he said that right now is a very difficult time, even more difficult than a war. Because there are enemies all around. Wreckers, spies, saboteurs, double-dealers, and so on. England and France, they say, are full to overflowing with German spies. Why then, he said, shouldn't we have them? We do, and even more than over there, but it's hard to expose them, because, he said, they use Party cards and past services as a cover. All in all, they camouflage themselves very cleverly, the creeps."

He fell silent, wrinkling his brow.

"Well?" asked Gorik.

"What do you mean 'well'? A well is a hole in the ground. If we took Volodka into a cave, and he blabbed to his father, and his father gave the information about the cave to the German General Staff. And caves play a very important role in war. Is that clear to you nitwits?"

The "nitwits" were silent. Everything that Karas had said was clear and wise, but because of that wisdom they suddenly felt depressed. The game was over. Something else was beginning. But they didn't want to believe in that. For almost their whole lives, a long one for the one and a short, unhappy one for the other, they didn't believe that *the game was over.*

Everyone divided up into two warring camps: some for Seryozhka's Valya, the others against Seryozhka's Valya. For—Grandmother,

Mother, Zhenka, Uncle Misha, Valerka, the maid Marusya; against— Father, Gorik, Aunt Dina, Seryozhka himself, Uncle Grisha, and his wife Zoya. Everything was understandable except for one thing: why was Uncle Misha for? Probably only because he invariably argued with Father and especially with Seryozhka. If they were against, that meant he of course was for. The hubbub started one evening, when Grandmother came home from work very upset and said that Seryozhka's Valya had come to see her at the Secretariat, had cried, *sobbed*, and complained about Seryozhka, and called him a scoundrel. All of that was told over supper to just the adults, but Gorik, who ran into the dining room several times with a geometry textbook—as though to ask father about a tricky problem—although he pretended that he didn't understand anything and wasn't interested in anything except for geometry, and although Grandmother lowered her voice every time that he ran in, he managed to understand everything perfectly well. What he heard stunned him. He had never seen people *sobbing*, but a picture of Valya *sobbing* immediately arose in his imagination. It was something majestic and at the same time frightening. The main thing that he understood was that Seryozhka no longer wished to be Valya's fiancé and had found himself another girlfriend. Gorik had already seen this other one, named Ada, three times or so. Seryozhka had brought her to visit, and they had once all gone to the movies together to see *Arsen from Marabda*, a terrific picture about bandits in the Caucasus.

Ada was much prettier than Valya. First, Valya wore glasses, was dark, with dark eyes and a swarthy, mulatto-colored face. And if you looked closely, you could notice a little black moustache on her, the kind that guys in the tenth grade have. Valya was a student, in the same class as Seryozhka, while Ada was an artist, worked at a film studio and could get tickets to any film without standing in line. Ada had light-colored, curly hair, played tennis, laughed merrily, loved to sing "The Morning Greets Us with Coolness." But some said that Ada couldn't be a real fiancée for Seryozhka, because she had a husband, an executive, who lived right here in this building, in another courtyard. But Seryozhka said that Ada didn't want to live with that husband and would leave him all the same. But Grandmother said that one shouldn't deceive a person, that is, Valya, the way Seryozhka had done. But Father said that no matter how relations shape up, one shouldn't come to the Secretariat about such a matter.

Valya came at one time and sat for a long time in Grandmother's room behind the marsh-colored door-curtain. The next day Ada came and spent a whole hour in Father's study, where first Mother, then Seryozhka would run in, but Grandmother would walk past the door of the study with an imperturbable and proud look, and Gorik heard her say: "No, there's nothing for me to do there!" Then Valya came to say good-bye. She was leaving for another city. She came first to the children's room—she had never been in there—and offering her hand to Gorik, said: "Good-bye, Gorik! I wish you all the best. I hope you grow up to be a happy and honest person." Gorik replied: "All right." He didn't know what else to say, and Valya didn't leave. She said: "Do you remember how we went skiing, at the country house?" He remembered. "And memorized Pushkin." "Uhuh," he said. He began to feel sorry for her, because he recalled how terribly she skied and how badly she memorized poetry. Her lips began to twitch, and her eyes turned bright, and Gorik was afraid because he thought that at any moment she would *sob*, but she nodded and went out.

A few days later Seryozhka was responsible for a new hubbub. He had yelled at Grandmother, quarreled with Mother, thrown his things out of his room into the hall and run off somewhere with a leather suitcase packed full of books and papers. He said that he couldn't live in a household where people didn't respect him and didn't believe a single word he said. And he also left for another city. But two days later he came back. It was stifling spring weather. Lawns had turned green. In the school garden there was an oppressively hot smell of earth and the fresh paint with which the benches and low wooden fence were being covered. During the breaks students were allowed to go out into the garden, and in the higher grades students could go out to the embankment and walk there along the granite parapet.

Gorik and Marat watched the students from the higher grades through the fence. No one below the ninth grade had the right to run out onto the nice, sun-warmed pavement of the embankment: they might be run over by a car. Gorik went up to the gate and yelled: "Hey, hairworms! It's the bell!" The students from the higher grades trooped across the street, continuing to talk with a pompous air. And only after they had entered the yard did they notice that no one was rushing to the school building. Gorik and Marat took to their heels, yelling: "Fooled you all, ha-ha!" One of the students from the upper grades, a big lug with the crimson-red face of a bandit, took off after Gorik and Marat. They ran to the rear yard, hoping that the lug would leave them alone for fear of the mud and puddles. But he chased after them, splashing through the puddles and snorting like an elk. His friends and the girls encouraged the bandit with shouts: "Catch them! Stop them! Go get them!" After running through the rear yard, Gorik and Marat flew into the rear stairway—thank God, some kind person had left the door open!—and like lightning raced upstairs, to the third floor. They imagined the lug was running after them. To tell the truth, they were frightened: the stairs were dark and empty of people, and the lug would have had no trouble *pounding them into a paste*. No one would have heard cries for help. On the third floor they stopped, scarcely able to catch their breath. No, it was all quiet. After running as far as the rear entrance, the crimson-mugged guy apparently realized that his attempt to catch up to them was unlikely to be crowned with success, and he halted the pursuit.

The crimson-mugged guy turned out to be Ada's brother. His name was Lyova. Their father was a deputy people's commissar, and lived at entrance eleven. Ada and this Lyova once came to see Seryozhka. They both had tennis rackets in cases, and they invited Seryozhka along— to go to Petrovka, to the Dynamo courts—and seeing Gorik in the hall, Lyova said: "Hah, caught you!" He didn't say anything more. Gorik went out onto the balcony and from up there watched the three of them walk through the courtyard: Ada's and Lyova's two light-colored heads, and Seryozhka's dark one. Seryozhka said that Lyova had played tennis with Henri Cochet himself when he had come to Moscow, and Henri Cochet had predicted that Lyova would go a long way.

On that April day, from up on the balcony, Gorik saw Lyova for the last time. On the eve of the May Holidays terrible news spread: Lyova had been arrested by the police, and he and four other guys would be tried. They were robbing apartments. Lyova had stolen his father's pistol. And Valka, David Shvarts's son, was also mixed up in this business. Valka was not arrested like the others, but he was summoned to the investigator and interrogated. He hadn't taken part in the robberies, but knew about them and had even helped the robbers in some way. He had allowed a fellow who had run away from home to live in his room for several days, and he told David that the guy's father, a former priest, beat him for the fact that the guy had joined the Komsomol. The mythical Komsomol member turned out to be practically the main ringleader in the gang.

David Shvarts came to get advice about what to do with Valka.

Everyone was sitting in the dining room except for Zhenya, who, sick with tonsillitis, was lying in quarantine in Grandmother's room. Grandmother was especially enraged, but for some reason she attacked Seryozhka: "I told you that I didn't like any of that whole family! You argued with me. Now you can see what degeneration..."

"What does the family have to do with it? His father is a respected man. He worked with Ordzhonikidze, by the way. Now he only comes home late at night, that's true, that's the kind of work he has. Ada is also a decent, honest woman, but as you know, she can't bring up her brother, because she's married and lives apart..."

"A decent woman, being married, wouldn't be about to..."

I don't think that's any concern of yours!" Sergey turned crimson.

"Yes, it is. It concerns the morals of everyone, of the whole family."

"What are you talking about? What nonsense!" Sergey seethed. "And how about Anna Karenina? You ought to be ashamed!"

"Seryozhka, don't try to brush things aside. Mother's right to a certain extent," Gorik's mother said reasonably. "Why did such a thing happen precisely in that family? I can't imagine, for instance, you or Gorik stealing a pistol from Nikolay Grigorievich's desk and going off to rob apartments. Is that possible? I think it's impossible. And in the same way I can't imagine how, after falling out of love with a man and betraying him, one can continue living in an apartment with him, seeing him daily."

"And what should she do?"

"Leave."

"Where to?"

"To the man she loves, obviously."

"To a six-square-meter apartment? She has canvases, frames, an easel—where will all that fit? And when you come down to it this is demagogy: neither you nor Mother wants Ada to come here. For you that's a nightmare. And she senses that. Why say things for no good reason?"

"All right, if not here, then let her go to her father's." Gorik's mother wouldn't give in. "He has a large enough apartment. There would be room for his daughter."

"Exactly! Yes, yes," Grandmother nodded. "I can't understand it either. Such lack of principles, such cynicism."

"How easily you solve other people's problems, damn it! And if *she cannot* go back to her father's? If that's how relations with her stepmother have worked out? What then? Jump off the Stone Bridge? Put a bullet in her forehead?"

Gorik sat and listened with enormous interest. They'd forgotten about him. And he tried not to call attention to himself with any sound or the slightest movement of his body. Grandmother tenaciously stuck to her guns: "What I want to say is that I find the family unpleasant. I know their father. He's hardly a principled person: first he signs platforms, and then he just as easily repudiates them. You can't trust people like that, you know."

"Well, and so what that he signed platforms? What immorality! It means he had his own opinion, even if it was mistaken."

"For some reason Nikolay Grigorievich and I didn't make mistakes *that way*: *against* the Party, *against* the Party line. We made mistakes together with the Party, perhaps..."

"Perhaps so! Well, all right!" Seryozhka cried, leaping to his feet. His face had suddenly broken out in red spots near his eyes, which meant that he was not in control of himself. "Here's David Alexandrovich Shvarts sitting here—right? Respected by all of us and besides us, by hundreds, thousands of other people. Right? And what happened to Valentin? Does that mean we should explain Valka's sins through some sort of... characteristics of David Alexandrovich's? Is that right?"

"Please explain that," Shvarts said hoarsely. "That would be smart."

He sat on the daybed, panting, and turning his bulging eyes, with yellowish whites, filled with tiredness, first to one person and then to another. He most likely wasn't listening to what was being said, but was thinking. Watching him was amusing. Bubbles would suddenly well up on his thick lips, he would suddenly start picking his nose, do so with concentration, then roll something between his fingers—in plain sight of everyone—unconcerned about that fact that doing so was unseemly.

Grandmother said that the most sensible thing would be to send Valka to a country boarding school. Gorik's father gave a low whistle: "How do you like that! And who was it that criticized Vanya Snyakin for sending his son to a country boarding school?" "Don't muddle things, Nikolay Grigorievich! I know what I'm saying," Grandmother replied sharply. And she promised to talk to her friend Berta, an ugly, bearded old woman, an unbelievable smoker, who worked in the People's Commissariat of Education and dealt precisely with country boarding schools. "The Snyakins had all the conditions for raising the boy at home," Grandmother said sternly. "But his wife was too fond of comfort and the easy life. Now, true, she's living without any comfort at all somewhere in the North. I'm not gloating, of course, but on the contrary, I pity her. But David doesn't have those sorts of conditions and never did." The question of a country boarding school was resolved. Mother, who loved to make everything neat and efficient, immediately proposed getting Valka into the Shabanovo Country Boarding School, because Aunt Dina worked in Shabanovo, at the composer's museum, and she could visit Valka, and he could come see her.

David Shvarts nodded, agreeing with everything, and then said: "That's a good plan. I just don't know whether he'll agree to it." Everyone was indignant over that sentence. Nikolay Grigorievich demanded that Valka be sent to see him, and he would have a firm talk with him, and Grandmother kept repeating: "There are the results of your policy!" But David Shvarts said that if Valka were his own son, he would treat him very strictly, but as it was, he was obliged to pity him. Then Mother said irritatedly: "Gorik, what are you doing sitting here? Go to bed immediately!"

On his way out Gorik heard Seryozhka say in an unnatural, impudent voice: "Why so? You could also be just the opposite—more severe. That also has its own logic." After that there was a silence. Perhaps they all fell to drinking tea and eating candy at the same time. But after he had gone far down the hallway, Gorik continued to sense a strange awkwardness in that silence. He thought about that silence while sitting in the toilet, then in the bathroom, and after the bathroom, when he went to bed too. And he was a little bit ashamed of Seryozhka, of his insolent tone of voice, and of something else that he couldn't manage exactly to identify. Gorik tossed from side to side and took a long time to fall asleep.

Seryozhka was the same sort of adoptive son for Grandmother as Valka was for Shvarts. Only David Shvarts had taken Valka from an orphanage recently, seven years ago, while Grandmother had taken Seryozhka after the Civil War, during the famine, when Seryozhka was five years old. He didn't speak Russian, because he was Chuvash and was born on the Volga, in a Chuvash village. But no one, of course—neither Grandmother, nor Mother, nor Uncle Grisha, nor Father, nor Gorik, nor Zhenka—gave any sign that Seryozhka wasn't Grandmother's own son. Gorik didn't even know about that for many years. Mother only told him last year. And now recently, when Gorik got angry at Seryozhka for something and quarreled with him, calling him "a hopeless fool," Mother said that he should never call Seryozhka names and say rude things to him. "But what if he does it first?" Gorik asked. "All the same you must restrain yourself and not say anything."

Late in the evening Sergey put on a suit, draped his coat over his arm, stuck a box of Herzegovina Flors in his pocket—he hardly touched those cigarettes, saving them for special occasions—and looked into the dining room so as to say: "Well, so long! I'm going to go for a walk before bed." David Alexandrovich and Grandmother were still sitting at the tea table. They looked up at him as though out of a deep sleep. It goes without saying that Anna Genrikhovna, Sergey's mother, whom he, like everyone in the household, called "grandmother" or even, in Gorik's version, "grammar," never demanded an accounting of where he was going to, with whom, for how long. But now he had pronounced his "so long" after eleven o'clock at night, and she looked at him very distantly. She seemed not even to understand that he was leaving. But Liza, who ran into him in the large hallway, understood everything, and she made a wry face sourly and weakly. She sighed: "Oh, Seryozhka..."—in reply to which Sergey mumbled curtly: "I'll be back soon. But lock one of the locks."

It was warm. People with little burning corners of cigarettes were standing in a circle on the pavement in front of the entrance and talking in low voices. Some words carried: "But there she's superb." "Where?" "In *Swan Lake*." "Oh, in *Swan Lake*—I don't deny it, but I'm talking about..." Walking down the paved path away from that bunch of people smoking cigarettes before bed and discussing ballet, Sergey wondered whether that was serious or for the sake of appearances. An awful lot of people pretended to be interested in nonsense. Half the guys in his class raved about soccer. All you heard was "Ilin, Starostin, backs, halfbacks." Others were crazy about chess. They drew tables, played even during classes. What do you think, who'll win in the postponed match: Levenfish or Yudovich? He really wanted to say to the fool: "My dear, I play chess, too, but I don't pretend that it's so insanely important for me to know who will win—Levenfish or Yudovich. Who will win: General Franco or General Walter? Meyerhold or Kerzhentsev? Stalin or Hitler? That will concern you personally, fool, that will roll over your life, while you'll be playing chess in heaven." That's what Sergey wanted to say, but didn't yesterday, when a fellow sidled up to him after an all-school meeting at which Professor Uspensky had been inveighed against as "a Trotskyite and ideological wrecker," and asked: "What do you think, who will win the postponed match: Levenfish or Yudovich?" He looked at the empty rabbit's eyes under glasses, and after being silent for a moment, said: "I think that all in all, Levenfish has a better chance." And the recollection of that moment of silence, of what he said and what he didn't say, drove him along, drove him down the pavement around the corner, to another courtyard, to the corner entrance.

When he approached this entrance he was always troubled by a nonsensical and stupid fear of the doorman. Of his indifferent and vig-

ilant gaze and of a possible question. Fortunately, at this same entrance, on the seventh floor—Ada lived on the fourth—lived a friend
from elementary school years, Boris Volodichev, now a student at a
legal institute. He hardly saw Boris, mutual interests had dried up, but
in response to the question "Where to?" he could answer—to see him.
They had never yet asked, not even once, because the doormen he
came across were ones he knew, who remembered Sergey from the
times when he really had come to visit Boris. Sergey would courte-
ously say hello, and the doormen, nodding in reply, didn't trouble
themselves to ask the unnecessary questions required by their instructions. All these taciturn, uniformed men wearing dark-blue tunics and
sitting bored at their official desks were undoubtedly employees of the
NKVD. The inhabitants of the building knew that and treated them
with customary caution, as they would, for instance, iron boxes with
the lettering "Dangerous! High Voltage!" They weren't exactly afraid,
but they avoided lingering in their vicinity. Sergey, of course, couldn't
have cared less, but there was a woman involved here.

He pulled open the heavy door, and an evil premonition made his
heart thump. It was very late, eleven-thirty. It was in fact a new doorman. Sergey said "hello," in two leaps bounded up the first stairway
and headed to the left, toward the elevator. The doorman stopped him
from down below with a peremptory: "Just a moment! Who are you
going to see?" Not ever before, not in a single entranceway, had he
been hailed so imperiously. Sergey looked at him closely: a young,
heavy fellow, closely shaven, with puffy, full lips. The face seemed
powdered to Sergey, and the gaze of the small eyes under the dark
brows somehow theatrically intense. That sort of person should come
out onto the stage and start singing in a tenor voice "Oh, Galina, oh,
maiden..." Smiling for some reason, Sergey said: "To see Volodichev."

"Don't you think it's maybe a little late?" asked the doorman, turning and going toward the telephone hanging on the wall. While so
doing the heavy fellow yawned, gently patting his wide-open mouth
with his hand.

That singularly unceremonious tone and the movements full of dignity revealed a person who knew his own worth. "Probably a lieutenant," thought Sergey. "He'll do everything according to the book.

And what if Borka isn't home?" The doorman dialed the number and was silent for a long while. They had obviously already gone to bed there. Sergey feverishly thought about what to say to Borka.

"There's a person to see you." The doorman tilted his chin toward Sergey inquiringly and showed little respect. "What's your name?"

"Virsky."

"Virsky." The doorman was silent for a bit, then hung up the receiver.

He didn't say anything to Sergey, didn't look at him, just silently headed from the telephone to his chair, on which lay a round, green, flat, cotton pillow. "Maybe even a senior lieutenant," Sergey thought with a tinge of respect, opened the elevator, and pressed the button for the seventh floor. The door to the Volodichevs' apartment was open. In the doorway stood Boris's mother, in a robe, obviously roused from sleep, with spots of white, sickly, crumpled skin around the gimlet eyes that bored into Sergey. Mrs. Volodicheva didn't say a word, but her whole stunned look cried: "What's this about? Tell me! But if it's something awful, you shouldn't have, you shouldn't have dared..." Sergey hastily explained that he had come to see Boris about an insignificant but absolutely urgent matter. He had once lent Boris the book *Masters of Art on Art*, Volume One, but the next day he would need the book for a seminar. Boris wasn't home, he hadn't yet returned from a holiday dinner at the institute. They went to his room, dug around in the bookcases, found the book, and then Mrs. Volodicheva, peacefully enjoying herself, asked about Grandmother in detail: they had worked together at the Secretariat. Mrs. Volodicheva always spoke about Grandmother with great respect. And Grandmother also spoke of Mrs. Volodicheva with praise: especially when speaking of her unrestrained love of work and unbelievable conscientiousness. Sergey had heard such phrases as "Our Maria Stepanovna is strong," "No one ever stays longer than Maria Stepanovna!" That meant that Mrs. Volodicheva could easily stay at work until twelve, until one, until three in the morning. Sergey at last extricated himself from Mrs. Volodicheva's inquiries—about Nikolay Grigorievich, Liza, her children, plans for the summer, the health of David Shvarts, whom Mrs. Volodicheva, in her words, "admired insanely"—and dashed out into the freedom of the stairway. His watch said five minutes to twelve. Sergey went down three floors and rang at the apartment located exactly under the Volodichevs'.

Ada opened at once. There was the familiar irritating smell of floor polish: in this apartment the floors always glistened. Ada polished the parquet herself, every day, even now, when the apartment had come apart, everything had come undone, dinner had ceased being made, the maid had left. But the hallway gleamed. Ada jumped around, enjoying herself, as good as a floor-polisher, mornings for the sake of exercise, and after meals so as not to put on weight. The apartment was a rare one for this building—small, two-room. And two people lived in it: Ada and Volovik. Ada said that it was all over with Volovik, but in the depths of his soul Sergey couldn't believe that, although he said he did. Volovik lectured at the institute where Sergey studied. He was the editor of a philosophy journal. He was on the way up. And this homely, fifty-year-old *nerd*, with the dark complexion of someone suffering from an ulcer, had the right to young, mysterious Ada, like Nastasya Filippovna in Dostoevsky's novel *The Idiot*. She could have been his daughter, but he made her his wife, seducing her with his mocking and bilious wit, enormous memory, ability to move up, and his unspent ardor, which had been canned for many reasons. Until the age of thirty Volovik was too busy to be interested in woman; he lived for ideas, illegal activity, the struggle; after thirty women lost interest in him, because he had too exhausted himself in the struggle, and only now, when he had turned into a *nerd*, did he decide to open that jar with a crude can opener. And a heavy stench had come flowing out of there. One shouldn't try to preserve anything forever.

There was no person on earth—not counting Hitler and a few other political figures—whom Sergey hated more than he did Volovik. He didn't ask Ada, but he was convinced for some reason that Volovik had placed her in a hopeless situation, stupefied her with guile, driven her into a trap. This was how it had been: last summer at Nikola Hill, where Sergey had gone to stay with a friend, he met Ada on the volleyball court. Then, in the fall, he had come to see Volovik to take a test: Volovik had a swollen cheek from an inflamed tooth and was staying home, with a wool kerchief tied around him, like an old peasant woman. And he saw Ada. Then they went to *Orpheus and Euridice* at the Conservatory. Then they would meet in the courtyard, walk along the embankment to the Point and back. All the real business had started recently. Volovik worked fiercely at the realization of the decisions of the February-March Plenum: he would be away from home until late at night at meetings, conferences; he inveighed, rooted out, exposed. His name turned up in newspaper accounts. Sergey couldn't read without clenching his fists that "Comrade Volovik exposed the hostile intent of the speech," "Comrade Volovik used facts to prove the rotten, Menshevik essence of the good-for-nothing theoretician's 'works.'" It was vile, perhaps, but when embracing Ada, he would suddenly recall Volovikov's phrases, and his passion would increase violently.

He tried to figure out what had united these people who were so different. And what had so suddenly hurled them away from each other? There obviously had been something shared, some strings that sounded in unison, but there had been something insurmountably alienating. This shared thing, as Sergey surmised, was sensuality—rash and immature on Ada's part, tardy and fierce on the part of the bald satyr. And in addition—ridicule of everything that surrounded them, people, words, things. And the thing that alienated them was the essence of each of them, which was gradually distilled and finally, toward the end of the fourth year, came to the surface: the essence of the one was counterfeit, a falsehood; the essence of the other, naturalness, truth. That was how it seemed to Sergey, and he passionately wanted that to be the truth.

"Let's go have some tea. Do you want some tea?" Without waiting for an answer, she led him by the hand down the little hallway to the kitchen. "Have a seat!"

He sat down at the table. He looked at her slightly curved, strong back with its round sides, a tireless volleyball player's back, as she bustled at the gas range, struck matches, rinsed out the teapot. All her movements were elastic, full of a mysterious power. She somehow spent too long bustling, silently, standing with her back to him, and he couldn't see her face, and suddenly he was seized by alarm. He said he'd come to an agreement with a friend of his lived on Dmitrovka, and that in June they could move to his apartment, for the whole summer.

"Sergey, I can't leave Iosif Zinovievich," Ada said, turning to him. He saw something wretched in her eyes, and realized that she was speaking the truth. "I can't right now..."

Stunned, he was silent for a moment, then made for the door.

"Wait! I want... to explain to you... Seryozhka!"

"Why? Good-bye! I see you really can't. As for why—that isn't so important."

But with a powerful arm she pulled him away from the door. He sat down again, on a stool. He didn't have the strength to listen or ask. She said that everything had changed in the last few days: Volovik was threatened by mortally dangerous trouble. Two members of the editorial staff and his assistant at the journal had been arrested. Three days ago there had been a meeting for the journal staff to hear reports and elect new officials, and Volovik had been trampled on by his friends. No one had interceded. No one had refuted the outrageous accusations. In the issue of *Izvestiya* from the previous day there was an article about the meeting. "Have you really not read it?" "No, I haven't." Ada went to the room to get the paper.

"Does she love him?" Sergey thought, horrified. "That windbag, that swindler? But after all, she said so much about how he was hateful to her, how unbearable his touch was, what bad breath he had... But I can't give her up, I can't, I can't!"

"Leaving him right now would be contemptible. It would be the same thing as..." She tossed the newspaper on the table. "I thought that the attacks on him were perhaps connected to me, to the business with Lyova, but he says that doesn't have anything to do with it. He said that criminal activity was a wonderful, pure business. He would be glad to steal someone's wallet and go to prison. To sit out a half a year, as he says. And when he was leaving for Nikola's Hill yesterday, he suddenly said: 'Remember: the only thing that I loved in life was you.'"

Sergey, having trouble concentrating, read the newspaper article on the last page. "The comrades who spoke used a number of examples to show how the relaxation of Bolshevik vigilance and the absence of self-criticism facilitates the vile activity of the enemies of the people. Thus, the former assistant editor Saltsmakher, now exposed as a Trotskyite wrecker..."

"Why did he go to Nikola's Hill?" Sergey asked.

"There are some important documents at the country house there that he may need. Something confirming his work during the Civil War years. And then—he needs to get to see Alexander Vasilievich, and our country houses are next to each other. Alexander Vasilievich has always treated him well."

"For some reason I'm not worried on Iosif Zinovievich's count," said Sergey, unpleasantly stung by Ada's words "needs to get to see" and "our country houses." She spoke like someone who held the same views as Volovik. Formerly she had always separated herself from him. Compassion? For people like Ada that was almost love. God forbid anything should happen to him. Then she would be lost forever, would go mad from compassion. He caught the name "Saltsmakher" in the bouncing newspaper lines.

For instance: "Several years ago Saltsmakher published a book teeming with anti-Marxist propositions. That concoction was not subjected to any criticism. Moreover, the journal's editor-in-chief, Volovik, considered it possible to keep the camouflaged enemy on as his assistant. The Bolshevik method of personnel selection was replaced right and left by the 'principle' of pragmatism and cronyism. Only in that way can one explain how such sworn enemies of the people as Smirnov and Urbanovich, who were complete nonentities as regards scholarship.... The idiotic disease of freedom from worry led to the fact that in 1936 the journal published an article about Comrade Stalin's struggle for dialectical materialism that was written by an enemy of the people.... It was with alarmed attention that people listened to the speech by Volovik, who spoke twice at the request of the most active members... The editor-in-chief's unprincipled, confused speech, lacking in genuine self-criticism, did not satisfy them... falling back on the positions of Menshevist idealism... in the conditions of the divorce of theory from practice... to definitely bring to an end, smoke them out of their holes."

"It's nonsense. I can't understand any of it." Sergey pressed his hands to his temples. His head had suddenly started aching, as happened in moments of great mental exertion. He really couldn't understand anything, hard as he strained. "After all, they need him. Why is this being done?"

Ada was looking out the window. From her frozen gaze he understood that she didn't hear him. He saw that she was seized by compassion, powerful and all-devouring, like heavy intoxication, like the pain in the whole body that occurs in the case of heart ailments, and he felt envy for Volovik and, with trebled force, hatred for him. Before he had envied him and hated him just for the fact that he and Ada slept on the same daybed, that their pillows lay next to each other, that he saw her in the morning in her robe and without her robe, and for the fact that Volovik had been her first man. But now his torment because of all of these feelings intensified enormously, because he sensed the pain in her soul, *which had been caused by someone else.* And it was strange, his own feeling of love also increased enormously and inexplicably and simply pulled him towards her: to hug her, to calm her.

"My darling, don't. It will all be all right. After all, he's such a true believer." And, trying to calm her down, he started telling about how Volovik had spoken at a meeting for the whole institute, how he had inveighed and stigmatized, without regard to authorities, precisely as Comrade Khrushchev had demanded at the last plenum of the Moscow Committee, "to criticize, without regard to persons and the feelings of those persons." And with what fear the director himself dealt with him, and a representative of the Moscow Committee repeated several times in his speech, "As Comrade Volovik has pointed out here." So that in Sergey's opinion, there was no reason to fear for Iosif Zinovievich. He should be just fine. He was one of those who attacked others, not one of those who was attacked himself. If he in fact had come in for a little bit of abuse, it was a mistake, a misunderstanding, which would definitely be corrected. Right now was a time when everyone was desperately criticizing everyone else. An epidemic. The fashion, if you will. Even reasonable people succumbed to a psychosis—take, for instance... And he told about what nonsense a friend of his, also a student, a smart fellow, had talked, but, who, as it turned out, was a big fool.

Ada calmed down and talked about what was going on at the studio. She told about it almost with laughter, because some sort of nonsense was going on at the studio. A cameraman, an old man, had been accused of subversive activity because he did a bad job of filming a shot of a visit by the members of the Politburo to the construction site of the Moscow-Volga Canal: a shadow from a tree had fallen across Stalin's face. The cameraman, at the same time the director of the film, himself rejected the shot and didn't include it in the movie, but someone had pulled the film out of the wastebasket—and the whole film had Stalin on it, the slightest little scrap is supposed to be taken stock of—and the question had arisen of criminal intent, a subversive attack, and so on. An article entitled "A Brazen Trick of the Enemy's" had appeared in the studio newspaper. The poor old man didn't know how to save himself, and had even rushed to Ada for help: he wanted Volovik to call the studio's director or Party organizer, but Volovik had refused. Something obscure was going on with Volovik. Little wheels of some sort had started running in reverse. That had begun in March. He had ceased understanding humor. He had gotten completely bent out of shape, had changed his opinions about everything and everyone. He had formerly respected David Shvarts very much, ordered articles from him for the journal, worked at getting the articles, but now he didn't call Shvarts anything other than "a hypocrite" and "an old fumbler." He had recently had a stormy quarrel with Ada's father, whom he had also admired and even loved. And a few days ago he had been visited by a friend of his by way of the Institute of Red Professors, a very dear man. Now he was an invalid, suffering from a very serious heart condition. He allowed himself to joke mildly and inoffensively about Stalin—something apropos of his height and that of Yezhov, saying that Yezhov, a tiny little thing, was shorter than Stalin, and that, he said, must please Stalin. And suddenly Volovik started yelling at him: "Don't you dare in my home! I refuse to listen!" The fellow rose, and without saying good-bye, left. That night Volovik couldn't sleep. He moaned, suffered torments.

"He's weak," Ada said. "And that's the most dangerous thing. He could admit anything at all, sign any confession, and—he won't come out of it alive."

"Your Iosif Zinovievich will come out of it alive. I assure you: he will," said Sergey. "He has nine lives."

In point of fact he wasn't so certain that Volovik would be all right. Volovik was close to Bukharin, and Bukharin was already openly being called an enemy, in the newspapers. But for some reason Sergey found it more pleasant to think precisely that way: Volovik was invulnerable.

"He's done for," said Ada. "I can feel it."

"Well and to hell with him!" Sergey suddenly exploded. He grabbed her by the hands. "What, then, if he is done for, are we too? Yes or no?"

She was silent. He repeated: "Yes or no! Answer!"

She answered: "Don't ask me about anything."

Then they went to Ada's room and didn't say anything more, because everything was clear and it was impossible to do anything, and it was also impossible to lose each other. Before going to bed Ada opened the window wide. The warmth of the night, along with the shuffling of people's feet along the pavement, entered the room. They began to forget about what had just worried them. They had a hard time forgetting, and did so gradually, but later they didn't notice how their forgetting had become total, final, forever, obscuring their consciousness and as stifling as the night. And they fell asleep. The doorbell awoke them. They leapt up at once, sat up on the daybed, listening numbly, hoping that they had both dreamed the bell. But the bell rang again. Sergey took his watch, which was lying on the wooden shelf at the head of the daybed. It was a quarter to four. He thought: "I'll tell him everything now. It's even better this way!" The fear and numbness had disappeared. He hugged Ada, pressed her to himself, saying: "It's even better this way. Let it happen! I'll go open the door!"

"My hands are cold," said Ada, freeing herself.

He could tell she was trembling.

"I'll go open the door."

"No. Stay here."

She went into the little hallway and flicked the light switch. Sergey went out after her and stopped in the doorway. The bell rang for a third time, for a long time, with murderous intensity. It was still ringing when Ada, holding her robe under her chin with one hand, turned the bolt with the other hand. Sergey suddenly thought: "But what if it isn't Volovik? We should ask." Above Ada's head of light-brown hair appeared a khaki service cap with a polished khaki peak, and when Ada stepped back, into the hallway came a stranger, a tall young man holding himself very erect and wearing a field shirt, belt, and boots. Without saying hello, he went directly toward Sergey, and behind him, his boots thudding, came in a second man, very much resembling the first, also tall, holding himself erect, also wearing a field shirt, belt, with the same sort of pale face totally lacking in expression as the first, and then—they were all alike, like brothers, with identically pale, rather sleepy faces—appeared a third, fourth, and fifth one. They immediately blocked off the whole hallway. The two who had come in last held rolled up empty canvas bags in their hands. Despite their swaggering bearing, they all looked tired. One of them yawned openly. At the first moment, while this coming out from the wings onto the stage by the new people lasted, nothing was said and nothing could be heard except for the thudding of boots. With her back pressed up against the coat rack, and still holding the edges of her robe on her chest with one hand, Ada read a piece of paper. Sergey saw her pale cheeks and the penetratingly burning gaze of her eyes as they ran down the lines.

"Where is Iosif Zinovievich?" Sergey heard her altered voice.

"Where he should be," answered the man who had come in first. He seemed to be waiting for Ada to finish reading what was written there, or rather, waiting for the four or five seconds prescribed for the reading of such documents to pass.

"What does it say?" Sergey asked, unable to restrain himself.

"It's a search warrant," said Ada, continuing to look at the piece of paper. "It says: 'Conduct a search of I. Z. Volovik's apartment and arrest him.' I don't understand."

"What don't you understand?" the first man said rudely now, apparently having lost patience now that the four or five prescribed seconds had passed. "Where's Volovik's study?"

"The study—it's here... But I don't understand. Where is Iosif Zinovievich?"

The five quickly broke up and went to the rooms, and the search began. Three of them worked in the study, and two went into Ada's room, where the unmade bedding still lay on the daybed. No one answered Ada's question. It was obvious that Volovik had been arrested. Apparently at the country house. Perhaps he was sitting down below in a car, or perhaps he was already at the Lubyanka. Going up to Ada, Sergey asked with just his lips: "Should I leave?"

"I'm afraid," Ada said scarcely audibly, although that wasn't at all obvious from looking at her. She behaved calmly, but she had turned very pale. He hugged her, letting her know that he wouldn't go anywhere. They didn't pay any attention to him. The unmade bedding didn't bother anyone either. Someone simply grabbed it by the corners, pulled it off, and threw it onto the floor with a single sharp motion. After pulling the daybed away from the wall, they started lifting the daybed pillows and tossing them onto the floor. Standing in the hallway, Sergey and Ada watched through the open doors what was going on in both rooms. Ada continually paced back and forth in the hall, while Sergey stood motionless. He smoked cigarettes from the Herzegovina Flor box one after the other. The idea occurred that they should know that Stalin liked to smoke precisely those cigarettes. Perhaps that was why they had treated him indulgently and weren't asking: "Who are you? Your documents!" He'd expected them to ask at any second. He didn't have any documents with him. Why should they ask for documents, however? They could guess what he was doing here. They'd probably guessed. That sphere of life didn't interest them. They were focussed on something else. If he suddenly decided to leave now, that might provoke suspicion, and they would take alarm: "And just why do you want to leave?" He should stand motionless, with an indifferent and calm look.

That was exactly how he stood, although his heart was pounding and everything in him was tense. He was afraid that if they asked him his name and found out it was Virsky, there would be trouble for Mother. He feared for her more than for anyone else. After all, she worked at the Secretariat.

In Volovik's study the desk drawers had been pulled out, placed on the rug, and two men were rifling through them quickly, efficiently, and at the same time casually, without stopping for long over any single piece of paper. They seemed to be looking for something in particular. Sergey wondered whether they were perhaps looking for letters from Bukharin. Some sort of secret instructions that Bukharin sent to his confederates?

They threw certain papers and whole files into a bag that the third man held ready. They shoved the typewriter and a pair of binoculars into the same bag. One of the agents took a bronze letter opener in the shape of a beautiful dagger from the desk, and after thinking for a moment, tossed it into the bag too. In Ada's room work was in full swing around her big desk, heaped with cardboard boxes, tubes, jars of paint, sheets, and fragments of white paper. The contents of the drawers were shaken out like trash from a trash bucket. Ada was about to point out that the desk belonged to her and that her personal things were kept in it, but the agent in charge, without offering any explanations, yelled from the study to his subordinates: "Continue the search, keep going!" The business was finished up around seven in the morning. A seal was placed on the study. The smell of dust, old papers, tobacco smoke, naphthalene, and the constant strain for three hours had made Sergey's headache worse again. He was exhausted, nauseated. And he was amazed at Ada, at how much stronger she was than he was. She had paced around the hallway the whole three hours, without sitting down even for a moment. On his way out, the agent in charge told her that she could get information about her husband at 24 Kuznetsky Bridge, the reception office for the NKVD. From ten to two.

Four of them, smoking cigarettes, went out onto the landing, while the fifth told Sergey that he wanted to wash his hands and asked for soap. Sergey showed him to the bathroom. The hands wouldn't come clean, because they were stained with oil paint. Sergey brought a bottle of turpentine. He did so involuntarily, not out of a desire to please, but simply because he wanted the fellow to leave as soon as possible. While the agent rubbed his hands with turpentine, soaped them and rinsed them under the faucet, Sergey looked at his plain face, with its prominent cheekbones and niggardly slit of a mouth, watched him purse his lips diligently and in a businesslike way, raising his brows while so doing and groaning slightly—not so much from tiredness as from some extraneous cares, no doubt—and Sergey thought: "A guy like that will do anything he's told. The most terrible things. And all he'll do in the process is groan and purse his peasant lips." But there was something empty in this malicious thought. The malice was diffused, unreal.

"You see, I have to go right from work to my mother-in-law's at Pavshino. My wife is staying with her right now," the fellow began to explain. "We haven't seen each other for a whole week. What do I mean a week! Longer." And looking at Sergey, he unexpectedly grinned: "Your girlfriend's husband is all wormy and rotten, but she's all right, good strong stuff." He winked, as though with approval, and took off running, on the tips of his shoes, down the hall to catch up with the rest of his group.

One of the four was waiting for him on the landing. They started talking in low voices. Sergey shut the door hard. Ada was sitting on the edge of the daybed, which had been turned upside-down, and was staring at the floor. Sergey sat down next to her and embraced her. They sat like that, without moving and without saying anything, for twenty minutes or so. It grew completely light. The sky was blue, heralding a warm day. On the Stone Bridge a lone tram rattled along distinctly. Ada said that she couldn't stay here, she would go to her father's, and got up. She didn't even get up, but darted off from the daybed somewhere. She began hurriedly getting ready, putting sheets of papers with drawings into a folder, and then suddenly tossed the folder onto the floor and said that she couldn't go to her father's. He was crushed as it was by the business with Lyova. What was she to do, finish him off? And there was that fool there, his wife.

"So," said Sergey. "We'll go to my place. Let's go!"

"To your place... You think Anna Genrikhovna will be glad to see me? And find all of this out?"

"Well, so what? All sorts of things happen." Sergey frowned. He could imagine the expression on his mother's face when she opened the door—she always got up before anyone else, even before Marusya—and at seven-thirty would see Sergey and Ada in the doorway: after a moment of confusion her face would acquire an expression of cold and somewhat contemptuous civility, and she would say: "How do you do?" And then he imagined the second expression on his mother's face, when she heard about Volovik: *disapproval*—that's what it would depict, very stern and direct disapproval, slightly softened by sudden human sympathy for Ada. She would immediately start offering something: "Perhaps you'd like to eat something, Ada? You must be hungry." Or: "Would you like a headache tablet?"

"We'll talk to Nikolay Grigorievich," said Sergey. "He knows Florinsky. And we can also work through Shvarts. He has connections in the Office of Justice."

"Work through him for what?"

"To find out..."

"No," said Ada. "I don't want to see your mother and your sister. And for that matter, I don't want to see anyone at all. Not even my father. I..." She covered her eyes with her hand. He sensed that she was about to say something bombastic, self-castigating, like "I can't stand myself," "I loathe myself," or "If I hadn't been unfaithful to him," but she fell silent, and he took fright. What she would have said aloud would have been a falsehood, but the fact that she had fallen silent testified to something else. A senseless feeling of guilt was tormenting her.

What he had been afraid of had happened: she was leaving him. She was leaving him for a man she had never loved. Whose whole strength consisted of his terrible weakness, of the fact that he was perishing, disappearing.

"Do you want me to leave right now?" Sergey asked after the silence.

"Yes." She nodded. "You leave right now, Seryozha. And at nine o'clock I'll go to Kuznetsky Bridge."

VIII

Nikolay Grigorievich put a heavy *holiday package* on the trunk in the entrance way. The package contained food, mounds of oranges, and something made of glass that clinked from inside. It was all tightly wrapped in glossy white paper and tied round with a ribbon. For the sake of these things, which the children needed, as did someone else, someone who required proof that the world, as before, was tightly wrapped and tied round with a ribbon, he had had to put up with a boring line in the cafeteria, ten minutes or so of marking time and of exhausting conversations. Nikolay Grigorievich knew how to cut off his feelings, however. He tried not to listen to the wisecracks, old jokes, pseudo-festive prattle about trifles, not to see the faces, on which there was nothing except serene and chaste smiles confidently looking into the distance. More than half the people crowding together in the line for packages were strangers to Nikolay Grigorievich. Perhaps they really were looking into the distance confidently. Fewer and fewer acquaintances were encountered in the cafeteria hall every day. But an end had to come to that sometime. It couldn't go on forever! The handing out of the package testified to a certain ephemeral well-being for today. Perhaps even for the day before, when the lists were approved in the Office of Goods and Services. Some people had not received packages, although they had the right to them. The few hours separating the approval of the lists and the receipt of the packages was an enormous period of time. And most important, night fell during that period.

The old man Isaychenkov, coming up from behind, whispered: "Klarin, Mironov, Sukhodolskaya." Fedya Lerberg had already told Nikolay Grigorievich about Klarin that morning, as they rode in the elevator. Klarin had to fall. There was nothing surprising there. On the contrary, people were surprised that he held on for so long. But Mironov? And Veronika Sukhodolskaya? Stalin valued that woman. During the second major purge David had wanted to expel her—some sort of machinations with the country house cooperative—but Stalin had defended her. Her husband was caught in machinations, and she was allegedly not involved, but all the same she wouldn't have survived if not for the support from above. Nine years had passed since then, however, and Stalin's attitude toward Veronika corresponded to the conditions that had caused him at one time to defend her, and it could have changed many times. But this hadn't slipped past Stalin. There could be two explanations here: he was presented with very serious disclosures, or... Or—he was losing control. Hadn't yet lost it, but was already losing it, things were getting out of hand. The most terrifying thing, as some people thought. Nikolay Grigorievich didn't feel that way. On the contrary, he saw a hope flicker there, a chance for salvation.

Nikolay Grigorievich wasn't thinking about his own salvation. He was forty-seven years old, he had lived his life. And besides, it somehow turned out that he had never thought about his own salvation; there was stuck in his soul a strange, inexplicable assurance, at first youthful, and then simply stupid, that nothing bad would ever happen to him personally. Well, if worst came to worst, he'd be killed. Or he'd come down with typhus and die in a delirium. He could be killed in a train wreck, like Volodka Krylov. But what else? All of those things had already nearly happened. No, he didn't fear for himself, but he did for Liza, for the children—but that was nearly the same thing as for himself, so that it could be said that there wasn't that fear in him either, it practically didn't exist—these things were all too personal, didn't concern anyone else—and that he was afraid for what his life had been spent for the sake of.

The evening mail was in the mail box: a bunch of greeting cards, *Evening Moscow, The Literary Gazette*, which Liza subscribed to, and three letters. The house was empty. The kids were out walking, Grandmother had warned everyone in the morning that she would be kept late at the Secretariat, and Liza, as always, was celebrating the evening of the first of May at the People's Commissariat of Agriculture: she spent the whole night making up poems for the wall newspapers and drawing cartoons. Nikolay Grigorievich looked through the newspapers in an instant. The cards didn't present any interest either. One letter was from an old friend from Kislovodsk, where the friend was being treated. It was the usual greeting. The second, written in a childish hand, was addressed to Gorik. And the third—without a stamp, without a postmark—was simply a white envelope: "To N. G. Bayukov." Someone had tossed it into the box without the help of the post office. On a piece of notebook paper, in a hand incomprehensibly familiar, feminine, flowery, that struck at his heart, stood: "Kolya, I came by, but didn't find anyone home. I need to see you very badly. Around 8 PM in the pharmacy on Bolshaya Polyanka. Forgive me. Maria Polub." Masha Poluboyarova! They hadn't seen each other in twelve years. How did she turn up here? After all, she lived somewhere in Bataysk or Taganrog. They had seen each other for the last time in Alupka, at a sanitarium, in 1925, and Masha at that time was already with her husband, a dark, unattractive fellow.

And why in the pharmacy on Bolshaya Polyanka?

Liza didn't know anything about Masha's existence. And no one knew, except for Mishka's wife Vanda and Mishka himself. But even they had probably forgotten: so many years had passed. Masha Poluboyarova had existed briefly, but formidably and ineradicably, in Nikolay Grigorievich's life. For several months: the fall and winter of 1920 in Rostov. The Nazarov Rebellion. The sudden news: a secretary for the Don Food Committee, a nineteen-year-old girl, given a job at the Don Food Committee by Nikolay Grigorievich at the request of Mishka's Vanda, was the sister of Colonel Poluboyarov, one of the leaders of the Nazarovites. Why had she concealed the fact? She was afraid she'd be shot and her nanny, a helpless old woman, would die. There was a person named Kravchuk in the Revolutionary Tribunal who pounded the table with the magazine of his Mauser and yelled: "And you, you rotten bourgeois, can't imagine life without nannies?!" Vanda had known Masha since childhood, from the Novocherkassk High School, but she grew quiet at that point, afraid to make a peep in her defense, and Mikhail was far away, with his Ninth Cavalry Division at the Polish front. Masha Poluboyarova lived with her nanny. Her mother had died long since, her father had disappeared on the German front without a trace, and her brother had left with volunteers. And suddenly—he turned up with a landing party. How could she have known? Nikolay Grigorievich saved the girl. He believed her eyes, her voice. And later, after he had gotten to know her better, he realized that he'd been right to believe: he had rarely met anyone with such frankness and naive goodness as this dark, blue-eyed girl with Cherkassk blood. And Nikolay Grigorievich was—how old then—twenty-eight, wore a beard, and was called "an old man."

On a wooden bench in the pharmacy sat an elderly, homely looking woman. She gazed around with fright. And seeing Nikolay Grigorievich, she immediately stood up and—without a smile—offered her hand. But the hand wasn't Masha's. It was coarse, red, the fingers wrinkled like carrots. And absolutely ice-cold.

"Are you frozen?" Nikolay Grigorievich asked. "Look, your teeth are even chattering."

"No," Masha said with effort. "I was worried about whether I'd see you. I thought you'd forgotten me or simply wouldn't come."

And she suddenly smiled, and he recognized her.

Masha was wearing a warm, checked overcoat with an edging of reddish fur and the same sort of cap. The coat was absurd for May. Nikolay Grigorievich asked why she'd decided not to drop by to see him at home again, why she hadn't called.

"I didn't much like having the man on duty at the entrance interrogate me about who I was, and what I wanted, and who I wanted to see. And besides, the building is unpleasant. It's like a prison." She grinned, but a tinge of fright again flashed in her eyes. "It would be better for us to walk around the streets for a while. The more so as it's a holiday, everything will be all lit up. It will be beautiful! I always dreamed of getting to Moscow for the holidays. I was just now riding the tram across Theater Square, past the Riding Hall. Such a delight! Everything sparkles and glows, like in the theater. It's great!"

"Let's walk for a while, if you want, but then let's stop in at my place all the same."

"Well, all right, that's fine. We'll stop in at your place." Masha took him by the arm. "You're a model husband, Kolya, huh?"

She laughed. He also laughed: he suddenly felt in a good mood and somehow amused. As though he had seen something pleasantly familiar and long since forgotten.

"Oh, yes!" he said. "Of course."

"We'll stop in, we'll stop in. We'll be sure to stop in. How old is your eldest?"

"Going on twelve. A big strapping ruffian, your height."

"That means he was born you know when? Precisely the year that we saw each other in Alupka, wasn't it? I was with Yasha already, and you played chess all the time with Shvarts, David Alexandrovich." She asked quickly: "Is Shvarts well?"

"Yes, he is," he said.

"It's just that I don't know your wife. What if she doesn't like the fact that I..."

"What?"

"Well, that I came for the holidays like a bolt from the blue, without having asked. A strange woman. Although..." She made a decisive motion with her hand. "It's important for me to see you. And everything else is nonsense."

They walked down the street in the direction of the Kanava. Masha said that she was staying with a distant female relative who was now sick. She had gotten medicine for her at the pharmacy. She said she'd sought out Vanda the day before, met her, found out about her troubles, misfortunes, hopes. So she had separated from Mikhail? Nikolay Grigorievich didn't know for sure. They seem to have separated, but then again perhaps not: sometimes they were together, then Mikhail spent the night at her place on the Arbat, then Vanda would travel to Kratovo to his place. He felt sorry for Valerka in this whole mess. But Masha had understood from what Vanda said that they'd separated for good.

The room on the Arbat was tiny—in an enormous communal apartment where there were twenty-eight neighbors, six families. But Vanda wasn't losing heart: she was hoping for a change of fate. She had somebody—yes, yes, Nikolay Grigorievich knew about that man—a diplomat, a widower, with two small children. Vanda, of course, had let herself go, had gotten heavy, but was still beautiful, nice, completely gray, like an eighteenth-century marquise. Entirely gray at the age of thirty-seven! But, as always, as twenty years before—there was a stunning indifference to anything that did not concern her person. To be more precise: her personal life. An absolutely antiquated and naive lack of interest in politics. She wasn't interested in anything, didn't know anything. She lived in dreams, in stuff and nonsense. The diplomat had turned her head, had promised that they'd go to France next year, settle on the Côte d'Azur, and she couldn't talk or think about anything else. She was worried that she wouldn't be allowed to go abroad because her older sister and her mother lived in France. In short, Vanda was Vanda, a bird of the air. But Masha had come to Moscow just to see Nikolay Grigorievich.

"Oh, go on," Nikolay Grigorievich grinned, as though he didn't believe her. But he surmised that she was telling the truth.

"Because, Kolya, you're the only person who can explain it. Last month Yasha was arrested." Taking him by the arm, she stopped him with an abrupt motion. He suddenly remembered her way of moving abruptly. They were standing on the bridge over the Kanava, and leaning on the railing, they looked into the black water. Here, on the bridge, it was rather dark, but the beginning of Polyanka, and especially the Shock worker Movie Theater, were ablaze with decorative lighting. The crowd near the Shock worker was lit from above by bright white and pink shafts of light from floodlights and the light of hundreds of garlands of hanging bulbs. Further on, on the enormous new bridge and on the embankment of the Moscow River, everything was also ablaze with light.

What could he explain? He listened. Time did strange things to people. No, it wasn't aging that was the most surprising, the enfeeblement of the flesh, but the changes that occurred in the make-up of the soul. There wasn't a trace left of that Novocherkassk high school girl, the admirer of Vera Kholodnaya, the volunteer's sister, who only by accident didn't wind up in Constantinople or Paris. In front of Nikolay Grigorievich was a Soviet lady, the wife of an administrator, who spoke sensibly and in a politically mature way. "I was told that Yasha is a Japanese spy. Well, what nonsense, for heaven's sake. What claptrap. There probably isn't another person as honest, another such a fanatical Communist, on the whole Vladikavkaz Highway. I managed, through acquaintances, by a very complicated route, to arrange an appointment to see the person in the regional NKVD office in charge of Yasha's case, a certain Sakharnov. But it turned out that it wasn't any Sakharnov, but instead, Boris Pchelintsev, a friend of my brother's from the Ataman Academy—I remember him very well—the son of a lieutenant-colonel. I recognized him at once, and he did me too. Of course he was surprised, because I was no longer Markova, but Slivyanskaya, and he expected to see some quite other Slivyanskaya. I said: 'Boris, I beg you to look into the case of Yakov Slivyansky, my husband, a very honest Communist...' He suddenly started yelling: 'Your husband is a Japanese spy, scum, an agent provocateur! We'll shoot him! And the same fate will befall you!' And he kept on shouting and shouting something. I don't remember getting out of there. I was advised to hide, to go away somewhere. I took the children to his relatives in Kamenka, and here I am here. But I'm not asking you for protection, I'm asking for an explanation. What does it all mean, Kolya? Why is Pchelintsev sitting in the regional office, and Yasha in prison? Has power shifted? Is there something people here in Moscow don't know? Nine of my acquaintances have been arrested this month. And you know what the strangest thing is? We're all thick-skinned until it touches us personally. And I'm the same sort of louse. Before Yasha was arrested I thought: 'Who the heck knows, maybe Bondarenko really is mixed up in something, and Fedya Kostrikov could have taken a false step somewhere, and Gnedov is from a family of former officers, so there's nothing strange here.' You understand? And Tseytlin worked with Pyatakov, his wife is from a Cossack family, the sister of a Nazarovite..."

The same things had occurred to Nikolay Grigorievich the last few months. People believed too easily in the guilt of others, that "there's something to it," and were too free of worry for themselves. It was an ominous fact, and it didn't bode well. But he shouldn't talk to unfortunate Masha about it. He had to calm her. But the only problem was how.

"I hadn't seen you for so many years. I sometimes heard things about you, your name would be mentioned in the newspaper..." Masha looked at him, smiling uncertainly. "I don't even know how you, all in all... Maybe you think otherwise? Why aren't you talking?"

Nikolay Grigorievich was seeing this woman as a young girl. That's why he was silent. And he saw everything around him as young.

"Let's go home. We'll have some tea and a talk." He tugged her by the arm.

"No, wait! First tell me what you think about all of this."

Nikolay Grigorievich sighed. Well, what does he think? He thinks that power has not shifted. And that in its general outlines people here know what's going on in the provinces. But knowing is one thing, explaining another. No, Pchelintsev alone doesn't decide anything. Not even a thousand Pchelintsevs decide anything. Not even Florinsky, Arsyushka, who is now an assistant to Yezhov—Did she remember him from Rostov? A young idiot in red German boots?—not even that Arsyushka, who is now so high up, means anything in and of himself. It seems to Nikolay Grigorievich that the real explanation for these strange political convulsions is fear of fascism. A provocation on the part of fascism is even possible. Hitler's influence is indisputable. There are no other explanations. But what else? But there has to be an end. This can't go on eternally, otherwise they'll all devour each other. The wave is subsiding, there is evidence that people are already being released...

Masha rejoiced: "Really? They're being released?" Nikolay Grigorievich confirmed it. He really had heard that a certain Zaltsman, an old Party member who was arrested in February, recently returned home.

He didn't manage to get Masha to his apartment that evening: she was in a hurry to see her sick relative. But she promised to be sure to come one of these days during the holidays.

Nikolay Grigorievich didn't especially insist. He had noticed how in recent years his interest in people had been waning, even in those he was once close to. The circle had been growing smaller and smaller. At one time an ocean of people had surrounded him, cities and years of underground activity, exile, and war had thrown hundreds of wonderful people his way, people who instantly became friends. But now there was no longer anyone—they still existed, but the necessity for friendships had disappeared—there was nobody, except for David, Mishka, and two or three others. And Liza and the children had remained in the circle. That was why Masha, who had flown in from afar, like a recollection, didn't arouse anything except business-like thoughts and the usual heaviness that gnawed from time to time at the middle of his chest, under his heart.

The children came running out to meet him. Gorik yelled: "We're going with Lyonka, with Lyonka! You promised!" Zhenya was silent, with an impenetrably gloomy expression. And Nikolay Grigorievich, as always, when he saw his daughter's small frowning face, thought of his own stern mother. Nikolay Grigorievich usually took three people to see the parade on Red Square: Gorik, Zhenya, and one of their friends. Arguments would arise because of that third place. His son won most often, with the help of the argument that a military parade was a masculine affair, that girls had nothing to do there. And true, the strength of their desire to make it to the reviewing stand was incommensurate. But today Gorik's yelling, his calf-like excitement, irritated Nikolay Grigorievich, while his daughter's gloominess, on the other hand, matched his mood, and he said coldly: "Stop yelling, or I won't even take you."

His son, offended, darted off to the children's room.

In the dining room they were having tea. Liza was excitedly telling about something, apparently the evening at the People's Commissariat of Agriculture. She was declaiming verses—her own, maybe?—and she was being attentively listened to by Grandmother and Grandmother's friend from work at the Secretariat, the old Party functionary Erna Ivanovna, Kolya Latsis's wife, whom Nikolay Grigorievich didn't care for, considering her a fool. But Grandmother valued her. She said she was a person of transparent honesty. Erna Ivanovna laughed in a bass voice, while Grandmother looked at her daughter with undisguised pride, and, when Nikolay Grigorievich entered the room, she made a sign with her finger that he was not to interrupt the declamation. Liza was reciting verses about a certain Ignat Ivanovich, "who had once been bold, but gradually, from year to year, lost his boldness in favor of the desire to live prosperously and quietly, even though boringly." Sitting right there was Mikhail, in a new commander's field shirt with a medal. He sipped tea loudly from his saucer, staring at the table through the fogged-over lenses of his pince-nez and not even raising his head upon his brother's arrival.

Nikolay Grigorievich sat down at the table quietly, trying not to make any noise, and poured himself some tea. Liza recited for several more minutes. The children also came to listen. When Liza had finished, everyone started clapping their hands. Erna Ivanovna declared in a bass voice, and as always, categorically, that Liza ought to have become a poet instead of a livestock expert, in response to which Grandmother noted that Nikolay Grigorievich was to blame, since he had made Liza go to the Timeryazev Institute.

"Kolya, where were you, I'd like to know?" Liza asked.

"I went to see someone. A woman," Nikolay Grigorievich answered, knowing that the reply wouldn't provoke anything except for a slight smile from Liza, a person who appreciated humor. He knew that she was completely at ease on his account, just as he was completely at ease on hers, and both of them, each taken separately, were completely at ease on their own account. But all the same, for some reason he wanted Liza to ask: "What woman?"—and he would have to say.

Liza didn't ask. Evenings she read *The Three Musketeers* to the children, and now they had all three clambered up on the daybed. Liza turned on the wall lamp, and Gorik, still with an expression of hurt and independence, ran past Nikolay Grigorievich into the children's room to get the book.

"Listen, brother," Mikhail said. "Those nincompoops from the Military Publishing House returned the manuscript to me. An idiotic resolution: 'We have planned a book by Division Commander Bogints on this topic.' But not a word from Mikhail Nikolaevich. Could you give him a call?"

His brother, as always, had come with dissatisfaction of some sort or with requests. His tone suggested that Nikolay Grigorievich had some connection to "those nincompoops from the Military Publishing House" or was perhaps even one of them. Nikolay Grigorievich said that Mikhail Nikolaevich was probably too busy just now to deal with the publishing matters. And he thought: "How can Misha not understand? Still and all, his being cut off from a responsible job and his hermit's life in Kratovo at the back of beyond have their effect... As though Mikhail Nikolaevich is about to deal with his manuscript!"

Mikhail looked at his brother with an air of suspicion: "Why too busy? I think he's doing just fine."

"Rumor has it that's not entirely so."

"Nonsense!" Mikhail gave a decisive wave of his hand. Well, of course, in Kratovo, after all, they knew everything firsthand. "That friend will always be just fine. I'm not worried on his account. Why not just say that you simply don't have the time to call?"

"No, I won't say that. I won't say it, because the point is not that I don't want to, but that it's inopportune. Inopportune, understand? You out there, on the farm, don't quite understand..."

"What? What don't I understand?" Mikhail raised his voice. He always overreacted, and rudely, to things his brother said jokingly that hinted at his life in retirement in Kratovo. "Cut it out! I understand everything perfectly well. And foresaw it long ago. Yes, yes, even before you did! I argued with you clever boys. Remember the conversation at Denisych's in 1925? In December?"

"There were lots of conversations. Let's go to my study."

But his brother was already gritting his teeth, his boots were pinching, his irritation seething. He stood up, paced up and down the room, with abrupt motions moving the chairs out of his way. And right then Erna Ivanovna entered in very felicitously: "Yes, by the way! Misha," she said, "where's your Valery?"

"At his mother's."

"Oh, so that's how it is. At his mother's? Is he staying with her now?"

The old fool's transparent honesty consisted of the fact that she meddled simple-heartedly and high-handedly in the personal lives of comrades, gave advice, and gave out marks.

"No," said Mikhail, looking at Erna Ivanovna gloomily. "They've gone to Leningrad for the holidays."

"When did they go?" asked Nikolay Grigorievich.

"They're going today. On the *Arrow*."

"The two of them?" Grandmother, who knew very well Vanda's laziness and stinginess, was surprised.

"I don't know," Mikhail answered even more gloomily. "I think with that gentleman from the People's Commissariat of Foreign Affairs. Why, is that so important to know?"

"Oh, now I really don't like that!" Erna Ivanovna, in vexation, struck the table with her palm and was already ready to give com-

radely advice, but Grandmother, who nevertheless had more percep-
tivity, interrupted her: "Don't worry, that's all right, they'll see
Leningrad."

"Are you going to let us read or not?" Liza asked from the daybed.

Nikolay Grigorievich pulled his brother toward the door.

But Erna Ivanovna wouldn't quiet down. She suddenly snorted del-
icately, giggled nasally, and exclaimed: "Misha, Misha! You know what
they're saying in our Center for Political Prisoners? That you've gotten
married? Is that true?"

Mikhail stopped in the doorway, and without turning around,
pointing his finger back, over his shoulder, at Erna Ivanovna, he said
to his brother: "You understand why I don't go to their meetings? Well,
do you understand? As it is, I've hidden forty versts from them, don't
see anyone, don't answer letters, and still this passionate interest in my
person. What a nightmare!"

"Maybe you really have gotten married?" asked Nikolay Grigorievich. "Confess, you villain."

Mikhail whispered something obscene, and with a wave of his
hand, left the dining room.

Erna Ivanovna, laughing, called out after him: "They say she's a
young thing! Well, is it true?"

The went into the study and shut the door. Mikhail asked for some
brandy. Nikolay Grigorievich always had a little cut-glass decanter in
the bookcase, camouflaged by books. They had two shot glasses each,
and Mikhail, who had turned pink and had relaxed, took a sword off
the wall, started chopping the air with it, and as usual, criticized
Nikolay Grigorievich for keeping a dragoon's sword instead of a
Cossack's: "Throw out this piece of junk! Or give it to me." He grunted
with pleasure, whistled, and the ceiling fixture was in danger. A
minute later he started gasping. Nikolay Grigorievich looked at his
brother gloomily. The heaviness in the middle of his chest had again
become noticeable. He thought: his brother was fifty-three, looked
sixty, had been ravaged by time, adversity, and still and all was a little
boy at heart. People who were old men in their youth become little
boys in their old age. And they wave toy swords around in their stud-

ies and on the porches of the country homes, where the pine boards thaw out slowly after the long winter.

They discussed what Masha had said about their home town. Masha herself did not interest them very much. His brother had trouble remembering her. Then they talked about Stalin, whom they had known and remembered much better, since years long passed. Nikolay Grigorievich had been in exile on the Yenisei with him, and Mikhail Grigorievich recognized him in Petersburg at the beginning of 1917, when they both returned from Siberia nearly simultaneously, and then worked together a year later at the Tsaritsyn front—the first quarrels, Stalin's threats, Mikhail's swearing, the ultimate rift. There had been a meeting of the brothers, when Nikolay Grigorievich was on his way from the South to Moscow, and Mikhail, laughing, had said: "Well, if Koba gets power in Tsaritsyn, he'll make a mess of things!" They laughed because they didn't believe it. He was neither a Cossack nor a military man—just a Party functionary. But he got power in Tsaritsyn very quickly. He pushed Minin aside, dismissed the Latvian Karl, packed Mikhail off to Moscow to military leadership courses. Before many others they realized what a Koba who had gotten power was. No one else had guessed. But they already knew. Heads crunched in his fist like ripe nuts dried in the sun. "You remember what I told you?" "It's me who told you, you old dummy!" But their secret hostility toward the other one, in the pince-nez, the prattler with the dark beard, who also knew how to crunch skulls in his fist, was stronger. Distrust of the one and enmity toward the other, intertwining, stretched through the years and filled them. And what had seemed a joke in Tsaritsyn had become a blunt and mighty truth, stretched out above the world like an enormous, measureless slab of iron. It hung unsteadily. People looked at it habitually, the way people look at the sky from below. But really, the time had to come when the truth weighing billions of tons would fall; it couldn't hang there forever shakily. Mikhail didn't know the details of the last plenum, where the Bukharin and Rykov case was investigated—how could he know in Kratovo? Even in Moscow few people knew. Nikolay Grigorievich had himself found out recently from David. The details were gloomy. It turned out that Bukharin had declared a hunger strike before the plenum. He had fasted for nine days. When he came into the meeting hall, Stalin asked him: "Just look at yourself, Nikolay! Against whom have you declared a hunger strike?" Bukharin answered: "What am I to do if they want to arrest me?" The plenum allegedly demanded that Bukharin cease his hunger strike. Bukharin spoke sharply, made accusations against the NKVD, said that outrages were occurring there. Stalin interrupted him maliciously: "We'll send you there, and you'll sort things out there!" The plenum appointed a committee to study the Bukharin and Rykov case—under the leadership of Mikoyan. Krupskaya allegedly was made a member of the committee. And when Bukharin was on his way out of the hall, Krupskaya hugged him and kissed him. That was somehow hard to believe. It was both unlike Nadezhda Konstantinovna and not in the style of Bolshevik meetings, too theatrical. But people said that was what happened. Style changed, after all. When their fate was being decided, the members of the Politburo were given ballots on which they had to write—briefly, in one or two words—how to deal with the accused. All the members of the Politburo wrote: "Arrest, try, shoot." But Stalin wrote: "Give them over to the NKVD."

Mikhail sat on the edge of the daybed hunched over, his face again having turned gray, and he listened with rapt attention. After a silence he said: "You know, Kolka, we won't make it through this year."

Nikolay Grigorievich didn't reply. He paced around the rug in soft shoes for a while, bent over, removed a stripe of dust from his pant leg—he didn't know where it had come from, perhaps from the children's bicycle that he dragged down today from the storage closet over the door?—and, straightening up, feeling a ringing in his ears, said: "That's quite possible. " And he said that somehow calmly, even absent-mindedly. "Quite, my dear fellow. But here's what the point is. There's a war on the way. And very soon. So that our internal squabbling will end willy-nilly, and we'll all put on army coats and go off to fight the fascists."

They started talking about that. Mikhail suggested—not a new idea, one that had already been heard—that perhaps this was a provocation on the part of the Germans. This whole campaign, the destruction of cadres. Nikolay Grigorievich thought that the Germans lacked the means for such a provocation. It was likely quality stuff of our own, Soviet-made. And based on ancient traditions, dating to the time of Ivan Vasilievich, when the boyars were chopped down so as to consolidate individual power. The only question was what to apply that power to. Toward what goal would it be aimed?

Mikhail waved his hand dismissively. "You keep needing a goal? You can't go anywhere without a goal? Do you drink tea or go to the john with a goal?" Nikolay Grigorievich, getting angry—because the conversation was getting close to a sore point—explained that he was used to seeing logic, a beginning and an end, in any movement. "Well, of course, you observe!" his brother mocked. "You see logic. But the movement drags you along like a puppy. You don't even thrash around and try to get away." "And what does your thrashing around and trying to get away consist of? Moving to a country house and tending a vegetable garden?" "At least, damn you, I don't participate, I don't serve, I don't ride around in a black Rolls-Royce, may all you observers go to hell." It ended, as usual, with cursing and new rounds of brandy. They started dragging out of their memories twenty-year-old matters, Rostov in 1918, just after it had been taken by Sivers's and Antonov-Ovseenko's detachments. None of this could excite them anymore, but they needed it for the argument. Mikhail kept trying to prove—and this angered Nikolay Grigorievich—that he too, the younger and less successful brother, was also involved, even if only obliquely, in the hideous mess, "sparing neither friend nor foe," that was now occurring. At work here were envy, which had been accumulating for years, and the disappointment with his whole, long life, essentially ruined, and even a bit of gloating, and sincere, deathly worry—that was the main thing that seethed in his heart—worry for the cause that had become his fate.

Nikolay Grigorievich realized that too and saw that very alarm behind all the irate attacks, unfairness, and rude words. That was why his own ire disappeared after it had barely arisen. He couldn't for long stay angry at his brother, the old rowdy, shouter from the same family, at this fantastic failure who had nothing left toward the end of his life—neither work, nor family, nor home.

There was a knock at the door. Nikolay Grigorievich opened it. In came Sergey, without saying hello and looking at them strangely.

"Have you heard that Volovik was arrested last night?"

"No," said Nikolay Grigorievich.

"Who is Volovik?" asked Mikhail.

"I was present during the search. Last night. But Volovik himself wasn't home. There were just Ada and me."

"I don't understand anything," said Mikhail, getting up from the day bed and pouring some brandy into his shot glass. "What Volovik? What Ada?"

"There's a fellow named Volovik. But why him?" Nikolay Grigorievich looked at Sergey with amazement. "Damn it, they're completely off their rockers. But where have you been these last two days? Today and yesterday."

"At Ada's. I called Mother this morning. She got so infuriated—"

"I don't know. She didn't say a word to me."

"Well what else could it be—a conspiracy! Our famous quality. May I?" Sergey poured himself some brandy and also drank it down. "We didn't sleep all night, of course. Didn't even get undressed. Ada was sure they'd come for her today, but, thank God, no one came. But at. dawn there was an incident. We were sitting in her room with the balcony. The window looks out on the other yard, where the steam plant is. The rear yard. And at about six in the morning we saw a woman dressed in black, an old woman with gray hair, go hurtling down outside the window. Absolutely without a sound, head first. In the morning the elevator man said that during the night an old man was taken, and that at dawn his wife jumped off the balcony, from the eighth floor."

"What was the name?" Nikolay Grigorievich asked.

"I don't know. Some very old woman, all gray."

"An old woman? Off the balcony?" Mikhail asked the same question, with a look of squeamishness. He was already very drunk. How little he needed that now!

"Tell you what, my dear friend, you shouldn't go see your Ada right now. Wait a week. Just friendly advice," said Nikolay Grigorievich.

"Meet in another place, on the street, wherever you please. Have her come here to our place."

"And here's my friendly advice to you too, Nikolay Grigorievich," said Sergey. "Get rid of all of this."

"What?"

"All of that stuff." With the tip of his shoe Sergey pointed to the metal box under the desk. In that box, under lock and key, Nikolay Grigorievich kept weapons, three pistols and cartridges.

"It doesn't make any difference," said Nikolay Grigorievich.

"Yes, it does."

"Not the slightest. And by the way, I have a permit for the Browning, and those two pieces are gifts from the Revolutionary Military Council of the front and the army. But..." He waved his finger contemptuously. "But..."

"I'm telling you... " Sergey whispered nearly with despair.

"All right, lay off. You don't understand much about this."

They were silent for a while. Sergey, after having a drink, lit up a cigarette. From the street, from the direction of the embankment opposite the social center, fragments of music carried up. Perhaps it was an orchestra playing, perhaps the radio.

Mikhail mumbled: "In no case..." and shook his finger meaningfully. "Not for anything... Never..."

"What are you talking about, Uncle Misha?" Sergey asked.

"He knows. Never..."

Grandmother came in and, looking at Sergey coldly and somewhat haughtily, called him to the dining room to have supper. Later, after the idiotic Erna Ivanovna had finally left, they all gathered in the study and talked for a long time. The children went to bed. Upstairs, where there was a new person, who had taken the place of Arsenev, who had been removed a half a year before, they were already celebrating the holiday: music and dancing could be heard, people were pounding the floor with their heels. Grandmother told about events at the Secretariat. As always, she kept quiet about the most important things. The main things were kept secret. It was her iron character, to which everyone in the household was accustomed and did not try to shake. The only thing she told them was: "Immediately after the holiday a huge article about the recruitment of spies, by a high-level member of the secret police, is to appear in *Pravda*." Then the conversation moved on to Silver Pines, because Nikolay Grigorievich also told them some news he had heard in the cafeteria: Arsyushka Florinsky had become a neighbor in Silver Pines too, had gotten a country house. Yes, behind the fence, the two-story one, with a solarium and tennis courts. Yes, yes, that one. Major figures in the OGPU always lived there: at one time Rauzer, then Rabinye, Tomson, and now Florinsky.

After that the conversation began branching off: to the fate of Pasha Nikodimov, into which Florinsky had promised to look, but there hadn't been a peep for three months now, and to Silver Pines, to country house concerns. The cooperative had sent a request to pay the rent for the first quarter and for the plumbing work scheduled for May. They didn't have the money and were wondering where to get it. Liza very cheerfully promised to get it where she worked, at the People's Commissariat of Agriculture, at the credit union.

Nikolay Grigorievich was ready to say, "What are you fussing about? What country house? What plumbing?"—but the women were discussing these matters with such honest enthusiasm that he couldn't bring himself to cut them off. At around eleven they went out for a walk before bed. The evening was warm. On the bridge were troops ready for the next day's parade. Mikhail, having sobered up slightly in the fresh air, began discussing the advantages of light tanks over heavy ones. Listening to him was boring, but arguing with him was dangerous. In the depths of his soul Nikolay Grigorievich was convinced that he understood military questions better than his brother, even though he had not graduated from a military academy.

The Kremlin was carved out of the darkness by floodlights, and in the black sky above it hung a portrait of Stalin attached to an invisible and camouflaged aerostat. The giant mustachioed face gleamed, iridescent in the silver beams of floodlights. It was almost motionless, just slightly swelling in the middle from a light wind, and past the gleaming portrait flew airplanes carrying smaller portraits of Marx, Engels, Lenin, and again Stalin. Everyone stopped on the bridge and looked at this string of familiar portraits slowly floating past in the clear sky, illuminated from below. The airplanes with the small portraits, roaring and keeping close formation, disappeared from the range of the flood-lights, the rumbling of the engines moved off into the distance, and the single huge portrait was left hanging in the sky above the Kremlin. Before there had been evanescence, temporariness, fleetingness, disappearance, while now there was stability, permanence. The portrait shone like a movie screen of incredible proportions. And at the same time its *being suspended* in the air seemed supernatural, was a miracle, and was remotely reminiscent of the motionless soaring of a little spider hanging on an invisible thread. The entrance to the Alexander Gardens was closed. Military traffic controllers pointed to the right. They had to turn toward the Lenin Library and then, via the Library, walk to the bridge and return home.

After midnight, when Mikhail was already snoring on the daybed, Liza was asleep with the children in their room, and Nikolay Grigorievich was coming out of the bathroom in his robe and slippers over his bare feet, the doorbell rang.

Nikolay Grigorievich quickly went to his study and began getting dressed. His heart pounded, his hands wouldn't obey. He felt a vile weakness somewhere inside, at the pit of his stomach, which he hadn't felt for a long time, perhaps since the years of his childhood. No one in the apartment had yet heard the bell. The people at the door were waiting. In a moment they would ring again, longer, harder. Should he destroy anything? Nothing. The hour was here. It had arrived. No one could avoid death, and this hour, which had arrived for him, does not pass anyone by. Why should he be more fortunate than others? No, he didn't want any special dispensations. He couldn't get the white shirt to button on his chest, couldn't find the cuff links. He had put them somewhere ten minutes ago. Really, they had just been here. Well, all right, he could make do without them. He had left his dirty socks in the bathroom, and he didn't feel like getting clean ones. There was no time, he was depressed, and already tormented by a terrible, feverish impatience. The bell rang again—this time long and tense, as prescribed. And someone was tapping at the door with a finger. Should he wake Liza up or go open the door at once?

Without having yet decided which would be better, he started off down the hall. He threw back the chain with a firm hand. It clattered, swinging.

On the landing stood Valerka.

"You? Where have you come from, you son of a gun?"

"From the train station. I ran away. Is Dad here?"

"Yes, he's here. Go on in. Take off your hat and coat. Get washed up." Nikolay Grigorievich waited for his nephew to remove his coat and cap, and, taking him by the ear, pulled him to himself and sweetly and firmly, drawing it out, smacked him on the crown of his head. Valerka even jumped a little, said in a whisper, "Ow!"—but apparently took it as something he had coming: he obediently ran off to the bathroom on tiptoe.

Red sailors stood in a white square, fliers in a dark blue one, frontier guards in a green one, and the Proletarian Division in a bright olive green one. Gorik had seen all of this many times and understood it perfectly well, because it was that way at all the parades. And similarly, at all the parades, at exactly ten o'clock, when the clock on the Spassky Tower had hammered out into the silence above the square its last, resonant, bell-like stroke, which penetrated into all hearts, Voroshilov would come riding out of the gates at a light gallop, and the "Ah... Ah..." would start. As though in the wake of the clattering of Voroshilov's horse an enormous carpet, consisting of a live, collective noise, would roll out. The noise rolled in waves. The carpet would unfurl and unfurl, encompassing the square. But every time again, although it was familiar, during the moments of the "Ah..." Gorik would be seized by a shiver, his stomach would tremble from delight, his palms sweat, contract into fists, and he would cry "Ah..." soundlessly with everyone.

In addition, he experienced the pleasant feeling of self-satisfaction from the consciousness that he had brought Lyonya to this wonderful spectacle and that Lyonya should be grateful to him. After all, very few people from their class could see a parade on Red Square. Perhaps only Katka Florinskaya and that new boy whose father was a deputy people's commissar. Sapog had used to go to parades, but now, poor

guy, he stayed home, Gorik looked at his friend from time to time, trying to read traces of gratitude on his tensely attentive, somewhat pale
face, but as yet he couldn't discover any. Karas even seemed to have
forgotten whom he had come with here. He watched the marching
troops without a pause. He didn't say a word, as though he had turned
to stone. While Valerka, on the contrary, wouldn't stay in one place,
fidgeted between the adults, constantly *tried to squeeze through*, once
disappeared for a long time, and after returning, said that he had
squeezed through to the Mausoleum, very, very close up, and had seen
Stalin, Molotov, Kalinin, and all the leaders. Uncle Misha yanked him
by the collar of his sailor jacket and said very irately: "If you run off
anywhere again, you rascal..." "Big deal!" answered Valerka. And, after
being silent for a bit, whispered, "Some commander..." Then Uncle
Misha smacked him soundly on the rear end. But Lyonya didn't hear
any of that, didn't even turn around.

The cavalry galloped, pikes fluttered, Cossack hoods dazzled the
eyes with scarlet and light blue, the people in the reviewing stands
rustled: "For the first time.. Cossacks... You know, for the first time
Red Cossacks are taking part in the parade." A woman laughed: "No, I
can't stand to look at them!" But everyone around applauded, and
someone yelled: "Hurrah, Cossacks!" Gorik wanted the people standing nearby—especially Lyonya—to know that his father was a real
Don Cossack, and he asked in a purposely loud voice: "Dad, are those
Don Cossacks or Kuban Cossacks?"

Nikolay Grigorievich, to Gorik's surprise, answered indifferently:
"Well, probably. I think they are."

But Uncle Misha explained that it was a joint Cossack division. The
Don Cossacks marched in front, second the Kuban Cossacks, and behind them the Terek Cossacks. Then noiseless bicycles sped along
over the flagstone pavement, damp from the morning rain, and then,
clattering in eager rivalry and roaring deafeningly, came motorcycles
with sidecars in which stood machine guns. That was something new.
That was terrific! Motorcycles with machine guns! A good little surprise for the foreign military attachés. They were probably grimacing
and blanching from fury on their reviewing stand. Gorik shouted:
"Hurrah, motorcyclists!" Heavy anti-tank weapons crept along on

caterpillar treads. Behind them came an avalanche of tanks—dwarf tanks and giant ones. Exhaust fumes filled the air. It was difficult to breathe, as in a real battle. The earth shook, the sky roared. From the thunder of the fighter plane and high-speed bomber engines it seemed that the people in the reviewing stands would go deaf at any moment. Women stopped up their ears, and their faces expressed horror, but Gorik and Karas stood there with imperturbable calm. They could have stood there two, three, four hours, as long as necessary.

And then, when their legs were giving out, and their hands were tired from clapping, when their heads were spinning from the noise, clatter, flashing, and music, when the athletes had marched past, the young Spaniards had run past in their amusing two-horned caps, which for some reason were called "sidecaps," when the radio had thundered: "We're on the air. The first steamships are blasting their horns! We're on the air to Madrid! Madrid is speaking! We're on the air to a train taking a detachment of Komsomol girls to the Far East!"—when the sun had come out, it had turned hot, and Father had said that it was time to go home, they were expecting them for dinner there, and Gorik, hardly able to stand on his feet, replied that he just had to watch it to the end... what happened then? Father said: "Never mind. You'll see the rest of it next time. Next year." And the thought suddenly occurred to Gorik that Father wasn't telling the truth, that there wouldn't be a next time. He couldn't understand where that idea had come from. He had simply felt it in his heart, which was exultant, half dead from tiredness. And perhaps Father had smiled that way and squeezed Gorik's hand. It had occurred to him, and that was all—for no good reason.

Gorik nodded, and they started making their way to the exit, in the direction of the Alexander Gardens.

In the evening there were many guests, about twenty people. Uncle Grisha and Zoya came from Kolomna. An old friend of Father's from the Civil War days, Aunt Marusya, from Rostov, a nice lady, came and brought gifts: the game "Aquarium" (with the aid of a magnet on a fishing pole you tried to catch paper fish) and a beautifully printed book, *Hubert in the Land of Marvels*, about a German Pioneer who had come to the Soviet Union. Gorik already had that book, but he kept quiet about that, of course, so as not to upset Aunt Marusya. Just before supper Valerka caused a scene, refused to take a bath—he had gotten very dirty when they were playing musketeers and crawling around on their stomachs in the rear courtyard, near the church—and Uncle Misha had edified him with a belt in the study. Valerka screamed at the top of his voice, the women tried to intercede for him, but Uncle Misha was furious, refused to listen, and drove everyone out. Suddenly the doorbell rang: Aunt Vanda, Valerka's mother, had come. Everyone was terribly surprised. It turned out that before reaching Leningrad, Aunt Vanda had transferred to a Moscow train and come back. Because she was very worried about Valerka, that scoundrel. After all, he had run away without her noticing, had deceived his mother by saying that he would stand between the cars until the train left, and she, such a fool, together with her Dmitry Vasilievich, remembered after the train had already left. Gorik knew what was going on: Valerka had not at all wanted to go with Dmitry Vasilievich, but Aunt Vanda had made him. She had promised to buy him a camera. Now Aunt Vanda was crying, hugging Valerka, and saying: "Oh, what a misfortune! My God!" She thought he had been run over by the train wheels. Valerka said that he wouldn't do that again and that he wanted to live with Aunt Vanda, and not with Uncle Misha, because "Father can't control his hands." Uncle Misha was enraged by such impudence and gave his son a good slap in the face. And was right to do so: he shouldn't be a traitor. Aunt Vanda cried again, yelling: "I can't live here. I'll go away from everyone! Masha, take me with you to Rostov. That's where I spent my childhood!" Aunt Marusya said she was willing. Things calmed down eventually, Grandmother and Grandmother Vera started playing piano pieces for four hands, and then everyone sat down to supper. There were three cakes, several bottles of cream soda, not counting the wine, and homemade ice cream, very tasty, although a little runny and reminiscent in smell of boiled milk: Seryozhka had spent half a day fixing the ice cream maker. During supper Gorik had an embarrassing moment. On the tablecloth, right next to his cup, he suddenly saw a bedbug and loudly informed everyone present about it. "A bedbug!" he yelled in a vigorous, and perhaps even joyful voice. "Look, a bedbug!"

It's hard to say what moved Gorik to yell like that. After all, he had opened his mouth for the first time the whole evening. For more than an hour he had sat amid the adults, constrained and depressed by his own silence, his inability to take part in the table talk—Zhenka was much more free and easy than him, not to mention Marina, who told all sorts of jokes without a let-up, and even Valerka squeaked out a joke—and then, tormented by his lack of talent and looking princi-pally at the tablecloth, Gorik saw the bedbug. And it seemed to him that that was amusing and could cheer everyone up. And he himself would somehow stand out against the general background. Actually, his joyful exclamation produced the impression of a bombshell. A hubbub arose, someone leapt up, someone started laughing. Aunt Dina and Grandmother Vera laughed especially loudly. Then, after ev-eryone had forgotten about the bedbug, Gorik happened to stop by the study and see his father standing near the window and looking out into the courtyard. It was half-dark. A single small lamp over the daybed was on.

"Dad..." Gorik began, going up to his father. His father suddenly turned around and slapped Gorik on the cheek painfully, saying, "Idiot!" Gorik realized that his father still remembered about the bed-bug. And that upset him. He couldn't get to sleep, and when Zhenka was fast asleep and Valerka was also snoring on the couch, he ran barefoot, in just a shirt, into the dining room, opened the door for a second, and called Mother. She came and sat down on the daybed. They whispered for a long time. At first, as a blind, he talked about all sorts of school matters, but then asked whether people would ever forget about the bedbug. "Of course they will," Mother said. "I think that by tomorrow or at the most the day after tomorrow. The main thing is for you to forget."

But many years passed...

COMMENTARY AND GLOSSARY

The following notes are based in part on A. P. Shitov's commentary in Yury Trifonov, *Otblesk kostra, Starik, Ischeznovenie* (Moscow: Moskovskii rabochii, 1988).

Agnivtsev, Nikolay Yakovlevich (1888-1932)—satirical poet

Agranov, Yakov Savlovich (?-1939)—deputy head of the NKVD under Yezhov; arrested and shot in 1939

Alexandrovsky Prison—famous prison in Alexandrovsky Zavod (Siberia)

Anatoly Vasilievich—see Lunacharsky

Andrey Sergeevich—see Bubnov

Arsyushka—form of the name Arseny appropriate for a child

bacha—Uzbek word denoting a boy who may provide sexual favors

Baratynsky, Yevgeny (1800-1844)—Russian romantic poet

Becker—make of piano

Benois, Alexander (1870-1960)—artist associated with the World of Art group

Brilliant—see Sokolnikov

Bubnov, Andrey Sergeevich (1884-1940)—Commissar of Education for the Russian SFSR 1929-1937; Bubnov served as the chair of the All-Union Pushkin Committee in 1937 and on 10 February of that year delivered the opening speech at a meeting held at the Bolshoy Theater to mark the hundredth anniversary of Pushkin's death

building—The building to which the narrator refers is the apartment building in the heart of Moscow at the intersection of Serafimovich Street and the Bersenev Embankment. Built in the 1930s to house the Party and government elite, it soon became known as either "the government apartment building" or "the apartment house on the embankment." The latter formulation serves as the title for a 1976 novel by Trifonov, who in fact lived in that well-known Stalinist landmark in his childhood.

The building in question additionally houses the Shock Worker movie theater.

Center for Political Prisoners—see entry on Society of Former Political Prisoners and Exiles

Cheka—Extraordinary Commission to Combat Counterrevolution, Sabotage, and Speculation, the earliest name for the Soviet political police, later the KGB

Chorny, Sasha (pseudonym of Alexander Glikberg, 1880-1932)—satirical
poet
Chuma—Russia word meaning "plague"
CPC—Commission for Party Control

Dinochka—diminutive of the name Dina
distribution center—a store to which only a specific and limited clientele has
access
Dynamo—stadium and sports complex in Moscow
dzhida—type of tree common in Uzbekistan

"Erlauben Sie mir, bitte, gehen dorthin, wohin der Kaiser zu Fuss geht"—
German for: "Please allow me to go to where even the emperor goes on
foot;" or, in other words, "I have to go to the bathroom"
expropriation—Bolshevik jargon for a bank robbery undertaken by
Bolsheviks as a means of raising money for the party coffers
February—the February Revolution of 1917
Feuchtwanger, Lion (1884-1958)—German writer whose *Moscow 1937* de-
fended the show trials
"From her *Monsieur* received the child..."—lines from the third stanza of
Pushkin's *Eugene Onegin*, as rendered by Walter Arndt

Gabay—beach in the Silver Pines section of Moscow
Gorik—diminutive of the name Igor
GUGB—Head Directorate of State Security

Inber, Vera (1890-1972)—poet
Industrial Party—a nonexistent underground organization, alleged member-
ship in which often resulted in engineers being tried
Iosif Vissarionovich—Stalin
Ivan Vasilievich—Ivan IV (the Terrible) (1533-84)
Izvestiya—the official Soviet government newspaper

Jeans, Sir James Hopwood (1877-1946), English mathematician, physicist,
and astronomist whose theory of the origin of the universe was widely discussed in the Soviet Union in the 1930s

Kamenev, Lev (1883-1936)—Soviet leader executed after show trial
Karas—Russian word meaning "carp"
Khatti—an ancient non-Indo-European people of Asia Minor

Khenkin, Vladimir Yakovlevich (1883-1953)—popular variety artist of the 1930s

Kholodnaya, Vera (1893-1919)—Russian movie actress

kilogram=2.2 pounds

Koba—one of the underground names used by Stalin during his early days as a Bolshevik revolutionary

Kolya—diminutive of the name Nikolay

Komsomol—Communist Youth League

Kozlovsky, Ivan Semyonovich (b. 1900)—distinguished Russian tenor

Krupskaya, Nadezhda (1869-1939)—Lenin's wife

Kyukhelbeker [Küchelbecker], Wilhelm (1797-1846)—Russian romantic poet

Lanceray, Evgeny (1875-1946)—Russian artist

Lena River Massacre—massacre of striking gold miners on the Lena River in 1912

Lenin Hills—the estate outside Moscow where Lenin spent his last years

Liza—diminutive of the name Yelizaveta

Lubyanka—NKVD, and later KGB, headquarters and prison in Moscow

Lunacharsky, Anatoly Vasilievich (1875-1933)—first Soviet commissar for education

Lyonka, Lyonya—diminutives of the name Leonid

M—a make of Soviet car

"making the sign of the cross"—Russian folk superstition calls for one to make the sign of the cross over one's mouth after yawning

Manya, Marinka—diminutives of the name Marina

Mayakovsky, Vladimir (1893-1930)—poet who wrote much satirical ideological verse

Metro-Vickers Trial—held in April 1933, it allegedly demonstrated the existence of a ring of saboteurs organized by British engineers

Mikoyan, Anastasy (1895-1978)—government official, Party functionary

Misha, Mishka—diminutives of the name Mikhail

Moyka—river in Petersburg/Leningrad

Nazarov Rebellion—unsuccessful White offensive on the lower Don led by Colonel Nazarov

Nezhdanova, Antonina Vasilievna (1873-1950)—distinguished Russian soprano

Nesterov, Mikhail (1862-1942)—Russian artist

NKVD—the People's Commissariat of Internal Affairs, official name of the Soviet political police from 1935 until after World War II when it became the KGB

OGPU—designation for the security police from 1922 to 1934
Ordzhonikidze, Grigory (Sergo) Konstantinovich (1886-1937)—close associate of Stalin; committed suicide during the purges

palvan—Uzbek folk hero
Pashka—diminutive of the name Pavel
personnel department—the de facto KGB office at any place of work, hence the presence of Major Oganov
Petya—a diminutive form of the name Pyotr
Pioneers—see entry for Young Pioneers
Piter—popular name for Petersburg/Petrograd/Leningrad
Plenum of the Central Committee—reference to the plenum of the Central Committee of the Communist Party held in February and March 1937 at which Stalin laid the ideological foundation for the great terror by promulgating his idea that as socialism was being successfully forged in the Soviet Union the class struggle would become more intense
Pyatakov, Georgy (1890-1937)—Soviet leader executed after show trial

Radek, Karl (1885-1939)—high-ranking Party member, purged
Remeykin-Skameykin—untranslatable punning on the last name "Remeyko"
RMC—Revolutionary Military Council (1918-1934)
Ruslan—protagonist in Pushkin's mock epic *Ruslan and Lyudmila*

Sakya-Muni—one of the names for Buddha
Sapozhnikov—last name formed from the word *sapog*, boot, and thus the real last name of the character introduced as Volodka Sapog
Sergo—see Ordzhonikidze
Sergunya, Seryozha—diminutives of the name Sergey
Shmidt, O. Yu. (1891-1956)—mathematician, astronomist and geophysicist, first vice-president of the USSR Academy of Sciences
Shock Worker—movie theater in "the apartment house on the embankment" (see entry for building)
Smilga, I.T. (1892-1938)—Party leader, Director of the Plekhanov Institute of Economics; purged, posthumously rehabilitated
Society of Former Political Prisoners and Exiles—organization formed in 1921 to aid its neediest members and to study the history of political pris-

oners in tsarist Russia
Sokolnikov, Grigory (Brilliant) (1888-1939)—Soviet leader imprisoned after
    show trial

"temporary insanity"—reference to the purges and show trials of August
    1936 and January 1937
tugrik—monetary unit of the Mongolian People's Republic

Uryuk—Russian word meaning "dried apricots"

Valera, Valerka—diminutives of the name Valery
Valka—diminutive of the name Valentin
Vanya—diminutive of the name Ivan
Vereshchagin, Vasily (1842-1847)—member of the group of artists known as
    the Wanderers. In 1847, stating that he considered "all ranks and honors
    in art harmful," Vereshchagin refused the title the Academy had bestowed
    upon him.
verst—old Russian unit of measurement equal to 3500 feet
Vyshinsky, Andrey (1883-1954)—chief prosecutor of the USSR 1935-39;
    conducted the show trials of the '30s
Volodka—diminutive of the name Vladimir

Yenisei—one of the major Siberian rivers
Yezhov, Nikolay Ivanovich (1895-1940)—head of the NKVD, i.e., the politi-
    cal police, from September 1936 until 1938; his name is thus associated
    with the height of the Stalinist terror
Young Pioneers—children's branch of the League of Young Communists

Zhenka, Zhenya, Zhenichka—diminutives of the names Evgeny (masc.) and
    Evgenia (fem.)
Zinoviev, Grigory (1883-1936)—Soviet leader executed after show trial
Zhukovsky, Vasily (1783-1852)—Russian romantic poet